A Table For Two

Janet Albert

Yellow Rose Books

Port Arthur, Texas

ISBN 978-1-935053-27-9
1-935053-27-2

First Printing 2010

9 8 7 6 5 4 3 2 1

Cover design by Donna Pawlowski

Published by:

Regal Crest Enterprises, LLC
4700 Highway 365, Suite A, PMB 210
Port Arthur, Texas 77642

Find us on the World Wide Web at
http://www.regalcrest.biz

Printed in the United States of America

Author's Comments

A Table for Two is special to me because it takes place in Philadelphia where I lived for many years and also because I love to cook. My mother was a simple but wonderful cook who passed her talent on to me. I think she would have been pleased that I'd paid attention all those years as I sat at the kitchen table and watched her prepare our family meals. My culinary skills have progressed way beyond those everyday foods and Sunday dinners she used to make. In fact, I've often been told I should open a restaurant. The long hours and stressful work of being a chef never appealed to me and since I preferred my other stressful career, I chose instead to settle for a fictional one. It was a lot more fun and a lot less work. I loved writing about Dana and Tracy and the dishes they created and I loved bringing Café De Marco to life. I hope you enjoy reading about it as much as I enjoyed writing about it.

Thanks from the bottom of my heart to my wonderful beta readers, Norma Serrato, Judy Underwood, and Donna O'Hara-Lewis. No one does this without help and I couldn't have done it without your valuable input, sound advice and keen eyes. All my love and thanks to Mary, who supports me in everything I do and encourages me to write in spite of attacks of self-doubt and a harsh and picky inner critic. You are all worth your weight in gold.

An affectionate thank you and a huge hug goes out to Pat Cronin, my editor, for putting up with me throughout the editing of this book. I appreciate your patience and understanding during a tough time for me, but most of all, I thank you for teaching me to be a better writer. The book as it is now is infinitely improved because of you.

A special thank you to Cathy LeNoir and RCE for taking a chance on me and for making my dream come true a second time. Donna Pawlowski came up with an amazing cover for the book and I am grateful for her efforts. Thanks to Brenda Adcock for her editing input and thanks to RCE author, Lori L. Lake, for her support as well as her handy guides and articles on writing. I'd also like to thank authors, Andi Marquette and Nann Dunne for their advice and encouragement. And thanks, Nann Dunne, for your amazing website, JAW. (Just About Write)

And, as I said in my first book and will say again here...my sincere thanks to all of you, the readers of lesbian fiction. You are the reason we writers persist in doing what we do.

For information about me, more on resources and useful websites for authors and places to purchase books, please visit me at my web site – www.janetalbert.com

To Mary, the woman who sits across from me at my table for two.

Chapter One

RIDLEY PULLED INTO one of the last spaces in the high school parking lot and sat for a minute with the air-conditioner running while she inspected herself in the rear view mirror. Her wavy auburn hair had curled thanks to the high humidity and she admired the way it fell around her face giving her that carefree, tousled hair style she wished she could have every day. She reached her hand to tame a wayward clump behind her ear and pulled off her sunglasses. In the morning light her eyes were as green as emeralds and she could easily see the tiny specks of gold scattered around the rims of the irises.

The long summer vacation had come to an end, the Labor Day celebrations and fireworks were over and she was about to begin her first day as the new physical education teacher in a high school not too far from where she lived. She was eager to get started, especially since her friend Laurie Morgan taught English at the same school yet at the same time she felt anxious, two conflicting emotions she accepted as understandable under the circumstances.

As soon as she lowered her long legs and planted her sandaled feet on the sticky blacktop, she heard Laurie yelling at her from the other end of the parking lot. Even though they were the only two people around, Laurie jumped up and down and flapped her hands in the air above her head as though she feared Ridley wouldn't be able to locate her without some sort of visual signal. Something about Laurie's hand movements reminded Ridley of a robin frolicking in a backyard birdbath on the first warm day of spring, but then it wasn't hard to think about robins when one thought of Laurie because she held the promise of spring in her heart and she was as reliable as she was pretty.

"Hey, Ridley, wait for me!" Laurie hollered.

Ridley waved back to acknowledge Laurie's request, grabbed her work bags from the front seat of her Honda CR-V and slammed the door shut. Near the rear bumper, she stopped to wait for her friend and pressed the button on her key chain that locked her vehicle. Although she heard the metallic clunk of the locks loud and clear, she pushed the button a second time just to hear the high-pitched beep that told her the doors were already locked. It dawned on her that it was a peculiar little habit and one she did quite often. Sometimes, she even pushed the button three or four times in a row to create a series of beeps.

Laurie half-walked, half-ran to catch up, her chest heaving as she struggled to inhale the heavy air of another hot and humid morning. Once she stood next to Ridley, she set her bags down while she stopped to catch her breath. "If it isn't my old friend, Ridley Kelsen," she said after fifteen or twenty seconds of deep breathing. "Imagine meeting you here."

"What do you mean, 'imagine meeting me here'? You're the one who told me to meet you in front of the school this morning, Ms. Morgan. Remember?"

"Sure I remember. Why wouldn't I?" Laurie's normally pale complexion was as red as the rising summer sun. "Is it hot enough for you?"

"Yeah, I'd say so. I hate September in Philadelphia and you shouldn't be running around in this heat. You look like you're going to self-combust." Ridley looked down at her sandals. "It's been so hot I think the asphalt's starting to melt. I thought my sandals would get stuck in it when I got out of my car." She bent her right foot up and inspected her sandal. "I think the bottom of my sandals might be melting."

Wet ringlets of medium-length, blond hair were stuck to Laurie's forehead and a stream of sweat wiggled a crooked path down the right side of her face. She swiped at it with her fingers, but that only served to send it trickling off in a new direction. "I think I'm melting."

Ridley touched Laurie's sweaty cheek and studied the thin film of moisture coating her fingers before she wiped it off on the side of her shorts. Even Laurie's cool blue eyes looked hot. "You're sweating like crazy. Too bad this school of yours doesn't have air-conditioning because after two weeks of temperatures like these, that old stone building's going to feel just like an enormous sauna inside."

"The entire city feels like a sauna," Laurie pointed out. "And the school has never had any air-conditioning except for a few select places." Laurie brushed at the stream of sweat on her face again. "The library isn't one of those places."

"The library isn't air-conditioned? Isn't that where we're having our meetings?" The staff was required to come in the day after Labor Day for two days of meetings before the official start of the school year. In these meetings they'd go over the District's goals for the coming school year as well as any changes in the curriculum and they'd be treated to a video pep-talk from the head of the school district thanking them in advance for their hard work.

"Yes, unfortunately," Laurie confirmed.

Ridley imagined how miserable her face must have looked as she absorbed the full impact of Laurie's words. "That's great, but I can't say I'm surprised. All the older schools in the city are like that. My last one was."

Laurie plucked at the front of her shirt. "Look at me, my shirt's soaked and we're not even inside the building. By the end of the day, I won't have an ounce of fluid left in my body."

Ridley groaned as she thought of how hellish the next two days would be. "I'm getting heat stroke just thinking about it—as if those meetings aren't intolerable enough."

As though Laurie felt she needed to offer Ridley a thread of hope, she added, "If it makes you feel any better, the weather report said it'll be a lot cooler by the weekend."

"Anything would feel better than this, but first we have to find some way to survive the rest of this week." Ridley lifted one of her bags. "I brought plenty of bottled water and I'm praying the teacher that was here before me left a fan in the gym office."

"If not, I've got an extra one." Laurie glanced briefly at her clothing and then at Ridley's. They both wore shorts and sleeveless polo shirts. "Thank God the students aren't here so we can get away with dressing like this. I don't know what I'll do if it's still this hot when I have to get dressed up to teach class."

"That's one good thing about being the Phys. Ed. teacher. I get away with casual clothes most of the time because no one expects me to dress up."

"And there's no need to. You'd just get dirty down in that gym." Laurie stared at Ridley for a moment and as she did she must have discovered something amusing which caused the corners of her mouth to turn up. "You couldn't pull off wearing a dress anyway. You'd look kind of funny in one. When I think of you, I think of handsome rather than feminine. It's not that you're super butchy or anything, but..." Laurie appeared worried about that last statement.

"Relax, I know what you mean," Ridley said, to put her friend at ease. She'd made it clear to Laurie on more than one occasion that she didn't like to dress too masculine or too feminine. She preferred a more neutral appearance and was attracted to the same kind of women although she did tend to favor women who leaned a tad more toward the feminine side. "And you're right, I would look funny. If I did dress up I'd have to wear dressier pants because I don't own a dress and I can't remember the last time I wore one— twelve years old, maybe?"

Laurie took a quick peek at her watch. "We'd better stop standing around chatting and get in there." She picked up her bag with one hand and took hold of Ridley's arm with the other as they started toward the main entrance. "When did you get back from the shore?"

"Last night around nine-thirty. I waited until the traffic thinned out before I hit the road. As you know, there's no sense in leaving any earlier on a holiday weekend because if you do, you just end up sitting in your car on the road while you crawl all the way home with everyone else who left early. You get home just as late."

"Bet you hated to leave. Is your Mom still down there?"

Ridley's nod answered Laurie's question. "September's one of her favorite months. It's still summer and still warm, but the vacation crowds are gone and it's peaceful again."

"It must be a lot more peaceful, but then we wouldn't know because we have to get back to work." Laurie let out a squeal after she said that and joggled Ridley's arm to and fro with gusto. "Speaking of work, I can't believe we're going to be working at the same school! I was thrilled when you told me your transfer was official."

"Back when we were in college, did you ever think we'd be working together someday?" The two of them had been friends ever since Laurie chose the seat next to Ridley's in their first freshman class at Temple University. Ridley's smile evolved into a wry grin. "I do hate to put a damper on your enthusiasm, but you'll be up on the third floor teaching English and I'm going to be down in the gym so we'll hardly see each other."

"So what? I'm just happy to have you here. We can eat lunch together and go to meetings together, can't we?" Laurie cocked her head, a habit Ridley was quite familiar with. "We can talk about the same people and we'll both know what's going on in the school. It'll be fun."

"When you put it that way, it sounds like a hell of a lot of fun." Ridley cocked her head to match Laurie's and mirrored her friend's silly smile.

Laurie straightened her head. "You don't need to make fun of me."

"I was only teasing you." Ridley covered her mouth and yawned. "God, I'm so tired today. I think I slept about four hours at the most. I couldn't get to sleep, I couldn't stay asleep and then I couldn't get up once I finally fell asleep. You know how out of whack our systems get after we've been off the entire summer."

"I didn't sleep much either," Laurie said. "Every September I go through an adjustment period for a week or two until I get back into my work routine."

"I go through the same thing, but on top of that I think I was anxious about going to a new school. I was happy to leave my old school, but..."

"I understand. Just don't be nervous about working here," Laurie said.

"I know, I know. You told me how much you love it here. Still, it is a new job and you can't blame me for being a little nervous and excited."

"No I can't, but I know you're going to love it here. That's why I called you the minute I found out our gym teacher was retiring. I..." Laurie didn't finish her sentence and her gaze became fixed on Ridley's. "I'm sorry, your eyes distracted me. I almost forgot how they change colors from one moment to the next. They can be different shades of green depending on the light and in the next second, they've got flecks of gold in them. They're so pretty they make you lose your train of thought."

"You should be used to them by now." Ridley was accustomed to other people's remarks about the color of her eyes, although she appreciated the compliment more when it came from Laurie or someone dear to her. "They probably have dark circles under them, today."

"Not really." Laurie paused on the sidewalk and inspected Ridley from top to bottom. "I haven't seen you in a few weeks and you may be tired, but you look fantastic and I love your tan. Not that you needed to, but did you lose a little weight over the summer? I didn't notice it when we came down to visit at the end of July, but now I can see it."

Ridley looked down at Laurie who at five feet five was a good two and a half inches shorter than she. "I lost about twelve pounds. I always lose weight in the summer."

"I usually lose a few pounds, too, but not because I'm as active as you are. I just don't feel like eating as much." Laurie stopped when they reached the high school's massive cascade of steps that led up to the main entrance. "Here we are. Nowhere left to go but up."

"My, isn't this is an attractive building." Ridley paused to study the dilapidated and dingy structure that loomed in front of them like an abandoned insane asylum. She'd seen the high school many times before, of course, but she'd never paid that much attention to it. In its day it must have been a stately building and in spite of its current state of disrepair, she could almost make out the ghostly image of the building's former grandeur.

"Isn't it? It's definitely seen better days."

"I'd say it's long past its heyday. Now I know what the 'P' stands for."

Laurie cast her friend a curious glance. "What are you talking about?"

"The P — the P in Calvin P. Hayes. It has to stand for prison."

"You're totally nuts. You know that, don't you?"

"Why do you say I'm nuts?" Ridley pretended to be wounded. "It looks just like a prison and look at the windows, they have bars on them. That proves my point." She pointed to the iron security bars on the ground floor windows.

"That doesn't prove anything. All the schools have bars on the windows."

"Laurie, I'm just teasing you and believe me when I tell you that I do not care how it looks as long as I enjoy working here. Anything would be an improvement over my last school. The last straw in a long line of last straws was that new principal we got last year. There's nothing worse than a bitchy woman armed with absolute power."

"All the principals are dictators. It's just a matter of whether you get a benevolent one or a malevolent one." Laurie climbed the first two steps and motioned with her hand for Ridley to catch up. "Hurry up. We don't want to be late or we'll miss out on the free coffee and bagels."

"In that case, we had better get moving." Ridley tucked her chin in, threw her chest out and squared her shoulders. "Are you ready to take on the challenge of another exciting and rewarding school year? I have no doubt it will prove to be more memorable than the last."

"I'm ready if you are, my fellow idealist." Laurie stood tall as she trudged all the way up the steps with Ridley and straight through the front door.

"Are you going straight up to the library?" Ridley asked once they were inside the main office. "It's cool in here. I wish I could stay in here all day."

"We've got about a half-hour to kill, so I'm going up to my classroom." Laurie reached inside her mailbox and removed some papers and a folder. After she did that, she pointed to another box one row over. "Check this out. They already gave you a mailbox with your name on it. Isn't that cute?" Without asking for permission, Laurie reached inside, grabbed the contents and handed it to Ridley. "Here are your materials for the meetings."

"Stealing someone's mail is a federal offense."

"So have me arrested why don't you?" Laurie's eyes drifted to the clock on the wall. "I've got to get going. I'll meet you in the library in twenty minutes. Save me a seat and get me a cup of coffee and a sesame bagel or a cinnamon raisin. And don't forget the cream cheese, regular not light." Laurie scurried out of the main office without another word.

"Anything else I can do for you?" Ridley mumbled to the wall.

AFTER LUNCH, THE staff was given the rest of the afternoon to get their classrooms in order and that gave Ridley an opportunity to check out the gymnasiums as well as her office. Horrified by a cluttered desk and closets stuffed with junk, she wasted no time launching her attack. Like any teacher who had to take over for someone who'd long ago lost their spark, she'd have to get rid of anything she didn't want or couldn't use and make the place her own.

"Those meetings bore me to tears." About an hour later, Laurie appeared out of nowhere and spoke from the doorway to Ridley's office. "It's the same old stuff every year and those group exercises..." She held her hands up to the ceiling. "Is there no mercy? Is there no God?"

"They drive me insane," Ridley said.

"Me, too," Laurie agreed. "Last spring at one of our meetings they made us pick someone we didn't know and take a walk with them. We were supposed to share something that we'd never told anyone. Now, if there was something you didn't want to tell to someone you knew why would you want to tell it to someone you didn't know?"

"They're definitely running out of ways to torture us." While she talked, Ridley kept on throwing huge piles of yellowed forms into trash bags. "Look at these old forms. Some are thirty years old. I'll bet you only the pentagon and the IRS have more forms than the school district." Ridley scraped an old wooden chair across the floor for Laurie. "Here, keep me company while I clear out this junk."

"I can't stay long." Laurie flopped in the chair with a sigh and gulped down the rest of the bottle of water she'd carried in with her. "How can you work in this heat?"

"I have to get it done before I get busy because I can't function in this mess. I have to have a neat and organized work space."

"This is such an appealing gym." A vinegary expression transformed Laurie's typically sweet face. "And it's so modern."

Ridley knew the reason for Laurie's sarcasm and although they'd both become accustomed to working in impoverished conditions, it never got any easier. She'd expected the drab green peeling walls, the exposed pipes and crumbling ceilings. It looked just like many other schools in the city and even better than some. "I'll never understand how the students can feel good about themselves in buildings like these."

"They always promise us new schools, but I don't see it happening," Laurie said.

"No money, that's the bottom line as the saying goes — a saying I've always hated, by the way." Ridley turned her attention to a couple of enormous cardboard boxes. She grabbed a filthy, deflated soccer ball out of one of them and shook it at Laurie. "Look at this." She threw it onto a pile of torn nets and cracked knee pads. "This broken junk has to be thrown out, but I'm afraid housekeeping will have a fit."

"They will if you put it in the regular trash. Call Ernie, our custodian and he'll send a couple of his guys over to get rid of it for you."

"Thanks. I'll do that." Ridley realized that Laurie was sitting around talking while everyone else was getting ready for school to start. "Don't you have to get your classroom in order?"

"I came in last week and did it." Laurie shrugged. "You know how I am. I hate doing things at the last minute. So what do you think so far—about working here, I mean?"

"I talked to Dr. Wilson after the meeting and she's very supportive about what I want to do, especially the health education part. She wants the students to take a half-year of health education as a graded course in addition to gym classes."

"I told you she's a great principal."

"Stay put, I'll be right back." Ridley walked to the other side of the gym and came back with a huge trash can bouncing behind her. She kept right on talking as she worked. "She said she welcomed fresh ideas and liked my enthusiasm."

"The guy who was here before you did as little as possible and I hate to say it, but the kids hated him. He was an odious man."

"Odious?" Ridley stopped what she was doing and put her hands on her hips. "You've read way too many nineteenth century novels."

"I'm a classics buff, what can I say? I love those Jane Austen words like 'felicity', 'condole' and 'trifle'. I don't know why we don't use any of those words anymore. They were so poetic and descriptive. I loved the way she wrote phrases like, 'you take great delight in vexing me' or 'I am excessively diverted'."

"Don't ever talk like that when the students are around. You'll never hear the end of it."

"Don't I know it?" Laurie remarked as if she'd had experience in the matter. "But be honest, doesn't 'don't trifle with me' sound better than 'don't fuck with me'?"

"I guess it sounds better, but..." Ridley hesitated and a mischievous smile formed in the corners of her mouth. "It doesn't feel nearly as good."

"I might have known you'd say that." Laurie sounded deflated.

"Sorry, but it's true. You know it is."

"Yeah, I guess so." Laurie leaned forward in her chair. "I hate to change the subject, but I want to know about that girl you were dating at the shore. Are you still seeing her?"

"You mean Melissa? No. It fizzled out and I let it. All she wanted to do was to drink and party with her friends and she made me feel like an ornament hanging on her arm. To tell you the truth,

I'm getting tired of the lesbian singles scene. Maybe I'm tired of lesbians in general."

"What a thing to say. You can't blame all lesbians for your dating woes."

"I don't know who else I'm supposed to blame."

"I'm sorry it didn't work out with her," Laurie said.

"Don't be. It doesn't matter and I only said I was tired of lesbians because I'm frustrated with the whole dating scene. It never seems to work out for me. Most of the women I've dated are only looking for casual sex and casual relationships and I guess I'm ready for more."

"I thought you enjoyed being alone and playing the field."

"Being alone is not a problem for me. My mother taught me to be self-sufficient and she taught me never to depend on someone else for my happiness." Ridley poked at her chest as she said the next words. "She said real happiness comes from inside here."

"I can't argue with that," Laurie said.

"She also told me that being able to survive on your own makes you stronger. Even as a young girl, I promised myself I'd never be one of those people who fell apart every time they found themselves alone. Being alone isn't such a bad thing, you know."

"I agree, but why do I get the feeling it's getting to you?"

"Because it is." Ridley took in a deep breath and forced it out. It wasn't easy to admit what she knew she was about to say, not to herself or to her best friend. "Look, it's not that I can't be alone, it's that I don't want to be, not anymore. I want someone in my life."

"I didn't know you felt that way. You've always been my single lesbian idol."

"Well, idols tend to disappoint. Toward the end of the last school year, I used to come home from work and dread the thoughts of eating another dinner alone or spending another evening with the only other voice I heard coming from the television. My apartment doesn't feel like my home anymore, if it ever did." Ridley grabbed a chair and straddled it so she was facing Laurie. "I feel like I'm missing something important, something I can count on."

"I think that something is love."

"My mother said the same thing to me, just the other day."

"You told her how you feel? I wish I could talk to my mother like that."

"I know you do and I know how lucky I am. I can tell her just about anything." Ridley took in a deep breath and made another admission. "Falling in love hasn't happened to me and I guess I'm having a hard time believing it ever will. I used to, but not anymore."

"Don't you ever give up hope. Love has a way of seeking you

out when you least expect it and it has a nasty habit of sneaking up on you when you're looking off in another direction. It shows up when you've decided you don't need it and worse yet, when you don't even want it."

"Do you really think so?" Ridley wanted so much to believe Laurie's words. She hated to acknowledge it, even to herself, but she had pretty much given up believing in love.

"I know so and I also know that when you fall for someone you're going to fall hard. In the meantime, while you're waiting for Ms. Right to come along, you should come over to our house when you're tired of being alone. You can have dinner with us anytime or you and I can have dinner together is closer to the truth since Karen is always working late."

"Thanks for the offer. You're a good friend."

Laurie laid her hand on top of Ridley's. "Karen and I always say how much we hope you'll meet someone. We'd give anything to see you end up as happy as we are."

"I'd love to have what you have with Karen, but I'm not sure I'll ever get it." Ridley hung her head. "Maybe I'm not destined to fall in love. Some people never do, you know."

"It has nothing to do with destiny. You just haven't met the right person. You're a real catch and someday, someone other than me and Karen is going to figure that out."

"You're a sweetheart." Ridley lifted her head and gazed into Laurie's brown eyes. "I know we've talked about this before, but don't you sometimes wonder why we never fell in love?"

"Yes, I do. I used to ask myself that same question before I met Karen."

"And what was your answer?"

"I don't have a clue, but I do know we have no control when it comes to love. You and I would have been a brilliant match, but we never had one single molecule of chemistry between us. One week after I met Karen, on our second date to be precise, I knew I'd fallen hopelessly in love." Laurie fanned her face with her hand. "Talk about chemical reactions. We would have burned the entire lab down."

"I think you still could. The chemistry is obvious to anyone who knows the two of you or is around you for any length of time."

"Things have cooled down a bit since then, thank God. You can't go around in that state for the rest of your life. That reminds me, how do you feel about going out with us this weekend? If you don't already have plans, that is?"

"I don't know. My mother wanted me to come back to the shore for the weekend, but I think I've had enough of the shore for a while. I'd rather stay home and get my life together before things get busy at work. I have nothing to eat in my apartment and I need to clean and tackle a mountain of laundry. What did you have in mind?"

"Karen and I have been invited to try a new restaurant on South Street. It's supposed to be one of the best new restaurants in the city. I wish you'd come with us."

"I don't know, maybe. What do you mean you were invited?"

"The owner is an old high school friend of Karen's. She just moved back here from Chicago to open this restaurant. We went to visit her a few years ago, but then Karen lost touch with her. We probably told you about her, but you may have forgotten. Say you'll go with us, please? It'll be fun." Laurie batted her eyelashes as she often did when she wanted to charm you into doing something. "Come on...please? Pretty please?"

"All right already. I can't stand to hear you beg. When are we going?"

"On Saturday. Our reservation is for seven o'clock." Laurie got up and stood by her chair. "I've got to meet with the roster chairman. Why don't you come over around six and we'll all walk to the restaurant together?" She walked out of Ridley's office.

Ridley hurried to catch her. "Laurie..." She waited for Laurie to turn and face her so she could look into her eyes because what she had to say was crucial. "Before you go, convince me this isn't another plan to fix me up. You know what happened the other times you tried to play matchmaker." Laurie's prior attempts to find the perfect person for Ridley had been disastrous and Ridley had made her swear she would never try again. "You promised, remember?"

"I remember and it's going to be just the three of us, I swear to God." Laurie made the sign of the cross on her chest, a residual habit from her Catholic upbringing.

"It had better be." Ridley glared at Laurie, her eyebrows drawn together.

Laurie raised her arms in the air as if to surrender. "I swear. I meant it when I said I'd never meddle in your love life again and I won't. You'll have to find that one special person who sets your soul on fire without any help from me."

"Good. I see you've finally learned your lesson."

"I have and I'm glad you're joining us on Saturday. Karen made me promise I'd ask you today. So, don't work too hard and I'll see you tomorrow morning?" Laurie managed to escape this time and hurried through the door that led into the hallway.

"I'll be here," Ridley said to the empty gymnasium.

Chapter
Two

"THEY HAD FRESH Chilean sea bass and the shrimp were so big and plump, I couldn't pass them up," Dana announced to Tracy the instant she burst through the back door of the kitchen at her restaurant, Café De Marco. It was close to nine on Saturday morning and she'd just returned from an early morning food-buying excursion to the wholesale markets located near the Delaware River in South Philadelphia. She loved going to the markets. As a matter of fact, she loved everything about food—reading about it, talking about it smelling it, preparing it and of course, eating it. "They had fantastic asparagus, so I got a lot of it along with our usual order of vegetables."

"Super. What do you want to do with it?"

"I've got something in mind, but I'll tell you about that later. First let me finish telling you what I got. I was excited when I saw what they had today and I think we should use a lot of Thai and Asian influence when we plan our specials for tonight. And before I forget to tell you, they had the most dazzling display of fresh flowers I've ever seen there so I bought big bunches of them so we could make bouquets for all the tables."

"You're talking a mile a minute, you're flushed and your hair's so windblown, you look like a wild woman." Tracy Morgan, Dana's sous-chef, leaned against the counter near the sink with a big cup of hot coffee cradled in her hands. She appeared as cool and collected as she always did and her gentle face left no doubt that she was quite amused by Dana's jabbering, albeit in the most loving way.

"I can hear myself, thank you very much, and I can tell by the look on your face that you think I'm way too hyped up and I need to slow down and you're right." As she took a moment to steady herself, Dana ran her fingers through her medium length dark brown hair in an attempt to smooth it into submission. It was fairly straight, but thick enough to take off on a whim when conditions were right. She tended to get overly excited when her creative juices were flowing and as soon as she felt her eyes darting from place to place and heard herself babbling she knew she needed to calm down. As of late, she derived most of her pleasure in life from buying food for the restaurant and coming up with interesting dishes. It was sad, but true. She took in a long deep breath and released it. "There, that's better."

"I hope you can also see the affection in my face."

"Yes, of course I can," Dana said. As usual, Tracy had her short, spiky brown hair wrapped in a bandana and she had a face far too cute to be capable of any real meanness. She could tease with the best of them and once in a while Dana detected a sparkle of mischief in her sharp blue eyes, but she was never cruel.

"Good." Tracy took a sip of her coffee. "So, are you going to tell me what you have in mind for these Asian-themed dishes? The suspense is killing me."

"Don't get carried away. We'll get to that soon enough." Dana planted her hands on her hips. She knew Tracy was teasing her, but she liked to play along and pretend she was a little miffed by it. "I got Thai basil, green papayas, a box of fresh coconuts, and a crate of perfectly ripe mangos and pineapples. I love working with those ingredients, don't you?"

"You know I do," Tracy said as she set her coffee cup on the counter. "Let me help you bring in the rest of the stuff and get it put away before we discuss the menu. I can't wait to see what you got."

"THESE RIPE MANGOES and pineapples smell so good, I can hardly stand it," Tracy said as she set the last box on the counter. "The entire kitchen already smells like ginger and basil and tropical fruits and my mouth is watering just thinking about what we can make with them." Tracy leaned into the box and inhaled through her nose. "Mmm, that is heavenly."

Dana held a piece of sea bass under Tracy's nose. "Smell this."

Tracy inhaled again. "I don't smell anything except a sweet hint of the sea."

"Exactly, and did you notice how clear their eyes are? Fish doesn't come any fresher than that. The shrimp is just as fresh." Dana helped Tracy put the fish and shrimp in the refrigerator and unpack the boxes of produce.

When they were done, Tracy fixed a cup of coffee for Dana and set it on the counter in front of her. Then she poured another cup for herself. "So, while we drink our coffee, let's talk about those specials you had in mind, boss?"

"Mmm, this is excellent coffee," Dana said after she'd tasted it. "I thought we'd do a shrimp appetizer like fried shrimp with an Asian sweet and sour dipping sauce. What do you think? With maybe just a hint of heat added to the sauce?"

"Perfect. Breaded in Panko?" Tracy suggested.

"That's even better. We have a case of Panko in the storage room and we should use some of it before it starts getting stale on us."

"What about the fresh ginger?"

"We'll use it in the sauce for the shrimp and wherever else we can use it. We could also use it for garnishing, maybe pickled or candied?"

In addition to the restaurant's standard menu, Dana liked to offer three or four additional specials based on what was available at the wholesale markets. Having to prepare the same entrées night after night got boring and in her opinion, it took all the fun out of being a chef. Having dinner specials also allowed her to make use of local products and ingredients when they were in season and at their peak.

She and Tracy collaborated each morning, always over a cup of coffee and sometimes over breakfast, to come up with the specials they'd make that day. Later in the day, when the other chefs arrived, they would review the recipes with them and go over the plating of each dish.

So that they became familiar with the specials, Dana required the wait staff to arrive an hour before the restaurant opened for a meeting with her and Tracy. That enabled them to answer the customer's questions and make informed suggestions.

Dana continued. "Also, I'd like to do the Thai green papaya salad we did about a month ago. I love that salad and we had a lot of positive feedback from the customers who ordered it. In fact, I loved it so much I'm going to have it for my dinner."

"I'll join you if you put a couple of those fat shrimp on top."

"But of course. It wouldn't be the same without the shrimp," Dana confirmed. "For one of the dinner specials, why don't we do a shrimp and red coconut curry on jasmine rice? We'll put onions, carrots, red peppers, green beans and chunks of pineapple in it. We could also offer it with chicken as an alternative."

"That sounds delicious. Would you like me to make a pineapple and coconut sorbet and serve it with those crispy little cookies you love with the fresh ginger in them? That would make a nice cooling dessert for these dishes."

Dana nodded. "That's a brilliant idea." Aside from her considerable skills as a chef, Tracy was also certified as a pastry chef and Dana thought she was a genius when it came to desserts. Her creativity seemed boundless. "Here's another idea I had. Could you do a pineapple upside down cake with rum whipped cream? If the customers like it, I might even keep it on the menu. It's something I've always loved and I think it goes well with our style of food."

"Uh..." Tracy scratched her head and paused as if to give the request some serious thought. "It's an old-fashioned dessert, but sure, I can do that for you."

"I know. My grandmother used to make it when we went to her house for Sunday dinner. What appeals to me is that you don't see it on dessert menus and it would be different."

"Anything that makes us stand out can only be good for business. How about if I put a new spin on it and make individual ones? You know...I could do a single gooey, rum-tinged ring of buttery, brown-sugary pineapple perched on top of an individual round cake made of delicate golden sponge? Your grandmother wouldn't object to that, would she?

"Hell, no. My Grandma liked rum." Dana's comment amused her as much as it appeared to amuse Tracy. "I'll give it to you. You always come up with the most wonderful ideas for desserts and you know how to give them an up-dated touch."

"I try, boss," Tracy said.

"We've got six ounce filets on hand, so why don't we do a surf and turf with beef teriyaki and shrimp? To vary it a little, we'll stir fry the shrimp and add a fresh pineapple and mango salsa next to it on the plate. It's unusual, but I think it will work."

"Sounds good to me and I'm seeing a garnish on top of the salsa and shrimp—just a few thin slices of pickled ginger. What should we do with the Chilean sea bass?" Tracy asked.

"I thought we'd pan sear it, finish it off in the oven and serve it with the asparagus and a side of Yukon gold fingerling potatoes. We'll arrange everything on a citrus and white wine reduction sauce. The sauce will complement every element of the dish."

"That sounds absolutely divine—simple but elegant."

"Why don't you ask Jimmy to make seafood bisque?" Dana suggested.

"Yeah, that's always popular. Are we doing a vegetarian entrée tonight?"

Dana nodded. "Yes, but it's not Asian. I bought leeks and butternut squash for that lasagna you love so much, but this time we're making twice as much because every time we put it on the menu, we run out of it half-way through the evening."

"That's because it's to die for," Tracy pointed out.

Dana bowed from the waist. "Why, thank you. You do flatter me so."

"It's the truth. You're the most talented and creative chef I've ever worked with, not to mention the nicest boss anyone could ever hope to have in this crazy business."

"Stop it before you make me blush." Dana fanned her face with her hand. "I like you, too. Now where do we stand with reservations? Have you checked?"

"We're totally booked again. In fact, we had to turn people away."

"Wow! It's been like that every weekend. I thought it was a fluke the first time it happened, but it looks as if it's going to continue."

Dana's mind drifted off for a moment as she thought about how much her restaurant meant to her and although the odds of making it in the restaurant business after the first year or two were abysmal, she wanted to beat the odds.

"Yeah, it does," Tracy said.

"Has the bread arrived yet?" Dana referred to her standing order of crusty Italian bread from Sarcone's, the best bread bakery in South Philadelphia. If there was one thing Dana hated it was a restaurant that served good food and mediocre bread.

"It should be here soon. If not, I'll call Vinnie and check on it," Tracy assured her. "Didn't you tell me that Karen and Laurie are coming for dinner tonight?"

"Yes, they are. This is the first time I've had a chance to socialize with them since I moved back here. You met them before, remember? That time they came to visit me in Chicago?"

"I remember and I liked them. From the looks of it, things are going to be hopping tonight, but I'll try to come out and say hello to them if I get a chance."

"I'll have to spend time with them, but I won't leave you alone the whole time they're here. That's why I want to get as much prep work done ahead of time as possible. I'll have all the lasagna done and the other specials aren't that complicated to make."

"Not a problem," Tracy said as she went over and poured herself another cup of coffee. "Would you like another cup of coffee, Dana?"

"Please. I need more before we get to work. I was hoping it would just be Karen and Laurie, but Karen called yesterday and told me they're bringing a friend of Laurie's along, another teacher that works with her. I'm not sure I feel like meeting someone new."

"It won't kill you, you know." Tracy turned her head and glanced at Dana as she poured a little milk into her coffee.

"No, I don't suppose it would."

"You say that, but I can see by that look on your face that you're not convinced."

"I'm not. They'd better not be playing matchmaker."

"Relax, will you? It's just dinner and maybe you'll like their friend." Tracy came over and set Dana's cup of coffee on the counter in front of her. "Why don't you make an effort to be more sociable? You need to meet new people."

"Why?" Dana asked.

"Because you're too attractive to hide away in this kitchen for the remainder of your days on earth, that's why. There's more to life than this."

"I know that." Dana picked up her coffee. "Thank you for the coffee and the unsolicited advice." She blew on the hot liquid as she lifted her eyes and focused on Tracy with what she hoped was a stern gaze. "Don't you worry, I'll be sociable." Although it was evident Tracy had her best interests in mind, Dana hoped she would heed her warning and refrain from making any further comments about her personal business.

"I'm not worried, I'm just saying."

Dana changed the subject in a hurry. It made her uncomfortable to talk about her lack of a social life and it embarrassed her even though she had no reason to be embarrassed in front of her very best friend. Over the last year, she'd become more and more withdrawn and she knew it wasn't good, but she wasn't ready to do anything about it. "When Jimmy gets here, we'll have him run over to Claudio's for mozzarella and provolone for the lasagna. I need more Parmigiano Regiano and I want some of those oil-cured black olives. We can always use them. And remind me to tell him to get the ones without pits. I don't want to pay anyone's dentist bills."

"Yes, boss." Tracy performed an exaggerated salute and clicked her heels together.

"I didn't mean to sound abrupt or anything. I just don't want to talk about my social life this morning. It makes me very upset and I don't feel like being upset today."

"That's okay. We don't have to discuss it." Tracy rinsed her cup and set it on the counter near the sink. "I have to run upstairs for a minute. I won't be long and when I get back, I'll get started on the prep work and the desserts."

Tracy made a quick exit through the back door and once she was gone, Dana took time to feast her eyes on her new kitchen. She'd enjoyed this private indulgence at least a hundred times since the workmen had completed the remodeling. Her kitchen contained professional, top-of-the-line appliances and every gadget and piece of equipment a chef could ever want. As she ran her hand over the mirror-like surface of the stainless steel counter in front of her, she caught a glimpse of her contented reflection and smiled at it.

Next, she sauntered over to her custom pot-filling faucet on the wall behind the largest and deepest sink and gave it a little push to the right. After opening each of the doors to the double wall ovens and peering inside, she moseyed over to visit the true love of her life, the professional gas range with its ten burners and immense ovens. With her right hand, she reached up to caress the salamander broiler mounted on the wall next to the gas range.

Three work islands were lined up in the center of the kitchen, one with a cool marble top for working pastry dough, the second with a durable composite stone top and the third with a butcher-block surface. An impressive collection of stainless steel pots and pans dangled from hooks attached to a wrought-iron ceiling rack above the islands.

Dana wondered what had become of her. She was in love with her kitchen, smitten by her sinks and stoves and thrilled by her pots and pans. Just as she began to contemplate what had brought her to this depressing point in her life, Tracy's voice drifted in from behind her, dug its way into her consciousness and yanked her out of her private thoughts.

"Earth to Dana, earth to Dana. Are you drifting in outer space or are you listening for the mother ship to contact you?" Tracy burst into laughter at her own joke.

Dana stared at Tracy until she settled down. "No, I'm telling them to beam you up so they can perform experiments on your cute little body. I told them to start with the anal probe and then work their way up to your brain if they can find it."

"Did you say anal probe? Ooh, baby, that sounds like fun." Tracy laughed even louder.

"You're such a riot." Dana waited again for Tracy to stop laughing. "If you must know, I was admiring my kitchen. I'm pleased with how it turned out." A wave of sadness swept over Dana as she thought about the other dreams that hadn't turned out the way she'd wanted them to and she looked away. When she turned to meet Tracy's eyes she was touched by the unspoken sympathy they held within them. Neither she nor Tracy uttered a word about what had happened to Dana in the past. They'd already talked it all out and there was nothing left to say.

"Your restaurant is perfect, honey and it's a huge success. Remember those reviews we got a month after we opened? They raved about the food, and that one critic said he thought it was the best new restaurant in the city? Remember that?"

"How could I ever forget?" Dana replied.

"Who knows? Maybe we'll end up on the front page of the Sunday Inquirer's food section someday," Tracy went on to say. "Can't you see our picture now? Right here in this kitchen with our arms around each other." Tracy closed her eyes and appeared to zone out as if picturing the article. Then her eyes popped open. "I'm assuming you'd let me be in the picture?"

"Sure I would. I like that fantasy. While we're in fantasy land, here's an even better one. We write a cookbook and it sells millions of copies and then we write a few more cookbooks and make more millions and then they offer us our own cooking show on the food network. Then we put out a line of pots and pans and kitchen gadgets and our own spice blends and sauces and scone mixes and quick breads and...and we'd be filthy rich."

"If you're going to dream, dream big, I always say," Tracy said.

"It could happen, you know." Kidding around with Tracy

helped Dana forgot her past, at least temporarily and that was always a good thing. "It has happened."

"I know, but it's not something you should count on if you live in reality."

"You're always telling me you don't like the word 'should' and too much reality can be so depressing, don't you think?" Dana asked.

Tracy seemed to consider Dana's question before she nodded in agreement. "I hate to cut you off, but we've got tons of work to do and seeing as we don't have to tape a television show today, maybe we could have some breakfast and get started? All this talk about food has made me so hungry."

"That makes two of us. Would a cheese omelet satisfy your hunger?"

"Right about now, anything would," Tracy answered.

As she reached for an omelet pan, Dana caught a glimpse of the guy who delivers the bread coming up to the back door. "The guy's here with the bread."

"That's what I call good timing. Now we can have toast with our omelets."

Chapter
Three

KAREN SWUNG THE front door open before Ridley had a chance to knock on it. She stared at Ridley for a moment with a strange expression that distorted her delicate features and crinkled her intense eyes. "I know what you're thinking, Ridley and no I do not have ESP."

"How do you know what I'm thinking, then?"

"Ah...quick witted as usual, I see. I just happened to be standing near the window and I saw you coming up the steps. Did you have a hard time finding a parking place?"

"Believe it or not, I found one right out front."

"Honest to God? That's unheard of around here, especially on a Saturday night." Karen stuck her head out the door as if she needed to confirm Ridley's claim. "Is there a riot, a fire or some other kind of emergency? Did the city order a mass evacuation?"

"Not that I'm aware of." Karen's remarks made Ridley smile. She enjoyed her friend's straightforward sense of humor. "I hope not, anyway."

"It's a little cooler out this evening, isn't it?"

"A lot cooler, thank God. I'm even starting to detect a hint of fall in the air."

"That may be a bit of a stretch, but it does feel good. So, why are we still standing here in the doorway? Come inside and make yourself comfortable. Naturally, our Laurie's not quite ready yet. You know her. Once she gets in the bathroom, you can't be sure she'll ever come out again. Would you like something to drink while we wait? We've got wine, beer, coke and I think there's a few bottles of iced tea in the fridge."

"No thanks. I'd rather wait until we have dinner." Ridley handed Karen the two bottles of wine she'd brought along. "Laurie told me it's a BYOB so I brought a couple of bottles of wine to take to the restaurant with us."

"That's what I was told." Karen studied the labels. "This is one of our favorite Chardonnays, but of course you know that don't you? That's why you bought it. I'm pretty sure we've never tried this Cabernet. Have you had it before? Is it good?"

"I haven't had it either. The guy in the liquor store recommended it."

Karen set the bottles on the table in the foyer and focused her attention on Ridley. "I'm glad you're going with us tonight. I haven't seen you in weeks. What's new? How was the rest of your summer? Are you happy you transferred to Laurie's school" How do you like working there so far? Karen fired one question after another at Ridley in rapid sequence as she walked with her into the living room.

Ridley held up her hand. "Whoa, slow down, counselor. I'm slow, so you're going to have to let me answer your questions one by one. I can't remember the first one by the time you've asked me the next three. Is this inquisitiveness a genetic trait all you lawyers are born with or do they teach it to you in law school?" Ridley said as she eased into a leather armchair. "It probably does come in handy, I'd imagine, especially during all that questioning."

Karen sat on the sofa. "I'm not a trial lawyer, so I really don't question people per se and you're as bad as Laurie. She's always ragging on me about being a lawyer." Karen feigned displeasure but a suggestion of a smile threatened to give away her true feelings. She pursed her lips as though trying to suppress it. "I'm not fooled by either of you. You're both jealous."

"You can't be serious? Do you really think I'd like to work eighty hours a week, memorize volumes of court cases that are written in what might as well be a foreign language and argue semantics with other lawyers?" Ridley dismissed the notion with her hand. "No thank you, not me. I just couldn't do it."

"It's not for everyone, I'll grant you that and for the record, I only work fifty or sixty hours a week on an average—give or take a few," Karen said. The smile she'd tried to squelch bubbled its way to the surface.

"Do pardon me." Ridley matched Karen's smile and then changed her tone. "I'm sorry about the teasing. All those jokes about lawyers have tainted my thinking. I hope you know how much I admire the work you do for the gay and lesbian community." Karen handled civil rights cases and she had served as a consultant to the school district to develop policies for the protection of LGBTQ students and staff members.

"Thanks for saying that. Now, stop trying to distract me and start answering my questions. I'll repeat them one by one, so you can keep up."

For the next twenty minutes, Ridley answered Karen's questions until she thought Karen's curiosity might have been satisfied. "If you're through with me, I've got a few questions of my own," she said when Karen had nothing left to ask her.

"Fire away."

"First of all, tell me about this chef friend of yours, the one whose restaurant we're going to this evening. I remember when you and Laurie went to Chicago to visit an old friend, but you never told me much about her. Laurie didn't even tell me her name."

"I guess I never had a reason to talk to you about her. Her name's Dana De Marco. We were good friends all through high school and right after we graduated, her parents moved to Chicago and she went with them, of course."

"Dana De Marco. That's a pretty name."

"And she's a pretty girl," Karen added.

"I'm fascinated by the fact that she's a chef. I've never met one and I've always been curious about someone who does that for a living."

"She wanted to be one as far back as I can remember. We kept in touch for a while after she moved away, but then I didn't hear from her anymore until she called me and said she was moving back here to open a restaurant on South Street."

"Have you seen her since she's been back?" Ridley asked.

"She came over once, right after she moved here, but this will be the first time we've had a chance to get together since then."

"I'm anxious to meet her and try her restaurant. Where is it?"

"It's between seventh and eighth on South. It's only been open two mon..."

"Hey you two, what are you talking about? Me?" Laurie rushed up to Karen, put her arm around her and kissed her. "You look nice honey and you smell so good." She let out a moan as she nuzzled her lips into Karen's neck. "Remind me to explore this area more extensively later on, when we're alone."

"You look nice yourself and no, we're not talking about you." Karen kissed Laurie on the cheek. "And I'll remind you if you're still awake. So, are you finally ready to go?"

"I'm as ready as I'll ever be. Give me a minute or two to check out my best friend here before we get going." Laurie hugged Ridley, then stepped back, holding her at arms length. "You've got that sexy, young lesbian thing going for you, but that's hardly newsworthy. That top matches your eyes and with that tan and all..." Laurie shook her head. "God, you have no idea how attractive you are, do you?"

"I don't know what to say. I wasn't aiming for any kind of young lesbian thing. I was just being me," Ridley replied. She knew her close friends found her attractive and she knew other women did because they told her often enough. What mattered most to her was that she be loved for the kind of person she was inside and since Laurie did love her for who she was, both inside and out, she took Laurie's compliments as they were intended.

"We all know how cute she is, Laurie," Karen said, heading for the door. "Now, let's be on our way before we end up being late. You two grab the wine, will you?"

Without further discussion, they strolled one block north and turned west onto South Street. Ridley was the first to break the silence. "I love South Street. I don't think there's another place quite like it in the entire world."

"You don't know that for a fact, do you?" Karen teased. "Have you actually been everywhere in the world?"

"No I haven't, counselor." Ridley glanced at Karen. "What's with you?"

"I'm simply paying you back for picking on me earlier. You know Laurie and I love South Street. That's one of the reasons we live down here, right Laurie?"

"Right, your honor," Laurie said. "I love all the funky shops and ethnic restaurants and it's great people watching. That's one of the best things about it."

"That's what makes it interesting," Ridley said. "I think South Street is one of the city's treasures. It would be hard to find a stranger collection of people gathered together in on place anywhere else that I can think of. Where else would you find people in business suits walking next to gothic teens and new age hippies?"

"And where else would you find stores like these?" Laurie asked.

"They're unique all right, but do you know what I like the most?"

"I don't believe you've ever told me," Laurie said.

"I like the hustle and bustle feel of it," Ridley said. "The way everyone darts around on the streets in every direction and seems to be going somewhere important."

Without responding to what Ridley had said, Laurie stopped in front of one of the stores and stared at the window display. She waved her hand to beckon Ridley and Karen over. "Hey, check out this display of penis shaped pasta. It says penis pasta, right on the boxes."

Ridley leaned in closer, her nose almost touching the window. "They didn't have them in there last week when I went by," she remarked. "I would have noticed that."

"What kind of sauce would you serve on those?" Karen's question sounded so serious, it made Laurie and Ridley laugh. Karen glared at them for a moment and then she joined in the laughter. They took one last look at the window display before Karen said, "Let's keep moving along, girls, we're almost there." She led them along for another block until they reached the corner. "Here we are. This is it."

Ridley paused outside the three story brick building. The name, *Café De Marco*, was painted in gold letters on the large downstairs windows and again on the awning over the front entrance. She followed Karen as she led them inside and listened as Karen told the hostess who they were. The hostess promised to let Dana know they'd arrived and then she handed three menus to a waitress who escorted them to a nicely situated table tucked away in a secluded corner of the main dining room.

"This is really beautiful," Laurie said as she and Karen took their seats.

"I'm not the least bit surprised," Karen remarked. "I'd expect Dana to have exquisite taste." She opened her menu and disappeared behind it.

Ridley scanned the room as she slid into her chair. One wall of exposed brick ran the length of the dining room. The other three walls were a heavily textured plaster, painted in a muted gold and decorated with hand-painted olive branches. Some of the branches followed the ceiling line or climbed the wall seams while others twisted randomly across the walls and reached up onto the ceiling. Brick-red table cloths were draped over black lacquered tables set with sparkling glassware and rich gold napkins. Small bronze lamps suspended by long thin black cables, cast a warm glow over the center of each table. "If the food is as good as the ambience suggests, we're in for a treat," Ridley said as she picked up her menu.

"This is quite a menu. It all sounds so appealing, I don't know what to choose," Laurie said. "Did you see the specials? They sound scrumptious."

"Here she comes now," Karen said. She got to her feet and Laurie did the same.

Ridley got to her feet and watched Dana De Marco as she walked toward them. One glimpse of her in her starched chef's jacket caused Ridley's stomach to dive to the floor where it landed with a resounding thud somewhere in the vicinity of her feet. For several suspended seconds, she wondered if her shaky knees would continue to support her in an upright position. All the other sounds in the room were obliterated by her thundering heartbeat and she felt a warm flush bathe her face and spill down into her neck. Dana was simply adorable. She was about an inch shorter than Ridley with dark chestnut hair and even darker eyes. Why hadn't she prepared herself for the possibility that she might be so good-looking? Karen said she was pretty, but this?

Dana swept Karen into her arms for a big hug and then she hugged Laurie. After greeting the two of them, she focused her attention on Ridley and acknowledged her with a nod. "You must be Karen and Laurie's friend. Karen called and told me you might come along."

"I'm glad I did," Ridley said. She could think of nothing else to say.

Karen took hold of Ridley's arm. "Dana, this is our closest friend, Ridley Kelsen. She and Laurie went to Temple together and I think I already told you she's a teacher." Karen turned to Ridley. "Ridley, I'd like you to meet Dana De Marco."

"I'm so happy you could make it tonight," Dana said. "I hope you enjoy my restaurant. She offered her hand.

Ridley shook hands with Dana and prayed her hand didn't feel damp or cold. She stood dumbfounded with Dana's hand in hers as Dana stared at her with lively, penetrating eyes. "It's a pleasure to meet you and I'm sure I will," Ridley said, surprised that she could speak coherently. She remembered to let go of Dana's hand when she heard Karen's voice.

"You haven't changed that much," Karen said to Dana. "Your hair's a little shorter than you used to wear it. I like it."

"Do you? When I first got here, I got it cut by someone new and she cut it shorter than I wanted. But after it grew in and I got used to it I decided I liked it a little shorter so I kept it that way. It's easier to take care of." Dana reached up and touched her hair.

Dana's eyes captured Ridley's again. "Karen told me that you and Laurie work at the same high school."

"We do. I just started there last week. I'm not new to teaching— I've been a teacher for years. I just left my old school and went to hers." Dana's eyes had a way of taking hold and Ridley had a hard time letting them go. After a brief pause, she said, "We brought wine."

"Great. Let me get someone to take care of those." Dana waved to the hostess who rushed right over as if the Queen of England had summoned her. "Open these bottles of wine, will you please, and put them on ice for my friends?" The hostess bowed slightly, took the bottles from Ridley, and hurried off to take care of them.

"Do you have time to sit and visit with us?" Karen asked Dana.

Dana directed her answer at all three of them. "Not right now. We're really busy and I have to get back to the kitchen. Why don't you go ahead and order? Your waitress will explain any of the dishes on the menu."

"Do you have any recommendations?" Karen asked.

"I highly recommend the butternut squash lasagna if you don't mind eating vegetarian. It's very popular with our customers. We have some nice specials tonight and I'd say go with what appeals to you because I think it's all good. At least I hope so."

"I'm disappointed. I thought you'd spend time with us," Karen said.

Dana took Karen's hand. "I will, I promise. I'll be out later." She squeezed Karen's hand as if to seal her promise and hurried away toward the kitchen. Karen sat down and picked up her menu again.

"I have to go over this. It's going to be tough to choose."

While Karen was absorbed in the menu, Ridley leaned over and hissed in Laurie's ear, "Why didn't you warn me she was so attractive?" It wasn't like Laurie to withhold that kind of information and Ridley wondered why she had. Maybe it didn't cross Laurie's mind that Ridley would think of Dana in any way other than friendship.

Laurie held her menu in front of her face to hide from Karen's watchful eyes and whispered to Ridley. "I didn't know you'd be interested in her and if I recall correctly, you warned me in no uncertain terms to mind my own business, so there." Laurie smirked as if she felt satisfied in an evil way. "So you like what you see, huh?"

"I sure do," Ridley answered. She thought Dana was the most delicious thing on the menu, but she did not share that particular thought with Laurie.

Karen pulled the top of Laurie's menu down. "What are you two whispering about?"

"Nothing," Ridley said firmly as she shot Laurie a warning glance.

"Nothing and we're not whispering," Laurie said with that smirk barely hidden beneath the surface. "We're just talking quietly."

After an hour or more of great food and spirited conversation, they waited as their waitress served dessert. Ridley stared down at the pineapple upside down cake as it was ceremoniously placed in front of her and then she made eye contact with the waitress. "This has been one of the best dinners I've ever had in my whole entire life."

"Thank you and I'll tell the chefs you said so. They always appreciate a compliment." She paused and then added, "I think our chefs are amazing. Our customers rave about the food."

"It's not hard to see why." Karen leaned back in her chair, her hands cradling her distended stomach. "I think I'm going to bust a gut."

"Don't even think of busting anything in here," Dana's smooth voice made an entry as she sneaked up behind Karen. "It would make an awful mess and it would be very bad for business, although we could use the publicity."

"So, exploding in a restaurant would be my ten minutes of fame, huh? Just what I always wanted." Karen groaned. "The Daily News would have a field day with that story."

"Can't you just see the headline?" Laurie asked.

"So, how was everything, ladies?" Dana asked.

Karen answered first. "Everything was outstanding. I had the beef and shrimp special and it was wonderful. The beef was tender and the shrimp were perfectly cooked and I loved the salsa. I cleaned my plate." Karen pointed to the dessert in front of her. "But as you can see, that didn't stop me from having dessert. I couldn't resist that sorbet and those ginger cookies. They were out of this world, by the way."

"You can thank Tracy, my sous-chef and pastry chef. She creates all of our desserts," Dana told them. "I consider her a genius."

"I can see why," Karen replied. "Tell her how much we loved everything."

"I will. She'll be pleased to hear it."

"Your lasagna was out of this world," Ridley said. "I've never tasted anything like it. Dishes like that could turn me into a vegetarian. I also loved my salad."

"Which one did you have?" Dana asked.

"I had the green papaya salad."

"That's an excellent choice. It's one of my personal favorites."

"The papaya reminded me of Jicama in a way. It has a delicate flavor and a nice crunch. Are green papayas just papayas that aren't ripe yet?" Ridley asked.

"No, they're actually another variety of papaya altogether. There are many different papayas and this salad is very common in Thai cuisine."

"I didn't know there was more than one kind." Ridley discovered she enjoyed having Dana's attention. Everything that came out of Dana's mouth fascinated her to no end and she wanted to know everything there was to know about this captivating woman even if it meant learning about every type of papaya on the face of the earth.

Dana broke the connection with Ridley and turned to Laurie. "What about you, Laurie. What did you have?"

"I had the Chilean sea bass. It was really fresh and the sauce was the best sauce I've ever had with fish. Not everyone can cook fish just right but this was flaky and tender. Everything was amazing—the asparagus, the potatoes, all of it. And it all went together."

"Thank you so much. I bought the fish this morning and it was very fresh." Dana pulled the empty chair away from the table and sat next to Ridley. "I'm glad you liked the lasagna."

Ridley got lost in Dana's eyes all over again. "You're an amazing chef." That was all she could come up with. She wanted to say just the right thing. She wanted to sound interesting and intelligent and irresistible, but nothing dazzling came to mind.

Dana saved Ridley by taking over their conversation. "I've loved cooking ever since I can remember. My mother's an accomplished cook and she taught me a lot." Dana paused and smiled as if she'd remembered something amusing from her past. "I think my Mom's classes were tougher than the ones I took in culinary school."

"I know what you mean," Ridley replied, thinking that Dana's smile would melt chocolate. "My mother loves to cook and she has tried to teach me how and I do mean tried. She has a rather extensive collection of cookbooks."

"So does my mother. She has tons of them. Have you ever read a cookbook, I mean aside from the recipes? Some of them are loaded with information about the history and culture of a country or a particular region within a country. You can learn a lot." This time Dana's expression hinted of an underlying shyness. "I guess that tells you something about me."

"It tells me you like to read about travel and food, but I confess, I've never read a cookbook in that way. I barely read any recipes," Ridley said between delectable bites of her pineapple upside down cake. "By the way, this cake is beyond description."

"I'll tell Tracy you said so. Do you do any cooking at all?"

"I can put together a basic meal and grill or roast a thing or two, but that's about the extent of it. I'm much better at eating than I am at cooking. You have a real gift, though. Everything we had tonight was delicious and I love your restaurant. It's so intimate and romantic." Ridley felt her face grow hot. Why did she have to use those words to describe it? With relief, she realized that Dana didn't appear to have any reaction to her choice of words. In fact, she appeared to be more than pleased with the description.

"I'm glad you think so. I put my heart and soul into it."

"I've never known a chef or anyone who owned a restaurant. I'd be fascinated to know what goes on behind the scenes."

"Would you like to come over sometime and see how we do it?" Dana asked.

"Sure. Yes, I would," Ridley answered right away. "I'd love to."

"Are you free a week from tomorrow? We're only open for brunch on Sundays so that would be a good day for you to come over. I'd have more time to talk to you."

"I'm totally free. I mean I don't have any plans on that day." Ridley didn't want to sound overly eager or make Dana think she had nothing to do. She felt so thrown off balance, she had to remind herself to stop blurting things out and to think before she spoke. She had to sound less excited. "What time would you like me to come over?"

"Around one-thirty would be good. We should be winding down by then."

"That's fine with me. Should I just come into the restaurant?"

Dana nodded. "I'll tell the hostess I'm expecting you."

"I can't wait—I mean, that sounds like fun," Ridley said.

Chapter
Four

ALTHOUGH IT FELT like it dragged on forever, the first full week of school finally ground to a halt. On Sunday afternoon, Ridley pulled up outside Café De Marco earlier than scheduled. Once again, she didn't want to appear too eager, so she parked on the street next to the side of the building and waited for fifteen minutes until the dashboard clock read thirty-five minutes past one. Only then did she allow herself to go inside the restaurant.

As Dana had promised, the hostess was expecting her and without delay, she led the way through the dining room and then through a set of double doors into the kitchen. Once inside, she asked Ridley to stand out of the way while she let Dana know she was there.

Ridley had no trouble finding Dana amidst the flurry of kitchen activities. She stood out in her starched white chef's jacket, a pair of baggy black and white checkered pants and black clogs. With each passing day, Ridley had begun to wonder whether she'd been unduly impressed that night she'd first met Dana. A handful of factors could have altered her initial assessment—one glass of wine too many, the excitement of an evening out with friends or even the subdued lighting playing tricks on her senses. But now, with Dana in plain view and cast in the light of day, she realized she hadn't embellished a thing. In fact, Dana was more beautiful and more attractive than she'd even remembered.

While the hostess whispered in Dana's ear, Ridley waited near the door and when Dana turned and dissolved her with her smile, she beamed with delight.

Dana hurried over to her. "Hi. You're here."

"I've been looking forward to this all week," Ridley readily confessed in spite of her resolve to come off as cool and reserved.

"And we've been looking forward to having you," Dana said. Her eyes roamed over Ridley before they settled on her silver bracelet with turquoise stones. "I love your bracelet. Where did you get it?"

Ridley lifted her wrist to afford Dana a closer inspection. "I bought it while I was on vacation in New Mexico a couple of years ago."

"I've never been there. How was it?"

"It was beautiful. The weather was perfect and this may sound strange, but it smelled better than any place I've ever been to. I forgot the names of all of them, but they have these shrubs and trees that fill the air with the most wonderful fragrances. A friend and I went to Albuquerque, Santa Fe, Taos and a few other places in between."

"That sounds like a nice trip. Do you like Mexican food?"

"I love it as long as it isn't too God-awful hot."

"How hot is too hot for you?" Dana asked.

"I don't like to have numb lips and I don't like to have my mouth on fire for a couple of hours. I like it when it just reaches the center of my ears. No hotter than that." Today, Dana's eyes were almost black and the light streaming in from the window brought out the natural sheen of her hair. Ridley's breathing increased as she thought about running her hands through it. "You look busy today."

"Welcome to a restaurant kitchen." Dana said. "We're always busy, but this isn't as bad as usual. Come with me. I want you to meet my sous-chef, Tracy Mathis. She made the desserts you guys had at dinner and the food, too, of course." Dana held Ridley by the arm and led her to the other side of the kitchen.

"Tracy, Ridley's here."

"Ridley Kelsen, nice to meet you," Tracy greeted her. After she wiped her hands on a red dishtowel tucked into the waistband of her pants, Tracy shook Ridley's hand. Her white jacket was the same as Dana's, but her pants were covered in a colorful red and green chili pepper print. She was tall and thin and short tufts of poker-straight brown hair jutted out from a bandana tied around her head, a bandana made of the same chili pepper print as the pants she wore.

"Nice to meet you, too," Ridley said. Ridley noticed that a section of Tracy's hair in the front had been turned white from an accidental dusting of flour or powdered sugar.

"I'm sorry I didn't have time to come out and talk to you guys when you came for dinner on Saturday," Tracy said. "I was too damn busy to leave the kitchen."

"Don't worry about it." An unwelcomed realization ripped its way through Ridley's mind and sent her insides into a knot. This very cute and clearly gay woman must be Dana's girlfriend. How could she have been stupid enough to assume Dana was unattached in the first place? It would be rare for a woman as fine as she was to be single unless it was someone who preferred to play the field and had no interest in settling down with anyone.

"I thought if I stayed in here, Dana would have more time with her friends."

"What on earth does a sous-chef do?" Ridley asked Tracy.

"I supervise the kitchen staff and the daily food preparation. I guess you could call me Dana's right hand woman." Tracy's eyes connected with Dana's and they shared the type of glance shared by two people who knew each other well and cared for each other.

"She sure is, in more ways than one," Dana said.

"How long have you two known each other?" Ridley asked. The fondness between them was palpable and seeing the way they interacted with each other convinced her that they were more than just friends.

"A long time," Dana answered. "We met in college."

"Is that where you both studied the culinary arts?

"Yes," Dana said. "You don't need a formal education to open your own restaurant or to call yourself a chef—something I think is all too obvious when you eat in some places, by the way."

"Boy, you're right about that," Tracy said. "We both thought it was important to learn all the classic cooking techniques. It comes in handy if you want to work in a really good restaurant."

"Or have a really good restaurant," Dana added.

Ridley watched the interchange between the two women with interest. The more Dana talked about being a chef, the more her face brightened and the more exhilarated she became. Her eyes sparkled, her skin glowed and her chef's hat sat on her head at a jaunty angle. Ridley found her enthusiasm quite contagious.

"Tracy's right," Dana said. That education made me a much better chef and learning about restaurant management helped me so much when it came to opening this restaurant."

"I absolutely agree," Tracy said. "And I'm glad I got certified as a pastry chef, too."

Ridley wagged her index finger at Tracy. "That's a wicked thing to be certified in. The pineapple upside down cake I had on Saturday was out of this world." It was easy to see how happy her compliment made Tracy. Her face said it all.

"I'm glad you enjoyed it. I wanted to put a new spin on an old homey dessert."

"You should try her other desserts." Dana patted Tracy on the back, her face brimming with pride. "Every one of them is to die for."

"I'll bet, but what a way to go," Ridley said.

"Death by dessert," Tracy replied. "That's always been my philosophy. You know, life is short, eat dessert first and all that."

"I basically agree with that philosophy, although I try not to indulge too often for the sake of my waistline," Ridley said.

"You don't look like you have a problem with that," Dana said.

"Not so far, but I'd like to keep it that way," Ridley said before steering the conversation in another direction. "Owning a restaurant has to be hard work. I don't know if I could do it."

"It can take over your whole life if you let it," Dana said. "Tracy and I decided we weren't willing to sacrifice everything for this. We're both able to run this place without the other one having to be here if either of us needs to take time off."

Tracy added, "We only serve dinner Tuesday through Saturday and on Sundays, we only do brunch. After brunch is over, we're closed for the rest of the day and we don't stay here and do work either. We really take the evening off."

"We're closed on Mondays," Dana added. "And I don't come down here at all unless I need something from the kitchen."

"Dana's the best boss," Tracy interjected. "I admire her as a chef and for the way she runs her restaurant. Everything we serve is top quality and she cares about what she puts in front of the customers from the soup to the nuts, so to speak."

"I feel strongly that every part of the meal has to be excellent," Dana said. "I won't have it any other way. I hate when a restaurant serves a good main course but has bad side dishes or when they put little or no effort into their salads and desserts."

"Even our bread is the best around," Tracy added. "And Dana's nice to work for. She gets excited sometimes but it doesn't make her irritable or mean. She's nice to everyone."

Dana put her arm around Tracy and drew her in for a side hug. "You're not so bad yourself, you know. How could I do all this without you?"

"Speaking of which...," Tracy said, addressing Ridley. "I'd better get back to work. I hope I see you again, sometime soon."

"Yeah, me too," Ridley said. "It was nice talking to you."

Dana grabbed Ridley's wrist. "Come on, I'll introduce you to the others."

AFTER THE INTRODUCTIONS and a brief tour of the kitchen, Dana left Ridley perched on a stool to observe as she and the other chefs plated their culinary creations in a controlled frenzy of practiced synchronicity. Like twin conductors who had memorized every note of the music and knew every nuance of the melody, Dana and Tracy orchestrated everything that went on in the kitchen and every now and then, one of them handed Ridley a small plate with a sample sized portion of one of the dishes. She tasted puffy apple French toast drizzled with a cinnamon infused cranberry syrup, a small serving of moist and creamy scrambled eggs garnished with herbs and goat cheese and accompanied by the most delicious hash browns she'd ever eaten.

"No more after this," Ridley said when Dana handed her a small pecan pancake topped with hot maple syrup and a pinch of orange zest. "Everything is delicious and I want to try it all, but I'm afraid I can't eat anymore."

"That means you'll have to come again," Dana said.

"I'd love to. The food is fantastic, but I'd come here just for the smells." The kitchen was permeated with the most wonderful sweet and savory aromas and every one of them made Ridley's mouth water. She could identify onions, garlic and peppers sautéing in butter and the salty smokiness of bacon. Now and then, little scented pockets of air floated by her carrying spicy scents like rosemary, thyme and nutmeg or sweet smells like apples caramelizing in brown sugar and butter. No matter what smells drifted by Ridley's nose, the essence of lemons, oranges and cinnamon were always present and she wondered if they'd become permanently imbedded in the kitchen's walls and counters.

Before long, the last customers were served and brunch was over. Dana removed her apron and hung it over a hook on the wall. After she washed and dried her hands, she said goodbye to Tracy and the kitchen staff and came over to Ridley. "Are you in a hurry to get somewhere?"

"No. I don't have to be anywhere," Ridley replied.

"Why don't you come upstairs and see where I live?"

"I'd love to." Ridley waved her farewell to Tracy and followed Dana through the back door and up a flight of stairs to the second floor apartment. "Laurie and Karen never told me you lived on top of your restaurant. I had no idea where you lived."

"It's very convenient and I love that I don't have to drive to work." Dana kicked off her clogs on a mat near the front door and pointed to the sofa. "Why don't you sit down? Would you like something to drink? I'm going to have some iced tea."

Ridley sat on one end of the sofa. "That sounds good to me."

Dana returned with two glasses of iced tea. She handed one to Ridley and then she sat down on the opposite end of the sofa and drank half of hers. "That's so refreshing. I didn't realize how thirsty I was." She propped her feet up on the coffee table. "It feels good to get off my feet. You have to stand all day in my line of work."

"Your place is nice. I love the wall color."

"Thanks. They called it "solitude" and I thought it was cool and soothing. The painters just finished last week. I bought more furniture than this, but it won't be delivered until the middle of next week and I'm still not finished unpacking some of my things."

"That takes time. Are you renting this building?"

"Believe it or not, I own it thanks to my more than generous father. He told me he considers it my early inheritance." Dana glowed as she spoke of her father. "I wouldn't have any of this if it weren't for him. I saved as much as I could, but no matter how much I put aside, it wouldn't have been enough to get this restaurant started, not without taking out a huge loan. I still had to borrow money, but it was a loan I can easily pay off."

"Aren't you the lucky one?"

"I am. My dad's a great guy."

"He must be awfully proud of you." Ridley thought of her own father and wondered if he would have been proud of her if he were still alive.

"He is. He's told me so more than once. He's banking on the fact that I'll be successful and he said he wanted to help me now so he could see how his money was being spent. I think he was joking about that last part."

"I'm sure he was, but what he said makes a lot of sense," Ridley said.

"I agree. He paid for most of the restaurant renovations and he and my mother got a huge kick out of helping me design and decorate it. That allowed me to use my own money to fix up my apartment and get new furniture."

"Well, everything came out great. It's all very nice."

"Thanks. Tracy and I love it. She lives here too."

"Oh...I didn't know." Ridley nearly choked as her last swallow of iced tea started heading down the wrong pipe. That clinched it. They must be a couple. Ridley couldn't help but be bowled over by her rotten luck. "It sounds like you have great parents," she said in an attempt to conceal her real reaction.

"I do. My father insisted on helping me and he had the money, so I decided, as his devoted and loving daughter, that I couldn't deny him something that would bring him so much pleasure. It was the least I could do, don't you agree?"

"Absolutely, and I think that was mighty big of you." Ridley extended her arm out so she could click the rim of her iced tea glass against Dana's.

"So, Karen said you were a teacher, but she didn't tell me what you teach."

"I teach physical education, but I'm not just an old-fashioned gym teacher. I teach health education classes and I'm going to coach the girl's varsity softball team at my new school. I've also coached volleyball in the past and track and field."

"No wonder you look so physically fit."

"I've always been physically active since I was a kid. I used to play softball and volleyball in college and I competed in track and field in high school."

Dana's cheeks looked as if they had rouge on them. "I never played competitive sports. I run three or four times a week, but I don't have time for much else."

"It must be hard to watch what you eat when you're a chef."

Dana had a nice trim body with feminine curves in all the right places and no matter what she did or didn't do to stay fit, Ridley thought she was fine just the way she was.

"Sometimes it is." Dana shrugged. "I love to eat, but Tracy and I don't eat a lot of the rich foods we serve in the restaurant and we rarely have dessert, or if we do it's just a small portion. We have to taste what we make, but we only eat a small amount and most nights, we just have a salad for dinner."

"I was pretty sure you couldn't eat like that every night."

"Good heavens, no. We consider it our mission in life to make other people overeat."

"And pay handsomely for it," Ridley added.

Dana raised her glass. "I'll drink to the pay handsomely part."

Ridley finished her iced tea, set the glass on the coffee table and got up. "I should be going. You must be tired and I've taken up enough of your time."

Dana stood. "I enjoyed having you here and talking to you."

"I enjoyed being here. Thanks for inviting me." Ridley paused. "I just had an idea. How would you feel about coming to my school to talk to the students about healthy eating? Maybe you could show them a few simple recipes they can make at home, something healthier than cheese fries and pop tarts. I know they'd like meeting a chef and it wouldn't hurt them to hear about some of the job opportunities in the food industry."

"I don't know. I've never done anything like that."

"You'd probably enjoy it. The kids are a trip." Ridley wondered where this insane idea had come from and why she was pushing it, especially now that she suspected Dana and Tracy were together. All she was certain of was that she wanted to see Dana again and she was attracted to her. In the back of her mind the voice of reason warned her she might be heading into dangerous territory, but she chose not to listen. She could handle it.

Dana took a while to consider Ridley's proposal. "Okay, why not? They used to make us teach classes and do demonstrations in culinary school, so I'm sure I can do the same thing with high school students. When would you like to do this?"

"Let's see..." In her head, Ridley checked her schedule and did a quick review of her lesson plans for the next two weeks. "What about Monday, two weeks from tomorrow? I have two afternoon classes back to back and we could do both."

"Stay here while I get my calendar." Dana went into another room and came back with a leather appointment book and a pen. She opened it and flipped the pages until she came to the day in question. "I don't have anything scheduled that day, so I'll write it in. Just call me if it doesn't work out." Dana pulled one of her business cards out of a pocket in the front of the book. "My e-mail address and the phone number at the restaurant are on this card." She flipped the business card over and wrote on it. "And my cell phone number is on the back."

Ridley took the card and slid it into her pocket. "Do you have a piece of paper and a pen? I should give you my numbers in case you need them."

Dana tore a piece of paper from a pad in her appointment book and handed it to Ridley along with the pen and as she did, her fingers brushed against Ridley's.

Dana's touch triggered a fluttering in Ridley's stomach and she had to keep her hand from shaking as she wrote on the paper and gave it back to Dana. "Here's my cell phone number, my home number and my work number in case you need to reach me. I have a direct line in the gym office and voice mail, so leave a message if I'm not there and I'll call you back. I'll have to make sure this is okay with my principal but I don't see why it wouldn't be. Consider it a date—well, you know what I mean." Ridley cleared her throat and shook her head, hoping to clear it as well. "I'll call you next week to discuss the details. Thanks for a great afternoon."

"I'll talk to you later. Be careful driving home."

RIDLEY WEIGHED THE pros and cons of stopping at Karen and Laurie's house on the way home to pump them for more information about Dana, but in the end, she resisted the temptation and drove straight home. Knowing them, they'd see right through her no matter how subtle she tried to be. She'd find out soon enough about Dana and Tracy now that they were all going to be friends and she could not bear to have her suspicions confirmed by Laurie and Karen. Having to endure their sympathy would be more than she could bear.

The attraction Ridley felt for Dana had flared up something fierce and now it burned deep inside of her like a chronic inflammation for which she could find no relief. For her sake and just in case it was all for nothing in the end, she decided it would be wise to keep her feelings to herself, at least for the time being.

AFTER RIDLEY WENT home, Dana felt too restless to stay in her apartment, so she went down to the kitchen to see if Tracy needed any help.

"How's it going down here?" she asked Tracy when she came through the door.

"I'm just putting these last few pans away and wiping the counters."

"Did everyone else leave?"

"They ran out of here like the place was on fire." Tracy stretched her arm up and hung a sauté pan on the pot rack above her head. "I like Ridley a lot, don't you?"

"Yeah, I suppose. She's okay."

Tracy stopped what she was doing and faced Dana head on. "She's okay? Are you out of your mind? She's totally cute as in the cutest thing I've seen in a hell of a long time. Did you check out those sparkling green eyes and that dark auburn hair? I don't think I need to point out that she also has a fabulous body, do I?"

"No. I did notice that, thank you very much." Dana stuck her tongue out.

"I'll choose to overlook that childish gesture," Tracy said. "She is gay, isn't she? I'm sure she is because she hangs out with Laurie and Karen and they are."

"That doesn't mean she is and besides, I don't know and I really don't care. I'm certain if she and I continue to be friends, there'll be no way I can avoid finding out all about her sexual preferences at some point." Dana picked up the dripping stock pot on the counter, dried it and set it on one of the back burners.

"Well, I'd like to know." Tracy said as she started wiping down the counters

"Why? Are you interested in her?"

"No, I'm not. I'm just interested in her on your behalf."

"Well then, feel free to ask her the next time you see her and if I happen to find out in the meantime, I'll report my findings to you immediately." Dana enunciated each word.

Tracy put her hands on her hips. "You don't have to get snippy about it."

Dana went over to the sink and wet a dish towel. "I'm sorry. She's definitely cute I'll grant you that, but she's nothing more than a potential friend. That's it, period. End of story."

"Hopefully it's not the end of your story."

"Listen to me, Tracy, I'm happy with my life the way it is and I don't want to mess it up." Dana shook the dish towel out and busied herself by wiping the counter tops with it. She wasn't sure why Tracy's comments had made her feel this irritated. Couldn't she meet an attractive woman and not have to think of her as a potential love interest? Why was it so important to Tracy that she have a girlfriend?

"I already wiped all that."

"You missed a few spots." Dana whipped her arm around so vigorously she knocked a large stainless steel bowl off the counter. She winced and covered her ears as it crashed onto the tile floor and shook noisily to a standstill like a renegade cymbal. She scowled as she bent over to retrieve it, embarrassed by her own actions. "If she is gay, you can bet she's not single. Someone like her would never be without a girlfriend."

"And she didn't bring this girlfriend with her last Saturday night?"

"Maybe she was out of town," Dana proposed. "Or maybe she had to work or she was sick or taking care of her ailing grandmother."

"Try this. Maybe she couldn't make it because she doesn't exist. I hate to break it to you, but I got the impression Ridley was interested in you. It was obvious to me."

"That's ridiculous." Dana felt her face heat up and she hoped Tracy wouldn't notice she was blushing. "She was just being friendly."

"Then why couldn't she take her eyes off of you?"

"So she's good at making eye contact. So what?"

"Did you see how nervous she was, how she kept fidgeting with her hands and stumbling over her words? I swear she was blushing just like you are now," Tracy pointed out.

"I'm not blushing, it's just warm in here and I think you're seeing things."

"You think so? Tell you what we'll do. Let's call Karen and Laurie and find out if Ridley said anything to them about you or about coming here today."

"We won't do any such thing. You're imagination's running wild, Tracy, and even if you're right, I'm not ready to get involved with anyone. I may never be."

"Dana, you can't avoid romance forever. It's not normal or healthy. I know you were hurt by Sarah, but don't you think it's time to move on? Don't you ever feel lonely? And what about being close to someone and being physically intimate? It's been a while, hasn't it?"

"You know it has, not that it's any of your business. I think the need for sex is highly over-rated. I do get lonely at times, but who doesn't? I'm busy, I have friends and I've come to realize that I'm better off alone. Relationships are nothing but trouble." Dana's words rang false in her own ears but she needed to hide in the safety of them and she'd recited those words to herself so many times she'd almost come to believe them. Right now, what she needed was to convince Tracy that they were true.

"You want to be alone forever? That's absurd. You're not that kind of person."

"I'm touched by your concern, really I am, and I love you for it, but you're wrong. I am that kind of person. I'm not unhappy and I have everything I've ever dreamed of. What more could I possibly want?"

Tracy shrugged her shoulders. "I have no answer for that. You obviously need to believe your own distorted logic. I just happen to know we all need love and I'm pretty sure that includes you. I'm convinced it's what life is all about and the longer I live, the more I think it's the only thing that really matters."

"I've heard this all before, but it's not for me. I can do without love." Dana rubbed her eyes to ward off the beginnings of a headache. "Once was more than enough. I don't feel like setting myself up for that kind of misery ever again." She stopped rubbing her eyes and blinked several times to bring them into focus. "What's wrong with being alone? Do we all have to be with someone in order to be all right?"

"Nobody has to be with anybody if you come right down to it. It's not about that."

"Tracy, please give me a break. For some reason, I feel like an emotional train wreck today and talking about this is upsetting me even more."

Tracy walked over to Dana and took her hand. "I'm sorry, I didn't know you felt that way. What's bothering you?"

"I wish I knew." She squeezed Tracy's hand.

"I'm here if you need me. I hope you know that."

"I do." Tears welled up in Dana's eyes.

"Hey, don't cry. I didn't mean to upset you. Sometimes I have a big fat know-it-all mouth." Tracy draped her arms around Dana's shoulders. "Why don't you go upstairs and do something nice for yourself to take your mind off things. You don't have to do anything for the rest of the day but hang out and take it easy."

"I think I will. Maybe I'll unpack a few more boxes." Dana wiped her eyes on her sleeve. "I think I'll call my mother and talk to her and then I'll give my sister a call. Do you want to come down later and watch a movie? I'll make popcorn."

"Sounds like fun, but I can't tonight. I have a date."

"You have a date? Why didn't you tell me?" Dana asked.

"I haven't had a chance," Tracy told her.

"Who is she? Where did you meet her?"

"Her name's Erika. She owns a little shop on the corner of Ninth and South. I went in there to buy some candles and incense last week and we got to talking. The next thing I knew, she was flirting with me and she was so cute, I flirted right back."

"Is it that great smelling shop with all the new-age stuff? The one that has the jewelry and crystals and the yoga classes upstairs?"

"That's the one and she's the yoga instructor," Tracy confirmed.

"Get out of here."

"It's the truth." Mischief took over Tracy's face. "I've heard they have amazing flexibility and can twist their bodies into some very interesting positions."

"Shame on you, Tracy, you are so bad." Dana tried not to smile.

"That's not bad, it's good." Tracy made no attempt to hide her wicked thoughts.

"I see your point and I want to hear all about it tomorrow — well, maybe not all about it. You can keep the sordid details to yourself."

"It's our first date, so there probably won't be any sordid details to report. However, if things should happen to go that way, I'll give you the R-rated version, okay?"

"Make it PG, will you? I don't want to get too worked up."

"Will you be all right this evening?" All the mischief vanished from Tracy's face.

"Don't worry about me, I'll be fine. You go out and have a good time."

"I will." Tracy glanced at the clock. "I've got to get going. Take it easy and be good to yourself, will you? I'll see you tomorrow."

Dana finished up in the kitchen, locked the door and climbed the stairs to her apartment. Snippets of her conversation with Tracy echoed in her mind and she kept going back to Tracy's suggestion that Ridley Kelsen was interested in her. She felt drawn to Ridley, a fact she had not shared with Tracy, and at the same time she wanted to run in the other direction as fast as she could. She hardly knew her and yet Ridley disturbed her in a way she didn't understand.

With a heavy heart, she unlocked the door to her apartment, kicked her clogs aside and went into the bathroom to take medicine to stem the headache gathering strength behind her eyes. As she swallowed the pills, she thought about the things Tracy had said about her being alone and needing someone in her life. Some of it made sense, but she didn't want her life to change, not when things were so easy and uncomplicated. She had her restaurant, her best friend was with her and she felt good. For the time being, she wanted things to stay the way they were. Her life made her feel secure and that was something she could count on. "I really don't need anyone. I really don't," she said to her reflection in the medicine cabinet mirror.

After washing her face, she went into the bedroom and climbed onto the bed. With her eyes closed, she thought about Sarah and their past and how much it would wear her down if she let it. She thought about how her dreams had evaporated into thin air in a single afternoon and how her plans had been destroyed by someone she'd loved and trusted, someone who had claimed to love her. The pain of the whole dirty mess had healed long ago, but she'd been left with something far worse. She'd been left with a pervasive sense of disillusionment.

Chapter Five

TWO WEEKS LATER on Sunday evening, Ridley climbed the steps to Laurie's front door. Last week, Laurie had called and invited her to a surprise birthday party for Karen. Ridley had promised to take her mother and aunt somewhere during the day, but as soon as she got back to the city, she showered and changed and left for the party. When she got to Laurie's house, she was relieved to discover that she was only half an hour late.

Laurie's cheeks were red and she sounded breathless as she opened the door. "I'm glad you made it." After Ridley stepped inside, Laurie shut the door and gave her the once over. "You should not be allowed to be out in public like that. It's not fair to the rest of us."

"Since I know you meant that as a compliment, I'll simply say thank you. How's the party going so far? Did you manage to surprise Karen?"

Laurie nodded. "Can you imagine that? I actually pulled it off for once."

"That's amazing. How did you fool her and how did you get her out of the house?"

"I took Karen out to dinner last night to celebrate her birthday, so she thought that was the end of it. Then I asked one of her friends to call this morning and beg her to go shopping to help her pick out a gift for her girlfriend. We weren't doing anything special and I pretended I had tests to grade, so Karen said she'd go. I don't think she suspected a thing. They got back about twenty minutes ago and by that time everyone was here except for you."

"You'll have to come up with a new trick next time you want to give her a surprise party. She'll never fall for that one a second time. I meant to ask you this when you called me, but I forgot. Why did you decide to have the party tonight when yesterday was her birthday? Wouldn't you rather have had it on Saturday?"

"Yeah, I would have, but I knew Dana and Tracy could only come if I had it on Sunday and I thought Karen would like it if they were here. Also, Dana offered to make something special for dinner and Tracy said she'd make the cake. All I had to do was buy salad stuff and provide the drinks and munchies. I couldn't turn that down."

"I thought maybe it had something to do with them."

"Come into the living room," Laurie said.

Ridley put her hand on Laurie's arm to hold her there. "Wait a minute. I want to ask you a question before we join the others. Did you get a chance to talk to Karen about our annual trip to the shore for Columbus Day weekend? Will she be able to get that Monday off? I promised my mother I'd call her tomorrow and let her know if we're going."

"Yes, I talked to her and everything is set. We wouldn't miss it for the world. Karen wanted me to ask you if it would be okay if we came down on Saturday morning instead of on Friday evening. She gets home late on Fridays and she's usually tired and grumpy and by the time we get down there, she'll be a mess. I think she'd feel a lot better if she had a good night's sleep."

"That's not a problem. I'm leaving right after work on Friday, but you guys can get there when you get there. Don't take too long, though. I want us to have a lot of time together."

"We'll be there by noon. Once she gets some sleep, she'll be fine. Now let's go in and join the others. Can I get you a beer or a glass of wine?"

"I'd like a beer." Ridley followed Laurie into the living room.

"Why don't you go say hello to the birthday girl? She's talking to some friends from her law firm." Laurie pointed to a group of people gathered near the fireplace. "I'll get you a beer and bring it out to you."

Ridley went to Karen and tapped her on the shoulder. "Happy Birthday, Karen."

Karen excused herself from the group and stood aside with Ridley. She hugged her and kissed her on the cheek. "Hey you, I'm glad you're here. Thanks for the nice card and the gift certificate. They came in the mail yesterday."

"You're welcome. I know you love book stores and I thought with a gift certificate, you could pick out your own books or get whatever you want."

"I can't think of a better gift for me. I love spending money in a book store and I love it even more when it's someone else's money." Karen hugged Ridley a second time. "I'll introduce you to anyone you don't know later on, but before we do that I want you to come with me. Tracy and Dana are in the kitchen and they told me to let them know the minute you got here."

In the kitchen, the first thing Ridley noticed was Tracy leaning against the counter with her arm draped across the shoulders of an unknown woman. Judging by the glances they exchanged and the way they touched, they had to be more than friends and that made Ridley so ecstatic she felt like jumping for joy. Dana and Tracy weren't a couple after all and she couldn't have been happier if someone had just told her she'd won the lottery.

Mouth-watering smells filled the kitchen and Ridley's eyes followed her nose to the stove where she saw Dana just standing there smiling at her. The sight of her made Ridley's heart dance inside her chest. It twirled and dipped and beat to a measure as old as time itself.

"I'm going back in the living room to talk to some of my friends from work," Karen said to Ridley. "Have a good time and I'll see you in a little while."

"Okay. I'll be out later." When Karen left, Ridley approached Tracy and the new girl. "Hi, Tracy, nice to see you again. Who's your friend?"

"Nice to see you, too and I'd like you to meet my date, Erika. Erika this is Ridley. She's the teacher I told you about, Karen and Laurie's friend."

"Hi," Erika offered her hand. "I heard about you."

Ridley shook Erika's hand. "Pleased to meet you."

"Well, thanks. I'm pleased to meet you, too. Tracy told me you came to visit her and Dana at the restaurant a couple of weeks ago. That must have been interesting."

"I enjoyed it," Ridley said. "I'd never been in a restaurant kitchen and I got to watch them in action. It was really something. Have you tried the restaurant yet?"

"Yes, I went to dinner there last week and I loved it." Erika glanced at Tracy and kissed her on the cheek. Anyone could see she was totally infatuated.

Ridley noticed a huge sheet cake on the kitchen table. "Laurie told me you were making Karen's birthday cake," she said to Tracy. "I can't wait to try it."

"Go over and see how I decorated it," Tracy said.

Ridley went to the table and checked out the cake. Tracy had used brightly colored icings to paint a likeness of Karen and Laurie's row house on the cake. The windows were tinted with yellow and white icings to suggest that warm lights were coming from inside the house and their street number was on the front door. Next to the house she wrote, Happy Birthday, Karen.

"It's a work of art," Ridley remarked. "Loaded with calories, too, I'll bet,"

"No need to worry. It's a carrot cake, so it's full of veggies and therefore, healthy. I also used a secret technique they taught us in chef's school that removes all the calories. It's highly technical, but it's worth it in the end, or should I say in the derriere?"

"Honestly, Tracy. Do you think Ridley's dumb enough to believe that?" Dana chimed in from her private corner of the kitchen. "Knowing the way you make cakes, it would be easier to believe that you used a secret technique to get even more calories into it."

"I'm deeply wounded that you would say such a thing about me, Dana." Tracy clutched at her chest and pretended to swoon while the rest of them laughed at her antics. "I know Ridley's not dumb and I would never do anything like that."

After the merriment died down, Ridley moved closer to Dana who was bending over in front of the oven checking on two large foil covered rectangular pans. Dana lifted a corner of the foil with a fork and dipped a finger inside and then she began to put what appeared to be several big loaves of garlic bread wrapped in foil into the oven alongside the pans."What's that you're making?" Ridley asked her.

"Chicken cutlets baked in a homemade blush sauce with thin slices of prosciutto and fresh mozzarella on top. I made it for Karen once, a long time ago, and she loved it so much she never forgot it, so I told Laurie I'd make it as a birthday gift. I made it earlier at the restaurant and now all I have to do is heat it up with the garlic bread."

"It smells luscious." Ridley inhaled deeply. "I can't wait to try it."

"I hope you like it," Dana said as she closed the oven door. After she straightened up and laid the potholders on the stove, she turned and met Ridley's eyes. "I'm happy to see you."

"Are you?" Ridley studied Dana's face. Standing this close to Dana made her feel giddy and weak in the knees. Those fiery brown eyes held on to hers and no matter how hard she tried, she couldn't tear her eyes away.

"Yes."

"That's good, because I'm happy to see you." Ridley's gaze shifted to Dana's mouth and she found herself fantasizing about what it would be like to kiss her. She felt it down to her toes as if her lips were actually touching Dana's and she shoved that thought out of her mind. What good would it do to think along those lines or to torture her mind with wild desires? Just because Dana wasn't involved with Tracy didn't mean she was interested in her. Ridley tried to focus her eyes on something else. "How's your apartment coming along?" she asked Dana, her heart racing and her breathing reduced to short little puffs.

Dana appeared to be unaware of Ridley's discomfort. "I got a lot done this week. They delivered my furniture on Wednesday and I finished unpacking the rest of my things. Now, it feels more like my home."

"My place is finished too, Ridley," Tracy called out. She must have been listening to their conversation. "In case you're even remotely interested. If you ever feel like climbing all the way up those stairs, you can come in and visit me."

"That's Tracy's indirect way of complaining about living on the third floor, Ridley." Dana gave Tracy a penetrating stare. "You need to climb up and down those stairs, because you're always sampling your pastries and licking the icing spoons."

"Don't listen to her." Tracy stuck her tongue out at Dana. "You're a lousy traitor. Here I thought you were my best friend. You ought to decrease my rent or increase my salary, or both, for forcing me to live all the way up on the third floor."

Dana waved her finger back and forth and shook her head to the same rhythm. "Your rent's as low as it's going to get and your salary's as high as it's going to get and that's that, at least for now. A barely detectable smirk peeked out from Dana's pseudo-serious facade.

Tracy folded her arms across her chest. "I don't know what to say."

"There's nothing you can say. I guess you're stuck with me." This time, Dana let everyone see without a doubt that her exchange with Tracy was all in fun.

"Yeah, I guess we're both stuck with each other," Tracy said. She kissed her palm and blew it in Dana's direction.

LESS THAN AN hour later, Dana and Tracy arranged the chicken dish, the garlic bread and a huge salad buffet style on the dining room table. The guests ate wherever they could find a spot and after everyone finished, Laurie and Tracy carried the cake into the dining room and led the others in a loud and discordant rendition of *Happy Birthday*. After Karen blew out the candles and made a wish, Tracy plucked the candle stubs out of the icing and cut slices of the cake onto small paper plates.

After dinner, Ridley talked to some people she knew and mingled with the other guests, but no matter where she was, her eyes roamed the area hoping to get a glimpse of Dana. Whatever it was that drew her to Dana was strong and something new to her. A few times, Dana happened to drift through her field of vision and when she did, Ridley took pleasure in the curve of her hip, the soft swell of her breasts, the sheen of her hair and the radiance of her skin.

"Are you having a good time?"

Ridley jumped at the intrusion and discovered that Laurie had sneaked up beside her. "Sorry, I was deep in thought. Yes, I'm having a great time. You really outdid yourself with this party."

"Karen said the same thing," Laurie said. "I couldn't help but notice the way you've been watching Dana. What's up with that?"

"Nothing's up. She's really attractive, that's all."

"Uh-huh, I also noticed that. In fact, I think she's quite special."

Ridley turned to her friend. "Laurie? Can I ask you something?"

"Sure. Go ahead."

"I assumed Dana was a lesbian and I assumed she was with Tracy, but now I see Tracy brought a date with her tonight and I wondered if I was wrong about Dana. Is she a lesbian?"

"Damn, I knew it! You're interested in her!" Laurie squealed quietly as she pumped her right fist a few times in front of her. "This is very good news."

Ridley pulled Laurie into a corner. "Will you please lower your voice?" she demanded in a hushed tone. "And do you have to squeal all the time?"

"You know I always squeal when I'm excited. I can't help it."

"Never mind that, just answer my question. Is she?"

"Is she what?" Laurie asked.

"Come on, Laurie, for God's sake!"

"I'm sorry. You're such fun to tease. Yeah, she is and she's available, too."

"I didn't ask you if she was available. I'm just curious about her, that's all."

"Uh-huh. If you say so," Laurie said.

"Well, I do say so and you're making too much of a simple question. Please don't mention this to anyone, especially Karen. I don't need anyone else to know I asked. "

"I won't. I promise," Laurie said as she held her right hand up.

"Thanks. I'm going to get another beer," Ridley said. "I'll catch you later."

Ridley hurried into the kitchen to get away from Laurie and that 'I know more than you're telling me' message on her face. Laurie's imagination was probably already running wild with the prospect of her being with Dana and all it would mean to their close-knit group of friends. The door that led out to the backyard was cracked open and through the screen, Ridley saw Dana on the back deck with her head tilted toward the sky. She grabbed two beers and quietly stepped onto the deck. "I thought you might need one of these after standing in front of a hot stove for so long." She handed Dana one of the beers. "Do you need a glass?"

"No, this is fine." Dana took a long swig. "Thanks."

"Care to share your thoughts?"

Dana turned to face Ridley. "Trust me, you wouldn't be interested in my thoughts." She tapped her head with the neck of her beer bottle. "Nothing much in here but a pile of worn-out memories and a few cobwebs, I'm afraid."

"But you're wrong. I would be interested."

"Just the same, it's not worth the effort." Dana glanced up at the sky again.

Because she sensed Dana was uneasy, Ridley moved on to a less personal subject matter. "That chicken dish you made for Karen was delicious."

"Thanks. I made that dish for Karen a long time ago when she and Laurie visited me in Chicago and she always remembered it so Laurie asked me to make it for the party. What did you think of Tracy's cake?"

"That was the best carrot cake I've ever had."

"She's the best. She never runs out of ideas." Dana was quiet again.

After a few awkward moments, Ridley said, "The stars are bright tonight, aren't they? You can't usually see them this well in the city because of all the lights. I love when the sky is that deep blue-black and the trees look as if someone sketched them in black ink."

Dana met Ridley's eyes in the darkness. "I love it, too. The universe is so timeless and it reminds us of how insignificant we all are in our little world, living our little lives. It kind of makes you put your problems in the proper perspective, doesn't it?"

Ridley dove without hesitation into the depths of Dana's eyes. A sadness lived in them and she got the impression that Dana was holding back the way people do when they're protecting themselves from being hurt. "What problems do you have?" she asked even though she knew Dana would never tell her.

It took Dana a fraction too long to answer. "I was speaking in generalities and not about myself. I don't have any problems."

"I thought..." Ridley wanted to know all about Dana and she wanted to be there for her if she was hurting, but they didn't know each other that well and it was wiser not to push. "Never mind. How are things at the restaurant?"

"Great. Business only gets better and better."

"I'm glad to hear it," Ridley said. This new topic had visibly lightened Dana's mood. Small crinkles flashed like flint sparks on both sides of Dana's mouth as she talked and when she smiled they burst into a dazzling display of dimples. Blindsided by a surge of desire, Ridley gripped the deck railing to stabilize herself. Her heart hammered in her chest and her legs felt unsteady. She'd never experienced this strong an attraction to anyone.

Ridley's hand rested on the railing close to Dana's. A strange energy made Ridley's fingers tingle and a force like a powerful magnet made her afraid her fingers would move without her permission and touch Dana's hand. She found it hard to breathe.

"Are you all right?" Dana asked.

Ridley's next words came out like a whisper. "Dana, I..." It took all the strength she possessed not to reach out and touch Dana. As if the railing had suddenly burst into flames, she yanked her hand away and stuffed it deep into the pocket of her jeans. She was in deep trouble.

"What did you want to say?" Dana asked.

"You're still coming to my school tomorrow, aren't you?"

"Of course I am. What time should I get there and where should I go?"

"Do you know where the school is?" Ridley asked.

"Yes, I've been by it many times."

"Why don't you come around twelve-thirty? Go to the main office. It's on the right, just inside the front entrance on 10th Street. I'll tell the secretaries to call me when you get there." Ridley was relieved to concentrate on something other than her physical response to Dana. "I'll come down and take you to the classroom so we can get set up. You'll be talking to my last two classes from one to one-fifty and from two to two-fifty. Is that okay?"

"That's fine. Where should I park?" Dana asked.

"You can park on any of the streets around the school or in the schoolyard if you can find an empty space. It's all legal parking."

"I came up with some ideas, but I'll let you be surprised."

"Do you need me to bring anything or pick anything up?" Ridley asked.

"No. Leave everything to me. I'm bringing one of my other chefs along. I've never talked to high school students, so I hope I won't be too nervous."

"You'll be fine. There's nothing to be nervous about. It will be informal and the students are going to enjoy it. I guarantee it."

"It sounds like we're all set then." Dana's pronouncement was followed by an awkward gap in the conversation and then she said, "Ridley?"

"Yes?"

"Thank you for asking me to come to your school. I..." Dana paused as if she intended to say something from the heart, but instead she said, "We'd better go in and join the others before we're missed." Dana held the back door open for Ridley.

Ridley went inside with Dana behind her. "I'll see you tomorrow, then?"

"You will. I'm going to go find Karen and Laurie. I've been so busy with Karen's birthday dinner, I haven't had a chance to talk to either one of them. Are you coming?"

"I'll be out in a minute. I need to use the bathroom."

"Okay. See you later." Dana left Ridley in the kitchen.

Ridley closed her eyes and wondered what the hell was happening to her. She wanted to spend more time with Dana, just to talk, just to breathe the same air and occupy the same space. How could she crave being with her this much when they'd only met a few weeks ago?

After she regained her senses, Ridley threw her empty beer bottle in the recycle bin outside the back door and went into the living room to find Laurie and Karen. They were in plain view, but Dana wasn't with them. Worn out and too tired to think about her feelings for Dana, she said her goodbyes, handed out kisses and hugs and went home. With any luck, a good night's sleep and a new tomorrow would bring her some blessed relief from the tempest of emotions she had to contend with every time she was anywhere near Dana De Marco.

Chapter
Six

THE NEXT DAY, during the free prep period Ridley had before her lunch, she and a few student volunteers were working to set up the health classroom for Dana's visit. She leaned against her desk as she gave instructions to the boys who had skipped part of their lunch period to assist her.

"Tyriek and Brian, please get that big folding table in the back and set it up down here in the front. And I want you guys to move the first row of chairs back about three or four feet so they're not real close to the table. Our guests need some room to move around."

Ridley had slept well after she got home from the party and some much-needed emotional distance had restored her to a more normal state. Today she felt confident she could be around Dana without the emotional turmoil she'd experienced while talking to Dana on the deck at Karen's house. Strong attractions were sometimes fleeting and they often fizzled out before they ever amounted to anything. At least that's what she told herself. Besides, Dana hadn't given her any reason to believe she was interested in anything more than being friends.

Just after twelve-thirty, one of the secretaries summoned Ridley to the main office where Dana waited with a young man Ridley recognized as one of the other chefs she'd seen at Café De Marco. They both wore white chef's jackets and black and white checkered pants.

"I'm glad you guys thought to come dressed in your chef's outfits. I forgot to tell you that I wanted you to do that," Ridley told them. She saw they had their names embroidered on their jacket pockets. The only difference in their outfits was that Jimmy wore black sneakers and Dana had on her black clogs.

"We wanted to impress the students," Dana replied. "We even brought chef's hats with us although we don't always wear them when we work."

"You had one on that day I came over to watch you work," Ridley said.

"That was because you were coming and I guess we like to put on a show," Dana said. "You remember Jimmy don't you?"

"I sure do." Ridley offered her hand. "Thanks for coming. I really appreciate it."

"No problem." Jimmy shook Ridley's hand. "I told Dana I'd do this with her because I like helping young people and it sounded like fun."

"I hope it'll be fun for all of us." Ridley glanced at the clock. "We'd better get upstairs and get the classroom set up. The first class starts in twenty-five minutes."

Dana had four large tote bags on the floor by her feet and she lifted two of them. "Do you think you can you carry these other two for me?" she asked Ridley.

"Sure." Ridley picked them up. "You need any help, Jimmy?"

"No thanks, I've got these." Jimmy picked up two large plastic containers he'd set on the office counter and balanced them in his arms.

"What's all this?" Ridley asked as they carried everything to the elevator.

"We brought all the ingredients to make a couple of easy recipes," Dana answered. "We're going to make a fruit salad with a yogurt dressing and a carrot raisin salad. They're both healthy things your students can make at home without too much trouble."

"I think they'll like that," Ridley said. "I know they like fruit and yogurt."

"I brought some utensils and a few unusual kitchen gadgets," Jimmy said. "I thought I'd show them how to use them and I also thought I'd do some carving."

"Jimmy's an artist when it comes to carving fruits and veggies into flowers and birds and any number of things," Dana said. "He thought that would be fun."

"What a great idea," Ridley said. "Thanks a lot, Jimmy."

"That's okay. Maybe I'll let a few students give it a try."

Ridley jumped all over that idea. "Just don't let them cut their fingers off. Our school nurse will kill me. And let me choose the students. I don't want you to get saddled with the trouble makers or the class clowns. They're always the first ones to volunteer."

Jimmy grimaced. "I didn't think of that."

"Don't worry. That's what they pay me for," Ridley told him.

DURING THE CLASSES, Ridley sat in the back of the room under the guise of being able to keep an eye on the students like a good teacher should. As true as that was, she also wanted to sit back and feast her eyes on Dana without being obvious about it. Her position assured her that no one would take notice of the way her eyes followed Dana as she moved around the room.

Dana's physical attributes were pleasing enough, but what drew Ridley to her even more was beyond the physical. Whatever it was, it was far more compelling and it touched her where nothing and no one had touched her before. As she watched Dana and Jimmy entertain the tenth graders, she knew one thing with total conviction. Her feelings for Dana were not going to fade away with time or distance or anything else and this raw aching attraction was not going to ever leave her alone. Not ever.

The class periods flew by and before Ridley knew it, the second session had come to an end. When the dismissal bell rang, the students jumped out of their chairs, seized their belongings and stampeded out of the gym like a herd of wild ponies pushing through a broken fence.

"That was certainly a big hit," Ridley said after all the students were gone. "Thank you both for doing this. I try to make things interesting for the students and I like to introduce them to something outside the boundaries of their narrow little world. Most of them never venture away from the ten block radius where they live and they don't know much about anything else."

"We were happy to help, weren't we Jimmy?" Dana said.

"Oh, man, it was fun. Did you see the bird that one girl carved? Couldn't have done it better myself. They paid attention, especially when we talked about the jobs you can get in the food industry. After the first class was over, one of the boys came up to me and said he wanted to be a chef. I told him he had to finish high school first and then I gave him some advice about what he should do after that."

"They don't always show that much interest. Maybe you'd think about coming again and doing a couple of other groups? The students switch for the second half of the year, so I'll have different students in the spring."

"We could do that, couldn't we, Jimmy?" Dana asked.

"Yeah, we could do that," Jimmy confirmed. "Just set it up and we'll be here. Do you need any help straightening up your classroom?"

"No. The students will help me tomorrow. I'm ready to get out of here." Ridley helped Dana and Jimmy carry their things out to Dana's car. It was only three-fifteen and she wanted to think of a way to spend more time with Dana although she didn't know what to do about Jimmy. Since Jimmy had just closed the trunk and they were about to leave, she came up with the first thing that popped into her mind. "Let me thank both of you by taking you out to dinner."

"Sorry, but I can't go," Jimmy said. "My wife made me promise to come right home as soon as we were done here and I'll be a dead man if I don't. I'm not home that much in the evening, so she's kind of possessive when it comes to my free time."

"That's okay. I understand," Ridley told him.

"I guess I'll see you another time, then." Jimmy went to the back of Dana's car and began loading the bags and containers into the trunk.

"Will you have dinner with me?" Ridley asked Dana. "I'd love it if you would."

"Uh..." Dana's face became tense for a moment and then it relaxed. "Okay, but I have to run Jimmy back to get his car and I want to put the left-over fruits and veggies away. I'd also like to change my clothes. I can't go out in this chef's outfit or they'll put me to work."

"Tell you what. I'll follow you to your place and help you take the stuff inside and put it away. Then you can change or do what you need to do. Why don't you leave your car there and come with me? I'll bring you home whenever you want me to."

WHILE DANA CHANGED, Ridley waited for her in the living room. Being in Dana's personal space filled her with a contentment that could only be described as coming home. The hopeless attraction she felt for Dana was one thing she'd have to deal with, but beyond that there was something more, something stronger and ultimately more significant. When she was with Dana, Ridley had a sense of being exactly where she was always meant to be.

She wanted and needed to be near Dana. They'd only known each other for a matter of weeks and yet Ridley couldn't change the direction her feelings had taken any more than she could change the direction of the earth's rotation.

Dana strolled into the living room wearing a pair of faded jeans and a long sleeved blue shirt with the cuffs rolled up a couple of times. Her dark hair had a slight curl to it and she deposited little whiffs of a pleasant scent here and there as she walked about the room. "I hope I didn't take long getting ready."

"We're not in a hurry," Ridley said as she inhaled Dana's intoxicating scent. She felt as lightheaded as she had the other times she'd been near Dana and she wondered how she managed to rise to her feet and get her legs to hold steady beneath her. "Are you ready to go?"

"As ready as I'll ever be," Dana said.

"Where would you like to eat? I've never given any thought to where a chef might want to eat or even if you enjoy going out to eat at all. It must be hard to find good places after the kind of food you make."

"It can be, but I enjoy eating out just as much as everyone else. I try to put the chef in me aside when I go out. The thing is, I haven't been to a restaurant since I moved here, so I don't know where to go or what to suggest."

"I have an even better idea. Why don't I make dinner for you at my apartment? I'm sort of famous for my chicken taco salad and you wouldn't have to lift a finger. I'd just have to stop at the store for a few things on the way."

"I like that idea. Are you sure you feel like doing it?"

"Yes, we've got plenty of time and I'd really like you to see where I live."

"That would be nice. We can get to know each other a little better."

"I'd really like that," Ridley said.

WHEN THEY GOT to her apartment, Ridley unpacked the groceries while Dana sat at the kitchen table and observed.

"Can I get you an iced tea or soda or something?" Ridley offered.

"Some iced tea would be great."

Ridley poured two glasses of iced tea, added a slice of lemon to each and set one on the table in front of Dana. "I have to grill the chicken so it can cool down before I make the salad." She opened the package of boneless chicken breasts, patted them with paper towels and spread them out on a platter. Then she sprinkled them with seasonings.

"What's that you're putting on the chicken?" Dana asked.

"It's a standard Tex-Mex spice blend. I mix my own and keep it in this spice shaker. Wait until you taste my lime vinaigrette. My mother gave me the recipe."

"I love limes and Tex-Mex." Dana searched the kitchen. "Where's your grill?"

"It's out on the balcony." Ridley opened a sliding door and stepped out onto a narrow balcony with the platter of chicken balanced on the palm of one hand. "I'll leave the door open so we can talk while I start the grill and get the chicken going."

Dana raised her voice so Ridley could hear her, the way people automatically do when they can't see the person they're talking to. "This is a nice apartment. You live close to your school and close to Karen and Laurie."

"I lived far from the school I was in last year. It took me forty-five minutes to get to work and that was only if there weren't any delays on the expressway. Now it's a short drive and if I had to, I could walk. I can also walk to Karen and Laurie's house which is nice." Ridley came inside and sat at the table. "I have to let the grill warm up."

"Tell me more about yourself, Ridley."

"What do you want to know?"

"How did you get the name Ridley? It's kind of unusual."

"I get asked that a lot. It was my mother's maiden name. Her name's Victoria Anne Ridley Kelsen. She wanted me to have her last name as my first name and she told me she thought it would be unique."

"She was right. Do you have a middle name?"

"I wish I didn't." Ridley had to pause to think. She'd never told anyone her middle name. Only Laurie knew and she wasn't sure she wanted to tell Dana. Her middle name was benign enough by itself, but when you put it together with her first and last names, it sounded terribly hokey. "It's Jean after my mother's sister." Before Dana could comment, Ridley jumped up. "Have to put the chicken on," she said as she escaped to the balcony.

"Ridley Jean Kelsen. That's so cute," Dana yelled.

"You think so?" Ridley hollered back. After she put the chicken on, she came back and sat at the table next to Dana. "You don't think it makes me sound like a country western singer?"

"Well...maybe just a little." The corners of Dana's mouth turned up. "I'm sorry. I just had an image of you on the stage at the Grand Ole Opry. I couldn't help it."

"See, I told you," Ridley said.

"How long have you been a teacher," Dana asked.

"About eight years."

"How old are you, if you don't mind me asking?"

"I'm thirty-one, almost thirty-two. How old are you?" Ridley asked even though she'd already figured out Dana had to be Karen's age since they went to high school together.

"I just turned thirty-three." Dana paused as if to consider what she wanted to ask Ridley next. "Do you find it hard working in the city schools?"

"On a bad day, I'd have to say it was close to impossible."

"And what would you say on a good day?"

"On a good day I'd have to say it was worth it."

"I'd have to say it was worth it every day," Dana said. "How could it not be?"

"I appreciate that. A lot of the students in the inner city schools come from some pretty awful home situations and many of them live in abject poverty. A lot of them have behavioral issues and all sorts of physical and mental problems."

"God, that's awful."

"Many of them aren't healthy because their mother's were drinking heavily or taking drugs while they were pregnant with them. They probably didn't get any pre-natal care or take vitamins or eat a healthy diet, either. Thank God we have a full-time school nurse or we wouldn't know what to do about their problems or the constant physical complaints they use to get out of class. And students get injured almost every day from fighting and fooling around."

"I wouldn't want her job," Dana said.

"Me either. Her name's Erin Lafferty. I don't know her that well yet, but so far, I like her. She knows all the students and she is so patient with them. Even though she's around our age, she's like a mother to them. You should see how she handles them when they get out of control and start acting crazy. I think she has a gift."

"I'm not sure I could deal with them at all," Dana said. "I'm not sure I'd want to."

"Some of them are tough to handle, that's for sure, but we do have a lot of great kids in our school. They have more than their share of hardships, but somehow they rise above it all. They remind me of fragile but beautiful little flowers that push their way through tiny cracks in the sidewalk and grow even though they've been rooted in the worst possible place."

"What do you think are the biggest problems they face?" Dana asked.

"I don't have to think about that. It's poor parenting or no parenting at all. A lot of students were born to mothers who were children themselves and many of them are on their own as soon as they learn to take care of themselves. The worst situations seem to happen when the parents are addicted to alcohol or drugs or they're incarcerated. Then there's abuse. Physical and sexual abuse is bad enough, but how can you begin to deal with emotional abuse?"

"Good Lord. Is it bad?"

"Bad enough and more frequent than I would ever have thought. Some students have one or two parents or somebody who cares about them, but many don't. It's common for grandparents or aunts to be raising them and I don't even want to tell you about some of the foster parents we come across. Erin told me that the city has thousands of kids who need homes and they can't place them, let alone be too fussy about who takes them in."

Dana grimaced. "God, I never knew that."

"I've had students tell me a parent was murdered in front of them or their mother died of AIDS or she's living out in the streets because she's a drug addict and — well, you get the idea. You name it, I've heard it. Every day I see students who act out because they can't keep up with their school work and some of our students can't read above a third or fourth grade level. A lot of them struggle for three or four years in the ninth and tenth grades until they finally give up and drop out completely."

"How do they get to high school without being able to read? That's shocking in this day and age and aside from that, you don't stand a chance without a high school education."

"You don't stand much of a chance with one. And another thing that drives me nuts is that they keep having unprotected sex.

Teenage pregnancy is a bigger problem than ever and so are sexually transmitted diseases. I go over all those things in my health classes and the nurse gives them classes, but they still don't get the message. Erin brings the public health department in to do voluntary STD testing."

"What happens if they have something?"

"The health department comes back to the school and treats them. They don't have to tell their parents, either. It's all confidential."

"Are some of the students HIV positive?" Dana asked.

"Yes, I'm sorry to say and I only know that because Erin told me, but I wouldn't know who they were unless they told me themselves. Erin said it's against the law for her to share that kind of information with anyone and she said that if a student told me, it would be against the law for me to tell anyone else."

"Jesus..." Dana drank some of her iced tea.

"I know. It's awful, isn't it?"

"Maybe you do reach some of them, but you just don't know it. I watched you with the students today and I saw how much they liked and respected you. You're calm and patient with them and you're a good role model."

"Teenagers are difficult to understand, but I happen to like them." Ridley shrugged and smiled as she remembered her mother's reply when she told her she liked teaching teenagers more than younger children. "My mother says I know how to relate to them because I'm still a teenager at heart. She's only teasing me, I hope."

"That sounds like something my mother would say." Dana drank some more of her iced tea and continued, "I admire you. You're an inspiration for the rest of us and I think it takes a special person to do the kind of work you do."

"I don't know about that. It's just..."

"I mean it, Ridley. People like you make the world a better place."

"It's just something I've always wanted to do—to make a difference."

"So why did you choose to teach in the city schools? Wouldn't it have been easier and safer to teach in the suburbs?"

"Yes, but these are the kids who need the most help and I don't want it to be easy. I know it would be better for me in the suburbs, but it's more challenging and interesting to teach in the city schools." Ridley got up and went out onto the patio to check on the chicken while she kept on talking. "The Catholic schools are better, but they should hand out tickets to heaven as a perk, because the salary and benefits stink. I get paid well in the city and I have excellent benefits." She came inside with the platter of grilled chicken and set it down on the table. "My mother's always asking me why I don't get a job in a nicer school district and if she knew what the city schools were really like, she'd have a conniption fit."

"Most people don't know what they're like. I know I don't," Dana admitted.

"Most people don't want to know."

"You're right, but I'd like to hear more about it."

"You will if you hang around with Laurie and me. Now that the chicken's done, why don't we move into the living room while it cools?" She poured Dana some more iced tea. "We'll be more comfortable in there and I want to wait a while before I put the salad together."

Dana followed Ridley into the living room. She settled on the sofa and stretched her legs out in front of her, her feet crossed at the ankles. "Nice living room."

"My mother helped me pick out the furniture and decorate." Ridley sat in a chair next to the sofa, tossed a throw pillow on the coffee table and put her feet up. "There, that's better. Tell me something? What made you want to move back to Philly?"

"This area feels like home to me and I've always loved South Street. That's where I wanted to open my restaurant." Dana had a far away look in her eyes.

"You could have opened one in Chicago," Ridley said.

"Yeah, I know, but I wanted to come back here," Dana explained. "Tell me more about your family? Where does your mother live?"

"She lives in Bucks County, near Newtown Square. That's where I grew up. My father died a few years ago so she's alone except for me and her sister my..."

"Don't tell me, your aunt Jean?"

"Yeah, that's right. You're paying attention," Ridley replied with a hint of teasing.

"Of course I am. I'm all ears and I'm sorry I interrupted you. Go on."

"We have a house on the Jersey shore in Long Beach Island and my mother spends a lot of time there. Her parents left it to her."

"I used to go to Long Beach Island. Where's the house?"

"It's in Loveladies. That's in the less populated North end of the Island."

"I think I remember where that is. I wish somebody would leave me a house on Long Beach Island. I used to love going there. It's a lot less crowded than other parts of the shore."

"You love it there?" Ridley was struck with a brilliant idea. "Then I've got a suggestion. Karen and Laurie and I go down every year over Columbus Day weekend. Why don't you join us? All we do is hang around, eat and drink and have a good time and I know I can speak for them when I say we'd all love it if you'd come along."

"I don't know. Are you sure I wouldn't be a fifth wheel?" Dana asked.

"A fifth wheel? What do you mean?"

"I just assumed that you—that you must have a girlfriend."

"A girlfriend? Me?"

"Yeah, you, Ridley Jean Kelsen. You are a lesbian, aren't you?"

"Definitely. I was born one as far as I can tell." Ridley didn't want to reveal the fact that she'd questioned Laurie and had already ascertained Dana's sexual preference, so she posed the next question as nonchalantly as possible. "Are you a lesbian, too?"

"Uh-huh. Always have been, just like you. I almost made a comment about Loveladies being an appropriate place for you to have a shore house, but I didn't want to say it without making sure you were a lesbian. I didn't want to put my foot in my mouth."

"Well, I would have thought your comment was funny and as for the girlfriend part, I don't have one. I'll just be the four of us that weekend."

"In that case, maybe I will think about going. I'd love to spend time with Karen and Laurie and I'd love to go back to the shore." Dana appeared to be considering the possibility for a few moments. "I'll have to make sure Tracy doesn't mind if I go. We said we could take time off if we wanted to, but neither of us has done that yet. Are you all going down together?"

"No. I'm leaving on Friday after work, but I could wait until Saturday morning if you want to ride down with me." The idea of sharing a long ride with Dana and having her all to herself on Friday evening was very appealing, but she didn't want to apply any pressure. "Laurie and Karen are leaving Saturday morning and you could probably go with them if you wanted to or you could drive down by yourself. It's up to you. We're all staying until Monday. We usually come home in the late afternoon or early evening."

"Let me talk to Tracy first and I'll let you know."

"I'll call you later this week and you can let me know if you're going. If you decide you'd rather drive down alone I can give you directions then." Ridley got up. "Stay here while I make the salad. I'll call you when it's ready." Ridley no sooner left the living room when she poked her head back through the doorway and asked Dana, "Do you like avocadoes?"

"I love them."

"Excellent." Ridley disappeared again. A matter of seconds later, she stuck her head in the doorway again. "Do you mind a little red onion?"

"Not as long as we're both having it."

After setting the table with the salad set her mother had given her as a gift, Ridley made the salad dressing. Then she created a bed of Romaine lettuce in the large serving bowl and arranged slices of avocado, cherry tomatoes, black olives and a small amount of thinly sliced red onions on top of the lettuce leaves. After spreading the cubes of chicken around evenly, she sprinkled cheddar cheese and crushed tortilla chips over the entire salad. Satisfied with her creation, she drizzled the dressing all over it. She placed the pitcher of iced tea with lemon slices on the table, inspected everything one last time and called Dana.

Just for fun, Ridley stood next to the table with a folded dishtowel over her arm and when Dana walked in, she pulled Dana's chair out and bowed at the waist. "Table for two?"

"Why thank you." Dana smiled as she took her seat. "I see you believe in good service, like I do." She tilted her head up. "I think I like it."

"It's your turn to be fussed over for a change. Allow me to serve you some of my special salad." With a flourish, Ridley used tongs to fill Dana's bowl and then she took her own seat and helped herself. "There's extra salad dressing if you need it."

Dana took a bite and chewed it thoughtfully. "This is really delicious. I'd like to have the recipe. Would you like to come and work for me—be my salad chef maybe?"

"Not unless you're planning on offering only one or two salads on the menu because that's all I know how to make. Well, three if you count plain old tossed salad. I'm afraid you'd live to regret it if you hired me because I'd crack under the pressure."

"We could teach you more salads and you'd get used to the pressure," Dana said.

"I wouldn't count on it. You've heard of two left feet? I've got two left hands. I'd ruin your shiny new kitchen or chop a few of my fingers off."

"That would be terrible. That kitchen means a lot to me."

"You're hilarious. I set myself up for that one, didn't I?"

"You did."

"I think I'd better keep my teaching job. My fingers mean a lot to me." Ridley dug into her salad and ate with gusto, a lingering smile on her face.

"Now I can ask you another question," Dana said. "How is it, being a lesbian in the school district? Are you out at work or do you have to be careful?"

"I'm the gym teacher. I'm supposed to be a lesbian," Ridley said, her smile getting broader. "Even if I wasn't, most everyone would automatically assume I was."

"I see your point, but in your case it's not all that obvious."

"Not to the untrained eye you mean. I'm new so I'm not out to that many people yet, but I will tell the ones who matter to me as I get to know them better. Some people will probably suspect it, but I've found most people won't ask or bring it up. At any rate, it's not something I have to worry about in this school district."

"What do you mean?" Dana asked.

"They have policies protecting students and staff from being harassed due to their sexual orientation and they're serious about it. An organization in the city helped them to develop the policies and train the staff to do sensitivity trainings in all the schools. Karen was involved in that process and I volunteered to be one of the trainers at my last high school."

"Wow, I didn't know that about Karen. You guys are something and I'm impressed that the school district would do that. It makes me think things are actually changing."

"They are changing," Ridley said. "I respect the school district for having those policies although I know they were motivated in part by some successful, multi-million dollar lawsuits against other school districts for failing to protect gay students. And get this, they named October gay and lesbian month on the school calendar. There it was in black and white, or green and gold to be exact. Some parents raised a stink about it."

"That doesn't surprise me. What happened?"

"Essentially, the school district said it was too bad if they didn't like it. Not in those words, of course. I'm sure they said it more diplomatically."

"Things really are changing," Dana said.

"I'm starting a gay-straight alliance at my school. I did it in the last three years and I loved it. Erin said she'd do it with me and we talked one of the guidance counselors into helping us. We invite gay and straight students to come together hoping they'll learn to respect each other and understand each other's issues."

"Now I admire you even more than I did a minute ago. People like you change the way people think and the way they feel about other people. Your principal supports that?"

"Absolutely. A couple of homophobic staff members were quite upset about it. They said the students were too young to talk about such things and one even said she thought it might make some of them 'turn gay', if you can believe that."

"I believe it—as if that could happen."

"I know. One of the teachers told me they went to the principal and complained so I went and talked to her myself to ask her what she thought I should do—if I should do it or not."

"What did she say?" Dana asked.

"She said she told them they could work someplace else if they didn't like it."

"Wow! Good for her," Dana said, stabbing a piece of chicken.

"I think she was sincere, but I also know she would hear it from administration if she stood in the way of having it because those are the kinds of thing the district wants the schools to do." It had been some time since Ridley felt this at ease talking to someone other than her mother or her close friends. Everything about being with Dana was comfortable and easy except for the physical attraction that never left her alone.

When they finished, Dana put her fork and knife on her plate and wiped her mouth with her napkin. "That was a great salad. Do you need help cleaning up?"

"No, there's not much to do. I'll clean up later."

"Would you mind taking me back? I've got some things I need to do."

"I said I'd take you home whenever you wanted me to." Although she hated to let Dana go, Ridley remembered her promise. "I had a good time and I enjoyed talking to you. Not that many people show an interest in my work."

"I enjoyed hearing about it. In fact, I enjoyed the entire day." Dana threw her a wink. "I think we're becoming good friends, Ridley Jean Kelsen."

"I believe you're right, Dana De Marco."

Being friends and nothing more wasn't what Ridley had in mind when it came to Dana. Given the attraction she felt for Dana, she knew friendship would ever be enough not unless her feelings changed dramatically. Just knowing they both existed on the same planet was enough to drive Ridley crazy. It was all too intense and way too soon, she thought. "Let me get you home. I have tests to grade and lesson plans to prepare."

Dana stood. "Tomorrow, I'll talk to Tracy about going to the shore."

"You do that. I'd really love it if you joined us."

Chapter
Seven

THE NEXT DAY, while they worked together in the restaurant kitchen, Dana talked to Tracy about Ridley's invitation to join her, Karen and Laurie at the shore the next weekend.

"I think you should go, Dana, I really do. All you've done is work since you moved here." Tracy pressed the pulse button on the food processor four or five times until the pastry dough formed itself into a ball.

"Maybe I should. I'd love to spend some time with Karen and Laurie."

"What about Ridley?" Tracy removed the ball of dough, patted it into a flat disc and wrapped it in plastic wrap. She put it in the refrigerator to chill and while she was there she grabbed another piece of dough she'd made earlier. "You enjoy spending time with her, don't you?" Tracy floured the marble counter and began rolling the dough out.

"So far, I've enjoyed her company very much." Dana leaned against the sink with her arms folded. "You're not going to start on that again are you?"

"No." Tracy looked up and met Dana's eyes. "You told me you used to love the shore."

"You'd have to do Sunday brunch without me," Dana reminded her.

Tracy went back to rolling the dough. "I don't mind. We agreed to cover each other, didn't we? We said we didn't want to work all the time and have no life, remember?" Tracy turned the dough clockwise and rolled it into a bigger circle. "It's not like I'd be here alone."

"I know, but we haven't done it yet." Dana knew Tracy was tossing out anything that came into her head that would persuade her to go. She also knew she should go. It had been too long since she'd taken any time off or gone anywhere with friends.

"Then it's time we did. How are we ever going to see how it goes? You know I can take care of things around here. Just plan the menu specials with me before you go and make sure we have everything we need. I'll do the rest."

"All right, if you're sure you don't mind."

"I don't mind because you're going to return the favor some time." Tracy laid the circle of dough she'd rolled out over a tart pan and pressed it into the bottom with her fingers. Then she ran the rolling pin over the top of the tart pan to cut off the excess dough. "I'm not going to spend the rest of my life working my ass off."

"Okay, you've convinced me and I will return the favor anytime you want me to." Dana went to the refrigerator and pulled out some leeks and carrots.

"Why don't you ride down with Ridley on Friday or at least think about going on Saturday morning with her? You told me she offered to wait for you, right?" Tracy poked holes in the tart dough with a fork and popped it into the oven. I can handle dinner on Saturday."

"I already made up my mind that if I decided to go I would drive down by myself on Sunday morning and come back on Monday. That's long enough for me and I want to be free to leave if I need to." Dana started peeling a carrot.

"Now why would you need to leave? Wait, don't tell me." The expression on Tracy's face mirrored the sarcasm in her next words. "You're thinking it might be difficult to have fun with good friends and spend time with an adorable lesbian."

"How do you know she's a lesbian?" Dana peeled another carrot.

"What? Give me a break, Dana."

"As a matter of fact, she is. I asked her," Dana said to annoy Tracy.

"You needed to ask? I swear, I think you've lost your mind."

"My mind's as sharp as ever." Dana paused and rested her hands on her hips. She looked at Tracy. "Now let's get back to me going alone. I'd feel better if I knew I could leave whenever I wanted to because I don't know what it's like there and I've never stayed with Ridley. Also, I don't want you to be stuck with dinner on Saturday. I know you're capable of doing it, but I'd feel better if I stayed."

"You know that's not the real reason."

"Okay, okay. God, it's a pain in the ass to have someone know you so well. I just think it's best to limit the time I spend with Ridley. I don't want our relationship, if we even have one, to get out of hand." Dana went back to preparing her vegetables.

"Why the hell not? Don't you like her?"

"That's the problem. I do like her and I don't want her to get the wrong idea."

"And what wrong idea would that be?" Tracy asked.

"The one where she gets it in her head that I might be interested in her. She's a very nice girl and it wouldn't be fair to lead her on." Dana felt a flush creeping up into her cheeks and that was always a dead giveaway that she wasn't being honest. She knew Tracy would notice.

"I think you really are interested in her and what's wrong with that? She's available and you're available and anyone can see she's interested in you." Tracy moved to the counter, next to Dana, grabbed a chef's knife and started helping her slice the leeks.

"Maybe she is interested in me, but you're wrong about me. I am definitely not interested in her, not in the way you mean. I swear I'm not."

Tracy stopped slicing for a moment. "Sure you're not."

"It's the truth, Tracy. You know I don't want to get involved. Besides, I..."

"Please don't tell me you still want Sarah?" Tracy slammed her chef's knife on the counter and turned to face Dana. "It's been over for two years for Christ's sake. You have got to get on with your life."

"Don't be mad at me," Dana whispered.

"I'm not mad at you. It's just that you make me crazy sometimes." Tracy took a deep breath and blew it out. "Sarah was a shit. Can't you see that? She never knew who the hell she was or what the hell she wanted. You should know better than to get involved with someone who isn't clear about their sexuality, especially when you are."

"I know, I know. It only leads to trouble. My head tells me you're right, but my heart tells me a different story. I loved her, Tracy. I planned my life around her. I can't switch it off just like that." Dana snapped her fingers in the air.

"But that's just what you need to do. Everyone deserves to be happy, Dana, even you, and you seem to have forgotten that. Please don't pass up this chance for happiness."

"I haven't forgotten a thing and I do want to be happy." Dana felt her eyes fill with tears.

"You're my best friend. I can't bear to see you alone and it breaks my heart to see you avoid relationships. You're too special to be doing that."

Dana gained control over her emotions and blinked away any trace of tears. "You worry about me far too much. I'm happy with the way things are." She went to the sink and filled a huge stock pot. "I like my life and I'm going to drive to the shore on Sunday morning all by myself. That's the way I want it and that's all I can deal with."

"Suit yourself. I guess it's a miracle that you're going at all. Just promise me you'll give some serious thought to what we talked about. You can't go on living in the past."

"Look, Tracy, I'm going, okay? What more do you want? And I intend to have a good time. Right now, I can't think of anything beyond that point."

Chapter
Eight

"RIDLEY, WHAT TIME did Dana tell you she'd be here?" Laurie asked as they sat around the kitchen table at the shore house on Sunday morning. They were drinking coffee and eating freshly baked blueberry muffins they'd picked up that morning from a local bakery. "I wish she could have come yesterday so we would have had more time to spend with her."

"We all do," Ridley said. "But when I called her on Thursday, she told me she preferred to drive down by herself on Sunday morning. I could tell she had her mind made up, so I didn't try to talk her out of it." Ridley had left straight from work on Friday afternoon to beat the rush hour traffic out of the city. That gave her time to unwind once she got there and make sure the shore house was ready before her friends arrived the next day. Every year she looked forward to her annual trip to the shore with Laurie and Karen on Columbus Day weekend, but now that Dana had agreed to join them for part of it, she could hardly wait for her to come.

"She was probably worried about the restaurant and maybe she felt a little shy about joining us for an entire weekend and staying somewhere unfamiliar. She seems more cautious than she used to be, but then we all get more wary as we get older, don't we?" Karen stood at the stove, stirring a pan of scrambled eggs. Next to her, on the countertop, she had a pound of crisp bacon strips draining between paper towels.

"She admitted to the first part and I think you're right about the second part, too, although she never actually said that," Ridley said. "And to answer your question, Laurie, she should be here any time now. She promised she'd get an early start."

"Is it all right if we go ahead and eat without her?" Laurie asked.

"I don't see why not?" Ridley answered. "Who knows when she'll get here and if she didn't eat, we can always make her something."

"Knowing us, we'll be eating again before too long," Laurie said.

"That's true." Ridley took another muffin from the white bakery box, peeled the paper off and took a big bite. "Why am I so hungry? Every time I come down here, I'm hungry all the time. Do you guys feel that way or is it just me?"

"It's not just you. I feel the same way. I think it's the fresh air."
Karen brought the frying pan over and divided the eggs into three
portions. Then she put the pan back and joined them at the table. She
stretched her arms far above her head and yawned. "I love it here in
the fall. It's so peaceful. Work has been so busy and it feels so good
just to mellow out."

"If you get any more mellowed out, you'll be in a coma," Laurie
commented.

Karen gave her partner a brief but meaningful stare and then
turned to her food.

"It's my favorite time of year," Ridley said between bites.
"People who only come to the shore in the summer don't have any
idea what they're missing."

"It's nice of your mother to let us use the house," Laurie said.
"She's very..."

"Very what?" Dana poked her head into the kitchen and looked
around. "You don't know how relieved I am to see that I'm in the
right place, because I just walked straight through the entire length
of this house and if it wasn't yours, I'd die."

"Hey, look who's here," Karen said.

"Did you knock on the door?" Ridley asked. "Sorry, we didn't
hear you."

"I tried, but no one came and I saw the cars in the driveway, so I
just came in." Dana looked at Laurie. "What were you saying when I
so rudely interrupted you?"

"Very generous, that's what I was saying when you came in,"
Laurie explained. "I was talking about Ridley's mother. She's nice to
let us come down here and take over her shore house several times a
year for our get-togethers."

"My mother loves that we come here," Ridley chimed in. "She
cleaned the place before she went back home on Thursday and she
left us food and beer and she left me a nice note telling us all to have
a good time. She's the greatest." Her eyes met Dana's and it was
enough to spark the first stirrings of desire. This attraction wasn't
going to leave her alone, just as she had feared. She smiled at Dana
and said, "I'm glad you're here."

"So are we. Laurie and I were thrilled that you decided to join
us," Karen said.

"What a nice greeting," Dana said. "Now I'm really glad I
came." Dana sat at the table. "It's nice to see all of you."

"Too bad you couldn't have joined us for the whole weekend,"
Karen said. "We were all saying that before you got here."

"Maybe next time I will."

"Did you have any trouble with the directions?" Ridley asked.

"The directions were very easy to follow and once I got close to the Pine Barrens there were hardly any cars on the road. Of course, I didn't expect there to be that many people out that early on a Sunday morning."

"Especially this time of year," Ridley added. "I always like it when I get to the point where the landscape starts to change. The dirt at the side of the road turns into sand, the terrain flattens out and those scrubby little pines stretch out in every direction as far as the eye can see. Then, when you get to the marshlands, the air's infused with the smell of fish and brine and decaying vegetation and you know you're close to the bay."

"I like that, too," Dana said.

"Can I get you some coffee?" Ridley asked. "Did you eat breakfast?"

"I ate before I left, but I'd love some coffee."

Ridley took her last bite of eggs, stood and picked up her coffee cup. "Stay there. I need another cup myself, so I'll get you one while I'm up. What do you take in it?"

"A rounded teaspoon of sugar and a splash of milk will be fine."

Laurie pushed the bakery box over to Dana. "Try one of these blueberry muffins. We just bought them at the bakery this morning and they're great."

Dana lifted the lid and peeked inside. "They look great. Maybe I will try one." Dana took one out of the box and put it on a plate that Laurie had placed in front of her. After Ridley brought her coffee over and set it in front of her, she blew on it and carefully took a sip. "This is excellent coffee." Dana took a bite of her muffin and washed it down with more coffee. "What have you been up to so far?"

"The same things we always do when we're down here," Ridley told her. "We hang around, talk our heads off, ride around the island, browse in the shops and walk on the beach." Ridley carried her coffee to the table and sat next to Dana. "Did we do anything that I forgot to mention, Laurie and Karen?"

"You forgot to tell her we do plenty of eating and drinking," Laurie said.

"And last night we went out to eat and took a ride along the bay," Karen added.

"Are a lot of restaurants still open?" Dana asked.

"More than you might think," Ridley said. "But mostly on the weekends."

"I remember a seafood restaurant I used to love, but I can't remember the name. It was in Harvey Cedars, I think—a small, very crowded place. They had the best French fries and their fish was always fresh."

"That would be the Harvey Cedars Shellfish Company. It's still there and it's open on the weekends. We could go tonight if you want to." Doing whatever made Dana happy had taken its rightful place on the top of Ridley's list of important things to do in life. "Is that okay with you guys?" she asked Laurie and Karen.

"I'd love to go there," Laurie replied. "What about you, honey?"

"That's always fine with me," Karen said. "I love that place." She got up, rinsed her coffee cup out in the sink and started to gather up the breakfast dishes. "I'm surprised you want to eat out, Dana. We all thought you'd be dying to cook dinner for us on your days off."

Dana laughed. "Think again. When I'm off, I try not to cook unless I really want to or have to. I had planned to make breakfast tomorrow, though, if it's okay with Ridley."

"You don't have to do that," Ridley said.

"I want to as a token of my appreciation for being invited here."

"We certainly won't stop you, right girls?" Ridley looked at Karen and Laurie.

"No way," Karen said. "I'm sure it will be something delicious."

"Then we'll need to stop at the supermarket sometime when we're out," Dana said.

"We should check to see what we have here before we go shopping. My mother stocked the refrigerator with basic necessities before we came down, so we might already have some of the things you need," Ridley said.

"We can do that, but I'm sure I'll need a few things you don't have."

"Don't worry, Dana," Laurie said. "If you're missing anything, I'll send Karen to the super market to pick it up for you."

Karen moved so she stood behind Laurie's chair and wrapped her hands around her neck as if to strangle her. "You're something. What do you mean you'll send me? And let me remind you that Dana came here to relax, not to cook for us. We wouldn't ask you to give us a lecture on nineteenth century novelists on your day off."

"No, but I'd be happy to oblige you if you're interested."

Ridley frowned. "And when you're done, I'll go over the basics of the most common sexually transmitted diseases. Now that's really fascinating."

"God no — please spare us," Karen and Laurie said in unison.

Dana visibly shuttered. "I'll pass on that topic."

"Seriously, Dana, Karen's right. Don't cook unless you feel like it," Laurie said.

"I'd like to do it. It's just breakfast and I'm not making anything difficult."

"I'll help you," Ridley offered.

"Me too," Laurie added. Laurie looked up at Karen who had released her death grip on Laurie's neck and had her hands on

Laurie's shoulders.

Karen smiled down at her. "Me three."

"I knew you'd all help." Dana smiled. "It's settled then."

"Goody." Laurie clapped her hands in the air.

Ridley got up from the table. "Dana, if you're finished with your coffee, why don't you come with me and I'll show you your room. You guys don't mind if we leave you alone for a little while, do you?"

"No, you go ahead. We'll clean up," Karen said.

"I LEFT MY bag out in my car," Dana said once they got into the living room. She touched Ridley's arm lightly. "I'll just run and get it. Don't go anywhere."

"Don't worry, I won't. I'll be right here." Ridley remained by the fireplace mantle and waited for Dana to come back with her things. The odor of burnt wood coming from the fireplace was one of the permanent smells that resided in the house, a collection of scents that nourished her soul and kindled her fondest memories. She breathed them in, the ever-present fresh sea air, the bouquet of flowers on the coffee table, the lingering aroma of bacon from the kitchen, freshly brewed coffee and just a trace of her mother's favorite cologne.

Over the years, she, Laurie and Karen had spent many a weekend at the shore house. Once in a while, if she met someone who lived down there or was staying for the summer, she might invite her to go out to dinner with the three of them or out to a club, but this was the first time someone who really meant something to her was going to stay at the house with them. She'd dated a few women for longer periods of time, but it had never been anyone special enough to bring to this place, even though she knew she had no right to think of Dana that way. Dana was just one of the gang.

"I'm back," Dana came back in with one overnight bag.

"You didn't bring much, did you?"

"I don't need much because I won't be here that long." Dana appeared to scan the room with her eyes. "This is a cozy room and that's a great fireplace. Do you use it much?"

Ridley nodded. "I thought we'd have a fire tonight. It's supposed to be chilly."

"That would be so nice," Dana said.

"Come on, I'll show you to your room." She led Dana down a hallway to one of the guest rooms on the first floor, a lovely room in shades of sea form green and soft pink with white wicker furniture. A large watercolor painting of sandpipers scurrying along the beach at sunset hung above the bed.

"This is a relaxing room. Did you buy the painting and decorate the room to match it or did you buy the painting to match the room?"

"Good question." Ridley thought a moment. "My mother did it a long time ago, but I think the room came first because I remember her looking for a painting to go in here."

Dana opened a door inside the room and peeked inside "Is this a bathroom?"

"Yes, you have your own. I hope you'll be comfortable in here."

"I'm sure I'll be very comfortable. This house is charming, what I've seem of it, and it's beautifully maintained both inside and out."

Ridley beamed. "That's my mother. She has good taste, doesn't she?" Ridley adored the older Cape Cod style ranch, so well-maintained its white cedar shake shingles barely showed any ill effects from the ruthless and constant battering of wind and salt.

"I'll say." Dana took a closer look at Ridley. "You look good. You've got nice color in your cheeks and your hair's all windblown. You look really cute."

Ridley ran her fingers through her hair. "We were walking on the beach before breakfast. I guess I should have combed it. You look good yourself. I'm glad you're here."

"I know. You told me when I got here. I almost changed my mind at the last minute, but now I can see that would have been a mistake." Dana opened her bag, took out a book and set it on the table next to her bed. She glanced at Ridley. "Where's your room?"

"I'm upstairs in the master suite. My mother added it on a few years ago."

"I thought I saw a new addition on the back of the house," Dana said.

"Did you go out there?"

"I went to take a quick look at the ocean and the beach when I got here and that's when I saw it. It must be nice to have an upper and lower deck overlooking the ocean."

"It is. We love to sit out there. The one on top comes off the master suite and connects to the one below it, the one that comes off the living room and goes down into the dunes. I'll take you up to see my room later. There's a whirlpool tub large enough for two people and skylights and another fireplace. At night you can hear the ocean and if the sky is clear, you can see the stars. I love that room, but I only get to stay in it when my mother's not here."

"If I owned a shore house, I'd want one just like this. It kind of reminds me of the houses around the Chesapeake Bay. I like the way the pine trees and bushes surround the house and make it feel secluded, like there aren't any other houses around."

"We actually have a triple lot. It's all worth a fortune now, the house and the land, but when my grandparents purchased the land it was quite cheap. Back then, there was nothing around and my grandparents weren't sure they wanted to build a house way down on this end because the island was so deserted. They thought they were making a big mistake, but they did it anyway."

"It looks like they made the right decision after all."

"They did, as it turned out. They left it to my mother when they died and now some parts of the island are crammed with expensive vacation homes and there's hardly a vacant lot to be had. We get some generous offers on the extra lots, but my mother would never sell them. She loves this place and she doesn't need the money."

"I don't blame her," Dana said. "I wouldn't sell them."

"Me either. I love the extra space around the house and the privacy it gives us. This house is precious to me and I wouldn't change a thing about it. It's the caretaker of my most cherished memories and a lot of my past lives in here."

"I guess this will all be yours someday?"

"Someday, but not too soon, I hope. I'd like my mother to be around for a long time yet. She's more precious to me than this house could ever be." Ridley looked away for a moment. "Would you like to go for a ride this afternoon and see some of the island?"

"Yes, I'd love to. I haven't seen the shore in a long time."

"On the way back, we'll stop at the supermarket and get whatever you need."

"Give me a few minutes to unpack and freshen up in the bathroom. Then we'll see what you have and make a list of what we need."

"Can you find your way back to the kitchen?"

Dana smiled softly. "I think so. If not, I'll yell for help."

"That was silly, wasn't it? It's not that big a house." Ridley smiled to herself and shook her head. "Well, I should go find the girls and see if they want to go out with us. They should be done washing the dishes by now."

Chapter
Nine

LATER THAT EVENING, after dinner and a ride along the bay, they returned to the house and gathered in the living room in front of a blazing fire. Laurie and Karen were snuggled close together on the sofa while Ridley and Dana sat in matching chairs on opposite ends of the sofa.

"What a great dinner," Dana said. "That restaurant was even better than I remembered. It's got the perfect shore ambience and they know how to prepare fresh seafood. Don't laugh at me, but I absolutely adore those French fries."

"I'm not laughing," Ridley said. "I love the French fries and the restaurant, but so do a lot of other people. It's so crowded during the summer you can't even get in on the weekends. They don't take reservations, so you have to either go very early or very late or just go whenever and be willing to wait in line for a long time."

"It's well worth the wait if you ask me," Laurie said.

"I agree," Karen said. "Don't you love sitting in front of a fire?"

"I could sit and stare at the flames for hours and hours," Ridley said. "And I often do. It's as if the fire puts me into a trance."

Without warning, Laurie stood up. "I hope you don't mind, but I'm going to call it an evening. I've had a nagging headache for a while and it's getting worse." Laurie had an odd expression on her face and she looked as if she was up to something. "Honey, didn't you tell me you were dying to get back to that lesbian mystery you were reading?"

"Uh..." Karen appeared confused, but it only lasted a moment. "Oh...yeah, I did. I hope you two don't mind. It's a really good book. You know how it is."

"Sorry you have a headache, Laurie," Dana said.

"I think I had a little too much wine at dinner," Laurie explained. "It's nothing a few Tylenol and a good night's sleep won't cure. I'll be good as new in the morning."

"That's a shame, Laurie." Ridley had an idea what her friends were up to. Laurie had looked fine all evening and rarely complained of headaches and Karen would never leave a group of friends and a good conversation to read any kind of book. Obviously, they were co-conspirators who had devised a clever plan to leave her alone with Dana. During dinner, Laurie had leaned over to whisper to Karen a couple of times and then when they got back to the house, she was whispering to Karen again. Ridley recognized a matchmaking scheme when she saw one and she reminded herself to be sure and thank them later on.

"See you in the morning," Dana said.

"Nighty-night you two. Hope you sleep well," Ridley called out to her friends as they started down the hallway to their room. "I hope you feel better, Laurie. Enjoy your book, Karen. See you both in the morning."

As soon as they left, Dana got up. "Will you excuse me? I'm going to my room."

Ridley jumped up. "You're not going to bed, are you? I thought we could go for a walk on the beach. There's a full moon out tonight." Ridley's heart raced as she waited for Dana's reply. God Lord, all that scheming by Laurie and Karen and as soon as she finally had the chance to be alone with Dana, she was going to bed?

"I don't want to go to bed yet and I'd love to take a walk on the beach. I just need to use the bathroom. Give me a minute to change my clothes before we go, okay?"

"I think I'll go change, too. Wear something warm. It'll be cool out there." Ridley fought to conceal how thrilled she felt to have time alone with Dana. "I'll meet you back here in about fifteen minutes."

DANA STOPPED IN her tracks as soon as they stepped onto the beach from the path that led through the dunes. "Will you look at that moon," she said. A full moon, the color of butter, smiled down upon them from the sky above the horizon. It lit up the entire beach, and made everything glisten under its glow. "The moon's amazing. You can see the face so clearly and it looks like it's watching us."

"It's a friendly face. You don't see a moon like that too often." Ridley walked a few feet behind Dana as they wound their way through the long dunes path so she could study her bathed in moonlight. She became more beautiful every time Ridley laid eyes on her.

Dana stayed ahead until they got close to the water and then she turned and waited for Ridley to catch up. "Thanks for suggesting this." For a few moments, she studied Ridley's eyes before she looked away at the ocean. Then she started walking.

"This is one of my favorite things to do. Over the years, I've walked on this beach with my family and friends more times than I can count. When my grandparents were still alive we'd walk on this beach after dinner in the cool crisp evening. Sometimes my parents would come along and we'd all laugh and talk and walk until it was too dark to see each other's faces. Those were days I'll never forget," Ridley said. "And walking on this beach never gets old for me. I feel certain I could do this for the rest of my life and still never have enough." Had she seen something there in Dana's eyes a moment ago or had she imagined it? Or had she merely wished for it?

"Have you ever brought a girlfriend down here?" Dana asked. "Someone special?"

"No, I haven't—no one that really mattered to me."

"I think walking on the beach at night is very romantic. It would be a great thing to do with someone you cared very deeply for, someone you loved."

"I agree, but I've never been in love," Ridley replied.

Dana stopped walking and studied Ridley's face. "You haven't? I'm surprised."

"Well, it's true. It's just never happened to me." Ridley wondered why she felt she had to reveal so much about herself to Dana. They hardly knew each other and yet she seemed unable to hold anything back or exercise even a sensible amount of caution. She asked Dana the next obvious question. "What about you? Have you ever been in love?"

"Yes, but only once." Dana looked off in the distance and said nothing more.

For the next ten minutes or so, they walked along the beach side by side in silence. Dana's earlier question made Ridley acutely aware that this truly was the first time she'd ever walked on this beach with a woman who meant something to her, someone other than her close family and friends. That fact she kept to herself.

Dana was the first to break the silence. "It was awfully nice of your mother to let us all use her house this weekend." Dana stood still for a moment and gazed into Ridley's eyes.

"My mother considers this house to be mine as well as hers and she loves it when I bring my friends here." Ridley found it impossible to tear her eyes away from Dana's. She longed to raise her hand and trace a line with her finger from the corner of Dana's eye, down her cheek and then to the corner of her mouth. "I look forward to this weekend with Karen and Laurie every year, but having you here has made it even more special."

Dana took a deep breath and as she released it, she sighed. "I love the way the air smells near the ocean, don't you? There are so many layers in it."

"I love it, too and I love the constant sound of the waves."

Dana looked out at the water. "I love everything about the ocean."

Ridley wanted to say that she loved everything about Dana, but she held her tongue and said something else instead. She felt dangerously close to doing or saying something she'd live to regret later on. "I never get tired of it no matter how many times I come here."

Again, they started walking and every now and then, the uneven terrain and soft yielding sand threw one of them off balance and caused them to brush up against each other. After a few minutes, Dana stopped and turned toward Ridley. "Please tell me if I'm out of line or if you'd rather not talk about this, but I'm curious about your father. You told me he died and I'd like to know what happened to him."

"He died of a heart attack." Ridley's voice barely rose above the sound of the wind and the crashing of the waves. She stared at her hands and twisted them together while she told Dana the story. "We were down here for the weekend and he went for a walk while my mother was getting dinner ready. He did that almost every day when he was here. Sometimes I went with him, but this time I stayed behind to help my mother and this time he never came back."

"God, I'm so sorry." Dana studied Ridley's face. "I can see how sad this makes you and you don't have to tell me any more about it if it's too hard for you."

"No, it's okay. It helps me to talk about it and it doesn't hurt as much as it used to." Ridley took a deep breath. "My mother had the phone in her hand and was about to call the police when they knocked on the door. Some man had found him on the beach and called 911. The man did CPR, but my father didn't respond and the paramedics couldn't revive him either. In the end, there was nothing anyone could do. The hospital told us he died of a massive coronary." Ridley's voice broke and tears pooled in her eyes. Her lips quivered and made it impossible to speak.

"It's okay." Dana wrapped her hand around Ridley's forearm. "Take your time and tell me more about him if you feel you can."

After some deep breaths, Ridley said, "He was a kind and wonderful man. I loved him very much. He worked hard to give us the life he thought we should have and he did so many nice things for me. When I was in college, I used to come down for the weekend and he and I would sit on the deck and drink beer and talk until late into the night. He was interested in everything about me. That's just the way he was."

"Good fathers are like that. Mine's the same way." Dana ran her hand down Ridley's forearm and when she reached her hand she grasped it firmly in her own. "What was his name? You never said."

"His name was Jeremy. Jeremy Paul Kelsen." Ridley held onto Dana's hand as if she were holding onto a lifeline. "My mother and I adored him. We'd both give everything we own just to have him back." Ridley dabbed at her tears with her free hand. "For a long time my mother was so sick with grief I wasn't sure she'd ever recover. I thought I'd lost both my parents. I took time off from work and then when school ended I stayed with her all summer.

Eventually she got past the worst part of it and she started to look better."

"That was a terrible loss for her and for you." Dana tightened her hold on Ridley's hand and moved in closer to her. "I can't imagine how hard it must have been."

"Sometimes I wonder..."

Dana waited and then asked, "What do you wonder?"

"I think about how tenuous life is and how someone's life can be snuffed out in a split second and..." Ridley paused for a moment. "And I wonder if my father just doesn't exist any longer or if he lives on in some other dimension or in some other form of life. I wonder if he cares about me or watches over me."

"Those are disturbing questions that have no answer."

"I know," Ridley said softly. "They make my heart ache when I'm alone in the dark and after a while I always come to the inevitable question — the most painful one. Does the fact that he was here even matter in the grand scheme of things? Does it matter for any of us?"

"Those are hard things to think about."

"Do you know what's even harder to think about? I..." Ridley stifled a sob and took a few seconds to gather her emotions. "I'm sorry. It hurts me to talk about this. " Although she didn't want to, she had to let go of Dana's hand and use her sweatshirt sleeves to soak up her tears.

"What hurts you so much?" Dana asked. "I want to know."

Ridley re-gained enough composure to go on. "I never told him I was gay. I wanted to and I almost did a few times, but I was too scared and too weak. He used to tell me he hoped I would meet someone special someday and get married. He couldn't wait for me to have children so he could have grandchildren."

"I'm so sorry," Dana said quietly.

"I let him down. I was his only child and..." Ridley's body shook all over and her hands trembled as she reached up to stem the never ending tide of tears. "I wasn't...I couldn't be what he wanted me to be. He died and he never knew who I was."

Dana reached into her pocket. "Here, I always carry tissues."

"Thanks." Ridley wiped her eyes and blew her nose. She put the used tissues in the pocket of her sweatpants and attempted a halfhearted smile. "Wiping my eyes on my sleeve is one thing, but blowing my nose on it would be disgusting."

Dana smiled gently and reached for Ridley's hand. "Your hands are trembling." She held it in her own and pressed their joined hands against Ridley's chest. "What about your mother? Does she know you're a lesbian?"

Ridley nodded. "I told her as soon as I thought she was well

enough to hear it. I didn't want to make the same mistake twice."
Ridley gripped Dana's hand tighter and held it to her, grateful for
the comfort of her touch. If she could control time, she'd make it stop
so she could stand on this beach and hold Dana's hand against her
chest forever. Dana's hand grounded her and held her in a place she
never wanted to leave.

"How did she take it?" Dana stared into Ridley's eyes.

"She was shocked at first and she cried a lot. It was tense for a
few days, but then she told me she'd already suspected it because I'd
never had any interest in men. Anyway, in the end, she told me she
loved me and she wanted me to be happy, no matter who I chose to
love. As it turned out, telling her the truth brought us closer
together."

"Did you tell her how you felt about not telling your father?"

Ridley nodded a second time. "She reminded me that he loved
me and he was proud of me and she told me she was certain that if he
knew he would still feel the same way. Then she said there was no
way I could ever let him down. She suggested I write him a letter."

"And did you?"

"Yes, that very night. I told him everything. I even put the letter
in an envelope, addressed it and put a stamp on it. I still have it in
my room at home."

"Did it help?" Dana asked.

"I think so. Too bad I didn't have the guts to do it while he was
still alive." Ridley broke down and cried softly. "I'm sorry I'm such a
mess."

"No, don't say you're sorry. You're not a mess. You're sweet,
you're honest, you're..."

"It feels so good to hold your hand. Please don't let go."

Dana squeezed Ridley's hand and brought their hands down
between them. "I'm not going to let go. Come on, we'll hold hands
while we walk." She tugged on Ridley's hand and they headed up
the beach.

A brisk, steady wind skidded across the water and it grew
increasingly colder. Before long, Ridley noticed that Dana had
started to shiver even though she'd worn a sweatshirt. She let go of
Dana's hand and took her hooded sweatshirt jacket off. She stood
behind Dana and placed it over her shoulders. "You're shivering. I
want you to put this on."

"Thanks, it's nice and warm." Dana pulled it around her. "But
what about you?"

"I'm okay. I've got another shirt on under this sweater."

As if some outside force had seized control of her actions, Ridley
kept her hands on Dana's shoulders and began to massage them.
And before she could stop herself, she pressed her chest against

Dana's back and embraced her from behind. A sigh escaped unbidden as she buried her face in Dana's hair.

Dana turned around in Ridley's arms. "What are you doing?"

"You're beautiful. I thought so the very first time I saw you."

"I don't know what to say." Dana lowered her eyes.

Ridley held Dana's chin in her hand and lifted it so she could see her eyes. "Please don't be upset with me for saying that." Ridley traced her fingers from the corner of Dana's left eye to the corner of her mouth exactly like she had longed to do earlier. After lingering at the corner of Dana's mouth for a heart beat or two, she brushed her fingertips over Dana's lips. Her touch was the lightest of touches and yet it unleashed a passion so wild it nearly swept her away.

"Ridley, please. I don't want you to do that. I..." Dana's lips parted and she touched the tip of her tongue to her lower lip.

Ridley moved closer until their bodies were touching. "Your mouth is so amazing." Her head inched closer and closer of its own volition until she felt Dana's breath on her lips. "Oh, Dana, I'm dying to kiss you."

"Then you'd better kiss me," Dana whispered back.

Ridley's kiss was hungry, desperate and fraught with all the longing and pent-up desire that had tormented her for weeks. As the kiss deepened, Dana moaned and parted her lips even more. That allowed Ridley to enter and explore the warmest, softest place she'd ever known. They were in each other's arms on the beach in the moonlight, but Ridley had lost all awareness of anything apart from the feel of their two mouths united in one breathtaking kiss.

Dana pulled her mouth away, placed the palm of one hand on Ridley's chest and pushed gently as if to create a little distance between them. She took a step backward as she struggled to catch her breath. "Ridley, listen to me. You..." She looked nervous as she brushed a piece of hair away from her eyes. "You can't be attracted to me, you just can't."

"But I already am, Dana," Ridley confessed between ragged breaths.

"I know and I don't want you to be." Dana lowered her eyes.

"I want to kiss you again. I don't want to stop," Ridley whispered.

"We have to. Please understand that this is not about you. I like you and I think you're a nice person and you're very attractive, but I don't think we should be any more than friends. I gave my heart away once and I think she still owns it. It's not finished for me, I..."

"You're in love with someone else?" Ridley grimaced. "I'm so sorry. She stepped back to create a greater space between them. "I've been so attracted to you since I met you and I thought maybe you felt the same about me. I never knew you were with someone. I had no idea or I would never have..."

"I'm not with her, not anymore. I used to be, but that was a long time ago. I'm not even sure I still love her." Dana folded her arms across her chest as if to protect herself. "I'm sorry if I gave you the wrong idea or did anything to lead you on. It's just that I don't want this with anyone. I don't need any complications in my life right now."

"I understand. It's just that..." Ridley struggled to gain control of her emotions. She was still recovering from that kiss and she didn't want to expose either the enormity of her desire or her anguish. In fact, she was shocked by the depth of her own reaction. "I wouldn't do anything to hurt you. We have mutual friends and I'd hate it if we had to avoid each other."

"So would I. We have good times to look forward to and I don't know about you, but I need all the friends I can get." Dana seemed to relax a little.

"I'd like to be your friend," Ridley said although she knew it was an out and out lie. She wanted so much more than that. In fact, when it came to Dana, she wanted it all. In spite of her hurt and disappointment, she managed a feeble smile.

Dana turned in the direction of the house. "Let's go back now. I'm tired and it's getting late and it's also getting way too cold out here."

"Okay." Ridley turned and walked beside Dana all the way to the house.

As soon as they got inside, Ridley grabbed Dana's arm to prevent her from making a beeline to her room. "Wait, please. I just want to say I'm sorry. I would never force myself on you. I promise it'll never happen again."

"I'm not worried and please stop saying you're sorry. You didn't force anything on me. You kissed me and it was nice. It was more than nice and I don't think you should feel bad about it."

"I won't be able to sleep if I think you're angry or upset with me."

"I'm not angry or upset, Ridley. You paid me a compliment and you don't need to apologize for being attracted to me." Dana looked into Ridley's eyes. "Trust me when I tell you this has nothing to do with you as a person. It's my problem. To be honest, I think you're incredibly attractive and if things were different..."

"I wish they were. You can't know how much." Ridley didn't know what else to do except to call it a night and escape to her room. She felt raw, on the verge of tears and if she couldn't be with Dana, she needed to be alone. "Good night Dana. I'll see you in the morning." Ridley turned and headed for the stairs.

"Good night. I hope you sleep well," Dana said behind her.

"I hope you do, too."

Once alone in her room, Ridley sat on the edge of the bed and let the reality of Dana's words sink in. Those words had hurt more than she would have imagined possible and she feared she'd done something irreparable. Why couldn't she have kept her feelings to herself? Why couldn't she have waited until she knew more about Dana? Usually, she didn't jump into things and she wondered what consequences she'd have to pay for her impulsive actions on the beach. Would Dana now try to avoid her? Had she destroyed any chance of a relationship with her? Questions like these tortured her as she washed her face, brushed her teeth and crawled into bed.

Kissing Dana had made her so aroused she knew she'd never get to sleep. Her taut nipples strained against the cotton fabric of her tank top and begged to be touched, so she reached under her shirt and touched them herself. They stiffened under her hands.

Never had she wanted anyone as much as she wanted Dana and never had she been this wet or this aroused. She needed relief even if it had to come by her own hand. She slid her hands over the warm smooth skin of her abdomen and under the elastic of her panties. Her moans filled the quiet room and the experienced strokes that had brought her relief so many times before soon tipped her over the edge. Sadly, the swift orgasm that coursed through her did little to diminish the fire that Dana had ignited. Hot tears stung her cheeks and out of pure exhaustion, she turned onto her side, hugged her pillow, and fell into a restless sleep.

Chapter
Ten

THE NEXT MORNING, the aroma of freshly brewed coffee smuggled its way into Ridley's senses with her first conscious breath of air. It had been a tough night, one of the toughest she'd ever had since the nights immediately following her father's death. All night, she'd tossed and turned in a state of semi-consciousness and now she would seriously consider doing just about anything for a cup of hot coffee.

Before heading downstairs, she showered and pulled on her favorite pair of worn-out jeans and an equally worn-out Temple University sweatshirt. As soon as she neared the kitchen, she heard Laurie and Karen talking and a horrible thought struck her. What if Dana had gotten up early and left because of what had happened last night? On the other side of the kitchen door, she whispered a soft prayer that she hadn't.

Laurie greeted Ridley when she entered the kitchen. "Hey, we thought you'd never get up. Need some coffee?" She got up and went to the coffee maker.

"Do I ever. How's everyone this morning?" Relief flooded Ridley when she saw Dana standing at the counter stirring something in a bowl. Her eyes stayed on Dana as she took the chair next to Karen.

Laurie brought Ridley a mug of coffee and hugged her from behind. "Here you go."

Ridley tilted her head up and planted a kiss on Laurie's cheek. "Thanks." She smiled at Laurie before she downed a hefty gulp. "What's that wonderful smell?"

"Dana's whipping up something delicious for us," Laurie said, taking the chair on the other side of Karen. "She's been at it since she got up."

Dana turned and faced them. Her eyes were kind and her smile warm. She showed no signs of being upset. "I hope you're hungry because I made one of my favorite breakfasts."

"I'm starving. What are we having?" Ridley took in a calming breath for the first time since she'd dragged her pitiful bones out of bed. Everything seemed friendly and although that came as a huge relief, she had to wonder how she would live with having Dana's friendship and nothing more? As hard as it was to imagine, she tried to convince herself that she could be friends and she could also get over this attraction. It didn't have to get the best of her.

"I'm making baked cinnamon apple French toast and we're having fruit salads with a lemon yogurt dressing. Does that sound good?"

"That sounds better than good. When do we eat?" Ridley asked.

"I hope it's soon, Dana. I'm famished," Laurie said.

"You'll only have to wait about ten more minutes." Dana placed a bowl in the center of the table. "Here's the dressing for the fruit salad. Why don't we start on them since you're all so hungry and then we'll have the French toast when it's done?" Dana sat at the table and spooned some dressing on her salad.

"Laurie, you're always hungry," Karen teased.

"I am when it comes to you, my honey pie." Laurie winked at Karen, leaned in, and smacked a loud kiss on her cheek.

"Honey pie?" Ridley laughed. "I've never heard you call her that before. And why are you two so hungry this morning? Is it from all that reading in bed last night?"

"It was a very stimulating book if you must know." Karen's devilish grin went well with her bright red cheeks. "Those lesbian detectives make me hot."

"Lesbian lawyers in power suits make me hot," Laurie said.

"Hey, stop it. That kind of talk is making me hot and soon I'll have to stand in front of that stove again," Dana said. She smiled as she ate a piece of fruit.

"I guess you got rid of that headache, huh Laurie?" Ridley said.

"Yes, I did. I took some pills and it went away as soon as I got in bed with Karen." Laurie put her arm around Karen and kissed her again.

"Okay, that's enough." Karen kissed Laurie and pushed her away, playfully. "Leave me alone and let me eat my fruit in peace."

"You two are so sweet." Ridley spoke to Karen and Laurie, but she watched Dana as she got up and went to the stove.

"Don't give up, Ridley. Some lucky girl is out there waiting for you to come along," Laurie reassured her. "You just haven't met her yet, that's all."

"I hope you're right," Ridley said, relieved to see that Dana had her mind on taking the French toast out of the oven and didn't seem to be paying attention to what Laurie had said. In order to get Laurie off the topic of her pitiable love life, Ridley announced, "It looks like the French toast is ready, girls."

Dana placed the baking dish full of bubbling hot French toast on a trivet in the center of the table and sprinkled the top with powdered sugar. While everyone watched, she lifted a saucepan of hot maple syrup and melted butter from the stove and poured its contents into a small pitcher which she then placed on the table.

Before she sat down, she filled everyone's coffee cups and said, "What are you waiting for? Dig in."

AFTER BREAKFAST, THEY all drove to the North end of the island to see the Barnegat lighthouse and take a walk by the ocean. Despite the moderate temperature and the cloudless sunny day, a stiff breeze made it feel a lot chillier by the water. Still, a few hardy souls ventured out onto the long jetty of massive slippery rocks that extended out from the southernmost tip of the island. Ridley suggested they take a safer route and stay on the cement pedestrian walkway that ran parallel to the shoreline.

Ridley and Dana walked together, a short distance behind Laurie and Karen. "I think this is one of my favorite places," Ridley said. "When I was young, I used to sit down here for hours watching the boats travel back and forth between Barnegat Bay and the Atlantic. I'd wave at the people on the boats and they would always wave back at me. I loved to watch the fishermen cast their lines from these massive rocks and I got an endless thrill every time one of them pulled a flapping fish out of the water."

"Did you ever go fishing?"

"My grandfather and father used to and sometimes they'd take me with them, but I hardly ever caught anything. I liked to watch, but I didn't like to do it that much."

Dana stopped walking and leaned on the metal railing that separated the walkway from the ocean. She stared out at the waves as they crashed relentlessly against the huge jagged rocks below. "It's been so long since I've seen the ocean."

Ridley stood beside her and let Karen and Laurie continue on ahead of them. She wanted to talk to Dana, alone. "Do you mind if I ask you something?"

Dana turned. "That depends on what you want to ask me."

"Are we, I mean are you..." Ridley shook her head as if to snap her thoughts into place. "I mean, are things okay between us after what happened last night?" The stiff wind whipped Dana's hair around her face and Ridley longed to reach out and touch it.

"We're fine as far as I'm concerned."

"I hope so. I got carried away. Nothing like that will happen again, I promise."

Dana smiled and touched Ridley's arm. "I told you that you didn't do anything wrong. You kissed me, that was all. I wanted you to and it happened to be very nice. It's just that..."

"I know. You told me you don't want to complicate your life. I was just worried that I might have ruined the friendship you and I have or the friendship the four of us have. I wouldn't want to do that because it means a great deal to me. I wouldn't want to mess it up."

"Nothing is messed up or ruined. I swear to God."

"You mean it?"

"I mean it." Dana tugged at Ridley's sleeve and started walking. "Come on, stop thinking about it. Let's catch up with the girls and have a nice afternoon."

"Okay." Ridley started walking. She should have been relieved, but she wasn't.

After a long walk, they spent an hour or so browsing in a nearby gift shop packed with shells and trinkets and every other shore themed souvenir under the sun. They all bought something to remember the weekend by and with their purchases in hand, they proceeded into the homey restaurant attached to the gift shop to have lunch.

Around four in the afternoon, they returned to the house and got ready to head back to the city. Everyone agreed they wanted to have time when they got home to unwind and prepare for the work week ahead. Laurie and Karen were the first to leave and after they said their goodbyes and pulled out of the driveway, Ridley stood in the driveway with Dana. "Will you come down here again some time?" Despite Dana's reassurances, Ridley still worried that Dana would stay away from her and be lost to her for good.

Dana nodded. "Of course I will. I had a good time and I wanted to spend more time with Karen and Laurie." She got into her car, fastened her seatbelt and rolled the window down. "And I enjoyed spending time with you," she added as an afterthought. "Thanks for everything and I'll see you around sometime, okay?"

Ridley leaned down near the open window. "I hope so. Keep in touch, will you?"

"I will." Dana smiled. "Goodbye."

"Goodbye." A heavy desolation dropped over Ridley like a dense cloud. She didn't want to say goodbye to Dana in the worst way and she wondered if Dana had just said goodbye to her forever. Once Dana had the chance to think, she'd change her mind about being around Ridley. That's the way things like this usually turned out.

Dana waved as she backed out of the driveway and as she turned into the street, she waved again. Ridley stayed in the driveway and kept Dana in sight as long as she could. "Why did I have to go and kiss her?" she murmured to the driveway as she kicked a stone with the toe of her shoe. Just the memory of that kiss made her aroused all over again. How many times would she feel that kiss and how long would she be tortured by a desire for someone she couldn't have? "Now that I have kissed her, how am I going to stand knowing I'll never kiss her again?"

Chapter
Eleven

AFTER SCHOOL LET out the following Friday, Ridley rushed through the school yard to get away from Laurie. She didn't need to turn around to know that Laurie was weaving her way through the crowd of students to catch up to her. Ridley had managed to dodge her friend every day since they'd come back from the shore, but on the way up the stairs from the gym, she had spotted Laurie outside the main office talking to another teacher. Laurie waved and gestured to her, but Ridley averted her eyes, skirted around a group of students and pretended not to see her. Without a backward glance, she made her getaway out the front door.

Dana's rejection was still an open wound and telling Laurie about it was an inevitability she wasn't prepared to tackle quite yet. Besides, Dana didn't actually reject her. She just didn't want her and that was even harder to accept. As soon as she reached the rear bumper of her car, she felt the tug on her sleeve at the same time she felt Laurie's presence behind her.

"Ridley, would you please hold still?" Laurie asked. "We need to talk."

Ridley obeyed and stood in place. "I'm holding still, so talk."

"What's going on? Are you mad at me or something? You've been avoiding me all week and it won't do you any good to deny it because I know you extremely well and I know when something's bothering you."

"I'm not mad at you and I haven't been avoiding you. Well, yes I have, but it's just because I've got a lot on my mind, that's all." Ridley moved toward the driver's door. .

Laurie stayed right behind her. "Wait a minute. I'm not done with you. Is that any reason to give me the brush-off at lunch and go hide in your office pretending you had things to do?"

"Maybe I did have things to do."

"That never stopped you from letting me sit and talk while you worked."

That statement rang true and it forced Ridley to turn around and make eye contact with Laurie for the first time. "You're right and I'm sorry."

"Are you going to tell me what's up with you or what?"

"It's nothing important. Nothing I won't get over soon enough."

Laurie persisted. "That may be so, but in the meantime..." Laurie sounded exasperated as she took a deep breath and let it out. "I'm your best friend. That gives me the right to care when you have a problem and the right to nag you until you tell me about it."

"I know you care, but it's nothing."

Laurie showed her increasing frustration by shaking her head. "Why do you always have to be so damned self-sufficient? Karen has to work late, so come home and have dinner with me and we'll talk about it." Laurie put her arm around Ridley's waist and leaned in. "Come on, we'll order Chinese take-out. Steamed dumplings and fried rice? An order of Sesame chicken and an order of Szechwan shrimp? Mmm..."

"That sounds really good. I'll meet you at your house."

"I'M SO BEAT." Ridley stretched out on Laurie's sofa and kicked off her shoes. "I haven't had one single decent night's sleep this entire week."

"Do you want to take a nap before we eat?" Laurie asked. "I can grade some papers for an hour or two and we can eat later on."

"That's nice of you, but I wouldn't be able to sleep anyway. I think talking to you would help me more and maybe I'll sleep better tonight."

"Let's talk, then. Would you like a cold beer?"

"Yes, please. The colder the better."

Laurie went into the kitchen and came back with the beers. After she handed one to Ridley she flopped into a chair next to the sofa and propped her feet up on the coffee table.

Ridley stared at her beer bottle and spun it around in her hands a few times. With her thumb nail, she picked at the upper edge of the center of the label. "This has been one hell of a week for me. TGIF doesn't begin to describe how glad I am it's finally over."

"Some weeks feel longer than others," Laurie said.

"This one did and it was only four days long. Honestly, I don't know how I made it. I must have been functioning on autopilot."

"Why don't you tell me what's bothering you?"

"Before I say one word, I want a promise from you." Ridley sat up and took a long drawn-out drink of beer. "A solemn promise."

"Okay. What is it?" Laurie asked.

"I want you to keep this between us. Don't tell Karen about anything I'm going to tell you. I don't want her to know, not yet anyway. Please?"

"Of course, I promise. Just because Karen and I are together, doesn't mean I have to tell her everything. You and I have been friends for many years and you've always been there for me. You've earned the right to confide in me and to trust me to respect your secrets."

"Thanks," Ridley said.

"Is this about last weekend by any chance?" Laurie asked. "Is it about Dana?"

"Uh-huh. It's about Dana."

"You're attracted to her aren't you?"

"That's not the half of it. Something happened to me the first time I met her. I can't get her out of my mind and I can't stop wanting to be with her, to talk to her and to touch her. It's like she's gotten under my skin. I can't remember ever feeling this way about anyone."

"Oh, Ridley, honey. You've got it bad, haven't you?"

Ridley closed her eyes and bobbed her head. "That's an understatement."

"But why are you so upset about it?"

"I'm upset because I made a fool of myself and she made it clear she's not interested in anything other than a friendship with me," Ridley explained. "Not ever."

"Why? What did you do? What did she say?"

"Hold on, I'm getting to that part. Sunday night at the shore, after you and Karen went to your room—and by the way, don't think I didn't catch on to your little plan. You faked that headache and made up the story about the book so I could be alone with her." Ridley leaned to the side, stretched her arm out and punched Laurie in the shoulder. "You think you're clever."

"Apparently, not clever enough to put one over on you," Laurie replied. "I want you to know I didn't tell Karen you were interested in Dana. I whispered sweet nothings into her ear at dinner and told her I had a plan to be alone with her when we got back. That's how I got her to play along with my scheme."

"Well, thanks for that anyway."

"You're welcome. So, go on with your story."

Ridley told Laurie about her walk on the beach with Dana. "While I was telling her about how he died I broke down and started to cry. She does that to me. She makes me feel ripped wide open and I can't seem to control my emotions whenever I'm with her. Next thing I knew, she was holding my hand and she was so sweet, so gentle, I..."

"Uh-oh."

"Yeah...uh-oh is right. It got colder and I put my sweat suit jacket on her shoulders and told her how beautiful she was and then I grabbed her from behind and held her and when she turned around, I almost begged her to let me kiss her."

Laurie moved to the edge of her chair. "Did she let you?"

"Yes, she did," Ridley turned away to avoid meeting Laurie's wide eyes.

"Don't turn away. Look at me."

"I'm a little embarrassed."

"What on earth for? You shouldn't be embarrassed to tell me anything. I don't see anything wrong with what you just said. It's the best thing I've heard in a long time."

Ridley met Laurie eyes. "Good Lord, Laurie, that was some kiss. It took my breath away. It's all I've thought about since. I can feel it in every cell of my body, as if it's happening all over again, right here and right now. I wanted her more than I've ever wanted anyone."

"Maybe I'm missing the point, but you're wonderful and attractive and she's wonderful and attractive and I just don't see why this is a problem?"

"It's not a problem for me, but it is for her." Ridley took another swig of beer.

"Why is that?"

"She told me she didn't want to get involved with anyone." With her thumb, Ridley peeled a long continuous strip of paper from the label on her beer bottle. "What she probably meant to say was that she didn't want to get involved with me."

"That is not possible. There's nothing wrong with you or the way you feel or with anything you said or did. Don't be so hard on yourself."

"What am I going to do?" Ridley asked.

"I don't know," Laurie said. "Karen told me that Dana had a bad experience with a woman she was in love with, someone she met in Chicago. She told Karen that was why she decided to move back here but Karen doesn't know exactly what happened between them because Dana never told her any of the details. Since Dana's been back, she hasn't brought up the subject again and we haven't asked about it."

"She did tell me she'd been in love with someone and it wasn't over for her."

"That must be the same woman. Did she kiss you like she meant it?"

"God, it felt like it to me," Ridley answered. "I thought I'd never feel this way about anyone. I've had my share of women but no one has ever touched me the way Dana has."

"Maybe she's that woman you've been searching for."

"I think she is. So why isn't she excited about finding me?"

"I think you should give her time. Once she gets to know you..." Laurie paused. "Well, let me put it to you this way. I think you're something special and I'm positive she will too. If she doesn't, she's out of her mind."

"I hope you're right. She said she wanted to be friends, but she might have said that to let me down easier. What if I don't see her again? I can't ask her out at this point and I'm pretty sure she won't be calling me. I feel so helpless."

"I think you'll see her again and I can tell you one thing I do know about her. She's a nice person and she's honest. I don't believe she'd lie to you just to be kind."

"Careful or I'll start to feel encouraged."

"There's no reason you shouldn't be. Why don't you give her a call? What have you got to lose? Friends get together, don't they? Ask her to do something and see where this friendship takes both of you."

"I'm not sure I can stand being her friend."

"I understand that," Laurie said as she got up. "Let me call in our order and while we wait for it, we'll put our scholarly minds together and see if we can come up with some fool proof plan to get you two together."

"Thanks. God knows, I'm open to suggestions," Ridley said.

Chapter
Twelve

ON THE SATURDAY after the weekend at the shore, Dana stood in the restaurant kitchen chopping soup vegetables on the butcher-block island. As usual, she'd shopped at the wholesale markets earlier that morning and she and Tracy had already decided on the dinner specials. Now, they had plenty of time to do some of the prep work before anyone else got there.

"Damn it all to hell and back again." Dana sucked on her left index finger after she cut it with her chef's knife. About twenty minutes ago, she'd nicked a small chunk of tissue off the tip of her left middle finger with the vegetable peeler. "I don't know what's wrong with me. I'm all thumbs today."

"It's not just today. You've been out of sorts all week since you came back from the shore." Tracy got a bandage from the first aid kit and brought it over, along with a paper towel. After Dana washed her hands and dried her finger, Tracy put the bandage on and went back to work at the counter. "You've done nothing but grumble and fumble and you've been cursing up a storm. Would you like to tell me what's going on?"

"No, I wouldn't, but since you won't leave me alone until I do, I might as well get on with it." Dana laid her knife down and faced Tracy. "I've been thinking about Sarah, okay? If you must know, she's been on my mind at lot."

"I should have known." Tracy stopped slicing carrots and stared at Dana as if she were trying very hard to keep from saying what was really on her mind.

Dana picked up her chef's knife again and proceeded to chop the living hell out of one of the peeled onions from the pile in front of her.

"Whoa! What did that poor innocent onion ever do to you?" Tracy came over and put her hand on top of Dana's knife wielding hand. "Stop before you cut your finger off and put that knife down while we talk this over. You have got to let go of that girl. I don't know what you were doing with her in the first place. We've been over and over this, haven't we?"

Dana laid the knife down. "We have, but I can't get her out of my system."

"Jesus, Dana. You seem to have forgotten how much she hurt you," Tracy said, not even trying to hide her anger. "She lied to you and cheated on you."

"I haven't forgotten, but anyone can make a mistake. She was confused and I'm not sure she knew what she was doing at the time. Did you ever stop to think she might be sorry for what she did? She loved me once and it was real, I know it was." Dana dabbed at her watery eyes. "I'm not crying...it's the onions."

Tracy shook her head. "You're hopeless. If Sarah loved you so much, where is she? I don't see her around here anywhere. Honestly, you could do so much better."

"I know you think that, but I loved her."

Tracy released an exasperated breath and said, "Losing your first love is always tough, but how are you ever going to get over her if you don't go out with other women? Why waste your time pining over someone you know you can't have, someone who clearly doesn't want you?" Tracy closed her eyes and rubbed the bridge of her nose with her thumb and index finger as if to soothe her frustration. "I don't know why I even bother," she said when she opened her eyes again. "If I had half a fucking brain in my head, I'd give up trying to talk sense into that thick skull of yours."

"I know you're frustrated with me and angry, but I can't help it. I tell myself to let her go. I know what she did was horrible. I know all that and I still can't move on."

Tracy's face softened and she waited a short time as if contemplating what to say next. "I think I know why you're having trouble letting go of her. You never had any closure. The whole nasty mess came at you out of the blue and when it was over, you were left hanging."

"You really think so? That kind of makes sense."

Tracy nodded. "I think if the relationship had lasted longer, you would have left her on your own at some point. I'm sure you would have figured out what kind of person she was and that would have been the end of that. You were always too mature for her."

"Too bad I wasn't mature enough to avoid getting involved with her." Dana turned away out of shame. Tracy was right about the lack of closure but she questioned the part about her having been more mature than Sarah. Whenever she let herself think about her relationship with Sarah, she never thought of herself as mature. She saw herself as foolish and naïve and she felt ashamed that she'd never suspected what Sarah was capable of. How could she not have seen it coming? She turned around again and addressed Tracy. "I'm glad you've figured this all out because I haven't. For a long time, I've avoided thinking about it or dealing with it by burying myself in my work and staying away from anyone except for you and my family."

"I'm aware of that. So, what started you thinking about this now?"

"I don't know, I..." Dana hesitated, unsure as to whether she wanted to tell Tracy about that night on the beach with Ridley. She'd gone over it in her mind a hundred times that week, but she'd kept it to herself thinking that if she did maybe it would be just go away. "No, that's not true. I do know what started this. It was the weekend at the shore with Ridley. We were walking on the beach the first evening I was there, just the two of us and..."

That got Tracy's undivided attention. She laid her knife down. "And what?"

"One thing led to another and we ended up kissing."

"So that's it. That's why you're all worked up." Tracy's face brightened and a faint smile began to elevate the corners of her mouth.

"I couldn't help it. She was sweet and nice and she was upset and..."

"Yeah, I get the picture." Tracy tightened her mouth as if to rein in her expanding smile. "So, how was it? Kissing her, I mean."

"I'm not going to lie. It was incredible."

"I can just imagine. And what else happened? What did she say?"

"She said she was attracted to me. She said I was beautiful."

"She's right about that and this is great news." Tracy's eyes lit up. "Damn, I knew that girl had good taste. How did you feel about what she said?"

"I'm not sure. No one has said that to me in a long time. I do know I wanted more, but it wouldn't have been fair to her. I don't think she's that kind of girl. She's very nice and kind and considerate and she's..."

"Very attractive," Tracy filled in the blank. "She's very attractive, Dana."

"Yes, she is. Even I noticed that, Tracy." Dana went back to chopping onions. "I'm not sure what there could be between us. I don't know if I could love anyone again and I'm not sure I want to. Besides, we have mutual friends and I wouldn't want to ruin that."

"Well then, let's stop making soup, because we need to get busy digging that hole you're planning on crawling into for the rest of your life. When we're done you can jump right in and drop out of the human race. No more problems."

"Tracy..."

"Dana...," Tracy echoed. "I can't figure you out. She's adorable and sexy and she obviously wants you. You're crazy to turn someone like her down. I sure as hell wouldn't." Tracy grabbed a stock pot from the overhead rack and set it on the counter. Then she went to the refrigerator and brought back two large containers of chicken stock they'd made earlier in the week. As she poured it into the pot, she glanced over her shoulder at Dana. "She's single, you're single and you're both consenting adults, so why not just go for it?"

"That's easy for you to say. What if she gets serious about me?"

"I think what scares you is that you might get serious about her."

For a moment, Dana had no reply. Leave it to Tracy to dig in that deep and extract her most carefully guarded truths. "It's better if Ridley and I are just friends. What if Sarah and I get back together in the future? What would I tell Ridley after I'd used her like that and what would she think of me? What would Karen and Laurie think of me?"

Tracy didn't attempt to answer Dana's questions. Instead, she lifted the pot of chicken stock and set it on one of the gas burners. After she set the burner on low, she went back to the counter and began peeling several large butternut squashes. "Okay, suit yourself. God knows you will anyway, no matter what I say. I still don't see why you can't get to know her better. Why don't you invite Laurie and Karen to brunch tomorrow and ask them to bring Ridley with them? That would be a nice safe way to see her again without any pressure."

"That's a good idea. Maybe I'll call Karen this afternoon."

"You do that. You won't get any answers to your questions by avoiding the situation. You have to take a chance and find the answers for yourself."

"Thanks, Tracy. You're the only person I know who'd dare to be so brutally honest with me and believe it or not, I do appreciate it."

"I'm not trying to be brutal. I just can't stand to see you waste your time clinging to the past. I think it's time you made a new life for yourself and you're going to need more in your life than me and this restaurant."

"I do have a new life and this restaurant keeps me plenty busy. What's wrong with that? Dana asked. "And I'll always need you in my life."

"And you'll always have me, but it's not enough and you know it." Tracy split one of the squashes in half lengthwise and began to chop it into uniform pieces.

Dana washed her hands and dried them on a kitchen towel. "These onions are ready. Why don't you finish making the soup? I have a few things I need to take care of in my office. I'll be back in about an hour. Maybe then I'll be able to get something done around here."

"Are you all right?"

"I'm fine. I just need to be alone for a while," Dana said as she walked away.

"Dana?" Tracy called her name before she reached the door to her office.

Dana turned around. "What is it?"

"I want to say something to you before you go." Tracy lifted her knife in the air. "I would cut off my right hand with this knife before I'd ever try to hurt you in any way. You're my best friend and I'll always love you." Tracy put the knife down.

Dana walked over to Tracy and stood close to her. "Come here, silly." She hugged her friend and held her in her arms. "I'm grateful that I have you and I wouldn't want you to be anything but honest with me. I love you, too, and I'm all right. It's just that I have a lot to think about and I feel a little overwhelmed at the moment. I'm not running away." What Dana told Tracy was the truth. What she didn't tell her was also the truth and was that Ridley had stirred up a hornet's nest of emotions inside of her and she needed to sort them out if she could. If she couldn't, she needed to follow her heart and buzzing around in her heart was the knowledge that she liked Ridley a whole hell of a lot and wanted to see her again.

"Okay, if you're sure," Tracy said.

"I'm sure. I really do have something I need to take care of in my office and I'll be back soon. Call me if you need me before then."

"I'll be right here. Take all the time you need."

Chapter
Thirteen

RIDLEY DARTED ACROSS South Street late Sunday morning to meet Karen and Laurie in front of the entrance to Café De Marco. On Saturday afternoon, Karen had called to tell her that Dana had invited them to come to brunch the next day and that Dana had insisted they bring her along. Naturally, Ridley had jumped at the chance. It would have been sweeter if Dana had called her directly, but she was so thrilled about seeing Dana again she decided not to get hung up on how she got invited.

As soon as Ridley caught up with them, Laurie grabbed the sleeve of Ridley's jacket to hold her back. "Honey, why don't you go inside and tell the hostess we're here," she told Karen. "I've got something in my shoe and as soon as I get it out, Ridley and I will be right behind you."

"Can't you wait until we get inside?" Karen asked.

"No, it hurts too much. It must be a sharp stone or something."

"All right, but don't take too long."

"How are you doing?" Laurie asked Ridley once Karen was out of the way.

"I feel a little better now. I picked up the phone to call her at least ten times yesterday, but each time I chickened out at the last second. You can't possibly know what she does to me."

"I think I do," Laurie said. "I was happy she called and asked us to come today. At least you'll get to see her again. How do you feel about it?"

"I'm thrilled and at the same time I'm terrified."

"Why wouldn't you be? If I were you, I'd take it one step at a time. See how she responds to you and if it seems right ask her to go to your mother's for dinner with you like we talked about. Just follow your instincts and your heart."

"I will. I'll be all right once we get in there."

"Speaking of which, I suppose we'd better get inside before Karen comes after us," Laurie said. "She's already suspicious."

The hostess escorted them to their table and as they walked to the back of the dining room, tantalizing aromas teased Ridley's senses. The smell of coffee, cinnamon, and sweet yeasty things baking in the oven registered in her mind and her stomach soon reacted with a series of hunger pangs. The pangs let her know she'd regained her normal appetite, something she'd been sorely lacking all week. "God, it smells good in here. I'm starving," she told Laurie.

"So am I. I can't wait to see the menu," Laurie said.

"There you are," Karen told them as they neared the table. "Did you get that rock out of your shoe, Laurie?"

"Uh...yeah, what a relief." Laurie glanced at Ridley.

"Uh-huh." Karen pursed her lips. "What are the two of you up to?"

"Not a thing," Laurie replied. "I just needed to talk to Ridley about something that happened at work and I didn't want to bore you with work talk." Laurie sat next to Karen and pointed to the chair across from her. "Sit over there, Ridley."

Shortly after they were seated, Dana came over to the table and sat in the chair next to Ridley's. After she spoke to Karen and Laurie briefly, she turned to Ridley and leaned closer to her. "It's so good to see you. I hope you didn't mind that I had Karen ask you to brunch today, but we've been so busy, I never had the chance to call you myself. I would have been very disappointed if you hadn't come."

"I was just happy that you included me."

"I wanted to," Dana said. Then she addressed all three of them. "I don't have to cook while you guys are here, so I thought I'd join you for brunch. Would you like that?"

"Very much," Karen answered. "We were hoping you would, weren't we Laurie?"

"Yes we were," Laurie confirmed. She picked up the menu and started to read it. "Wait until you see this menu, Karen. It's going to be hard to pick just one thing."

"I guess that means we'll have to come here again and again," Karen said.

"I hope you come here a lot," Dana told them.

A young girl from the wait staff came to their table and filled their water glasses with ice cold water. "Your waitress will be right with you," she announced.

Ridley took advantage of the fact that Karen and Laurie were discussing the menu choices and reached over to touch Dana's arm. Touching Dana may have been a poor choice under the circumstances, but she found it intolerable not to. "I'm glad you have time to sit with us." She stole a glimpse of her hand on Dana's arm and envisioned taking Dana's hand and bringing it to her lips. That image not only aroused her, it startled her back to reality.

"I wanted to see you again." Dana carefully withdrew her arm from beneath Ridley's grasp and clasped her hands together on the table. "I had a good time at the shore."

"I'm glad, but I wasn't sure you'd want to see me again, after..." Ridley kept her voice low and leaned closer to Dana. "After what happened."

"I wish you wouldn't worry about that," Dana said.

"I'll try not to. Did you mean what you said about wanting to be friends?"

"I'm not in the habit of saying things I don't mean," Dana assured her. "Besides, you're a nice person and I like you. Why wouldn't I want to be your friend?"

Right then, Ridley made a decision. On Friday, she and Laurie had come up with a few ideas to get her and Dana together and now Dana had supplied her with the perfect opening. She was sick of long agonizing weeks wondering when or if she'd ever see Dana again. After taking in a slow steadying breath, she tested the validity of Dana's words. "Okay, since you say you want to be friends, I'd like you to do something with me. I'm driving to my mother's next Sunday for dinner. It will be a beautiful drive now that the leaves are changing and I know she'd love to meet you."

"She would?" Dana asked.

"Yes. I told her about you and I think she'd enjoy talking to a real chef. Besides, she loves to meet my friends and have guests over for dinner."

"I could go as long as we go after brunch is over."

"That would be perfect timing. I could pick you up around three-thirty or four. Would that give you enough time to get ready or is that pushing it?"

"I think that would be okay," Dana said. "Can I bring anything?"

"You don't have to."

"I'd like to bring your mother a hostess gift. Does she drink wine?"

"Yes. She loves it."

"What's she making? Do you know?"

"No, I don't but I could find out and call you."

"No, don't bother. I'll just bring a red and a white."

"I'm sure my mother won't call the wine police if we drink white wine with meat or red wine with chicken," Ridley said. As long as Dana agreed to go with her, she didn't care if they drank a bottle of dirty dishwater. For the first time since they got there, her muscles relaxed and she felt her insides slow down. She could breathe again.

"I think people should drink what they like and to hell with the rules," Dana said.

"I'll drink to that." Ridley held her water glass up. "Rules are made to be broken."

"What rules? What are you two talking about?" Laurie asked.

"What wine to drink with what food," Ridley explained.

"Drink what you want. That's what I say." Laurie dismissed the subject with a wave of her hand as if she'd just said the final word and went back to talking to Karen.

"Let's talk about what you guys want," Dana said when the waitress arrived at their table. "If you're in the mood for Tex-Mex, try the frittata with the green chili cheese grits. That's one of our best recipes and everyone goes crazy over it. And before I forget, Tracy told me to tell you that she made her hot cinnamon rolls especially for you. I have to warn you, though, they're totally addictive."

"So that's what we smelled," Ridley said.

"I know I speak for all of us dough addicts when I say, bring on the cinnamon buns," Laurie said. She looked at Karen and Ridley and they both nodded. "We'll all have coffee, too, right?" she asked. Again, Karen and Ridley nodded.

"Why don't you bring us a carafe of coffee for the table while they decide what they want to order," Dana said to the waitress. "Anyone want juice?"

"I'll have a small grapefruit juice," Laurie replied.

"None for me," Karen said.

"Small orange for me," Ridley said.

The waitress scurried off to get the beverages.

"Dana, how's your hollandaise sauce? Is it really rich?" Karen asked.

"I don't think so. We make it a little differently than the classic French version, so it's nice and lemony and quite a bit lighter. I think it's good."

"Well then, I'm having the Café De Marco eggs Benedict," Karen announced.

"You'll like that. It's a variation on the classic. Instead of English muffins we use Italian bread and instead of Canadian bacon, we use Italian ham."

"That sounds good to me," Karen said. "But put the sauce on the side."

"I'm having the Greek omelet," Laurie said.

"Another good choice," Dana said. "What are you having, Ridley?"

"I'll try the Tex-Mex frittata thing."

"Great. I think you'll like it. It's a tiny bit spicy, but very tasty."

"Are you eating with us, Dana?" Karen asked.

"No. I was up early and I got hungry so I had to eat, but I'll have coffee and one of Tracy's cinnamon buns." The waitress came back with coffee and juices and Dana placed their orders. After the waitress left, Dana said, "I'm happy I decided to move back to Philadelphia. It's nice to be here again and to have friends around. I enjoy it when we all get together."

"We're glad you're back, too," Karen said.

"Tracy promised to come out and say hello if there's ever a lull in the kitchen." Dana held up her water glass. "I want to make a toast to all of you." First she faced Laurie and Karen, and said, "Here's to renewing old friendships." And then she held her glass toward Ridley and said, "And here's to making new friends."

"We'll drink to that," Laurie and Karen said in unison.

"Here's to our friendship," Ridley said as she clicked her glass against Dana's. Then she half stood so she could click Karen's and Laurie's glasses since everyone knew it was bad luck to skip a glass during a toast. When she clicked her glass against Laurie's, their eyes met and Laurie gave her a meaningful glance.

Chapter
Fourteen

AT LAST, SUNDAY rolled around, the day Ridley and Dana were going to have dinner at Ridley's mother's house. Dana had just made it up to her apartment from the restaurant kitchen a few minutes before Ridley got there, so she asked Ridley to wait while she took a quick shower and changed her clothes. Ridley took a seat on the sofa and allowed herself to settle down from the excitement that had been building inside of her for the past few days. As of late, everything in her life revolved around one crucial consideration. When would she see Dana again?

Ridley stood when Dana entered the living room. The sight of her was enough to blow Ridley away. Dana wore dark jeans that hugged her trim body and a ribbed turtleneck cotton sweater in a beautiful shade of steel blue. As Dana moved around the room, Ridley stole secret glimpses of her firm backside and perfectly proportioned breasts. Hands down, Dana had to be the cutest women on the face of the earth and knowing she'd have the rest of the day with her made Ridley dizzy with delight.

"I was worried about wearing jeans, but when I saw you were wearing them, I decided I would, too," Dana said. She sounded slightly breathless as she spoke and her cheeks were rosy.

"My mother will probably be wearing them, too. She's a classy lady but she's not formal. How was brunch today?"

"Busy and more crowded than usual," Dana answered.

"That's good. Were you able to finish and get cleaned up before I got here?"

"Not quite. As soon as the last customers were served, we all hustled to clean up and put everything away. The staff didn't even talk or fool around like they usually do. Everyone had plans and they all wanted to get out of there as fast as they could. They knew I had plans, so they told me to leave and they would do the rest."

"What's Tracy doing tonight?" Ridley asked.

"She's taking Erika out to dinner and then to a concert at the Kimmel Center. By the way, she said to say hello and she hopes we have a good time."

"The Kimmel Center? That's mostly classical music, isn't it?"

"Erika's a classical music fan," Dana said. "And Tracy isn't."

"The things we do for love." Ridley glanced at her watch. "Are you ready to leave? I told my mother we'd be there in an hour and we'll just make it if we leave now."

"I'm ready. I just have to get the wine." Dana hurried into the kitchen and returned with two bottles of wine. She held them up so Ridley could see the labels. "I chose a couple of my favorites. Do you think she'll like them?"

"She'll love them."

"Good. Let me grab a jacket and we'll be on our way." Dana opened the hall closet and took out a navy blue polar fleece. "What did your mother say when you told her I was coming?"

"She was thrilled. She's looking forward to meeting you."

THE DRIVE WAS as lovely as Ridley had promised it would be. The maple trees showed off their most dazzling reds and shouted out from among the spectrum of colors that painted the autumn landscape. As each leaf surrendered its fragile hold on life, it flitted to and fro in the air until it reached its final resting place where it would nourish the earth and allow the cycle of life to begin all over again. The autumn air was chilled by a gentle breeze and it smelled crisp and burnt around the edges.

As she drove, Ridley pointed out places of interest and threw in an anecdote from her childhood whenever a memory surfaced. In no time at all, they turned into a long driveway which led to an elegant, two-story stone house with white trim and black shutters."

"This is the kind of house you see on magazine covers," Dana said.

"It's nice, isn't it? My father had this house built for my mother. It was their dream home and she swears his heart and soul still live in it. She feels him in the house and that's why she won't sell it and get a smaller place."

"It would be like losing him all over again."

"I think that's true. She can't bear to part with it." Ridley pulled up in front of the garage door and turned to Dana. "Are you ready?"

"I'm ready if you are." Dana opened her door.

Ridley reminded Dana to take the wine bottles and she and Dana walked to the front door. "Mom, we're here," Ridley called out as they entered the house.

Vicki's voice floated out to them. "I'm in the kitchen, sweetheart."

Ridley led Dana into the kitchen where they found her mother at the counter cutting green beans. "Hello, Mom." Ridley went over to her mother, gave her a side hug and kissed her on the cheek. "How are you?"

"I'm just fine. How was the ride? Were the trees pretty?"

"The ride was nice and the trees were as pretty as I've ever seen them." Ridley went back to Dana's side, took her by the arm and brought her closer. "Mom, I'd like you to meet my new friend, Dana De Marco."

"Nice to meet you, Dana. I'm pleased you could join us for dinner."

"So am I. It's nice to meet you, Mrs. Kelsen," Dana said.

"I'd prefer it if you'd call me Vicki."

"Okay, Vicki. Thank you for inviting me."

"Ridley told me a little about you. She said you're a chef and you have your own restaurant in the city, on South Street. Is that right?"

"Yes, that's all true," Dana said.

"Ridley also told me you're a talented cook. I hope my amateur cooking skills will meet with your approval. I'm just an ordinary housewife, or at least I used to be."

"I enjoy it when someone else cooks for me." Dana handed Vicki the bottles. "I brought you some wine, but I didn't know what you were making."

"How nice of you, Dana," Vicki said as she read the labels. "This white will go well with what we're having for dinner and I'll save the red for another time, unless you girls want me to open both of them."

"No, the white is fine with us, right Dana?" Ridley asked.

"That's fine with me. It's one of my favorites."

Ridley's mother put the red wine on the counter and handed her the bottle of white. "Would you put this in the refrigerator to chill, sweetheart? Dinner won't be ready for another hour and I can't think of anything you can help me with. While I finish up here, why don't you show Dana around the house and take her outside to see the flowers. They're pretty this time of year."

"Okay, Mom."

Ridley gave Dana a quick tour of the house and then took her outside to see the garden. Stone pathways like spokes in a wheel ran through the flower beds and led to a central gazebo. Ridley stepped up into it and sat on the bench that lined the interior. "Sit here with me." She patted the empty stretch of bench beside her.

"Your mother's a good-looking woman. Now I see where you get your looks," Dana said as sat next to Ridley. "And she's nice like you or should I say you're nice like her?"

"Either way is okay and thank you. I'm lucky to have a mother like her."

"I feel the same about my mother," Dana said. "Maybe you'll meet her someday."

"I'd like that very much." Ridley inched a little closer to Dana.

"This is a lovely garden. Does your mother do this all by herself?"

"She putters around when she's at home, but no, she pays someone to maintain it and to do the heavy work. I like it in the fall when she puts in the mums and ornamental kale."

"What are those blue flowers, next to the sage?"

"Those are blue asters. You should see this in the spring when the azaleas are in bloom and the pink and white dogwoods are out."

"I'll bet it's pretty. Does your mother spend the entire summer at the shore?"

Ridley shook her head. "No, she goes back and forth. She has friends here and her sister and she comes up to see them and to check on the house. Her friends also visit her down there and my aunt comes down a couple of times for a week or so."

"What about you? Do you spend the summers there?"

"I'm down there a lot, since I'm off. I come home if my mother's friends are coming and if Karen and Laurie are coming for a weekend, she goes home and lets us have the place to ourselves. She's thoughtful like that."

"She must trust you," Dana remarked.

"I've never given her any reason not to. Besides, she raised me to be independent and she knows she doesn't need to run my life. She doesn't want to either."

"You seem like the independent type. I thought that right away."

Ridley met Dana's eyes. "That doesn't mean I don't want to be with someone."

"I just meant that you seemed strong and self-reliant."

"I guess you could say that about me. The funny thing is, I love to spend time with my mother even more because she doesn't demand my time and attention."

"It kind of works that way, doesn't it?"

"Yeah and I think my mother knows that."

"Has she gone out with anyone since your father died?" Dana asked.

"She says she's not interested in dating but that could change. She's attractive and she's only fifty-four, so she might want someone in her life someday and if she does, I think that's great. If not, I'll respect her choice either way." Ridley paused for a moment and then she said, "Tell me a little about your family."

"My mother used to be an elementary school teacher until she had my younger brother, Danny, and then she decided to stay home until we all left the nest. She's still at home but she keeps busy being a homemaker and a grandmother. My father owns his own financial consulting firm. My older sister Donna and her husband Wayne have three children and they live in the Chicago suburbs, not far from my parents. My brother Danny's in grad school in California."

"Donna, Dana and Danny. How cute," Ridley said with a smile.

"It's cute all right, but I'm afraid it gets worse. My father's name is Dino."

"What's your mother's name? Don't tell me...."

Dana laughed when she saw Ridley's expression. "Don't worry, her name is Maureen. You were expecting another name beginning with a D weren't you?"

"I have to admit I braced myself, just in case." Ridley laughed along.

"My mother always messed up our names when we were kids, especially when she was mad or in a hurry. She'd get tongue-tied and yell all the names out. Of course, we laughed like hyenas when she did that and then she'd get even madder."

"Kids are horrible. How did you like living in Chicago?"

"I loved it. It's an interesting city with lots of culture and wonderful places to eat."

"Did you enjoy living there?" Ridley asked. She would have loved to sit here forever just talking to Dana, getting to know her and just being with her. For the life of her, she couldn't think of anything else she'd rather do.

"Yes, but I always felt I was like a tourist. It's awfully big and it never felt like home. I'd much rather be in this area where I grew up."

"Karen said you moved there after high school."

"Two months after I graduated. My mother and father wanted to live closer to my sister and her children. My mother had a friend who owned a catering business there and she offered me a job. That's what made me decide once and for all that I wanted to be a chef. After I worked for her for a year she suggested I work for a chef she knew who owned a well-established restaurant in the city. He hired me as a prep chef. It's a good idea to work your way up from the bottom and learn all the different jobs in a restaurant before you become a chef. Culinary school teaches you theory and the basics, but it can't prepare you to function in a busy restaurant and take the heat, so to speak."

"What did you do after college?" Ridley asked.

"I worked in another restaurant in downtown Chicago. I started as a line chef and then worked my way up to garde manger."

"What on earth is that?"

"That's the person who creates the salads, appetizers, garnishes and any sandwiches if the place serves them, and believe it or not, the table decorations."

"How long did you work there?"

"About three years and then I took a job as an assistant chef in a popular restaurant on Lake Michigan. That's where I learned about running a small upscale restaurant like the one I opened here." Dana studied Ridley's eyes as if searching for something. "Are you sure you're interested in all this? I feel like I'm reciting my résumé."

"I'm interested in everything about you." Ridley had become completely beguiled by Dana's dark eyes. Arousal gripped her insides and made her feel lightheaded, a sensation that seemed to have become her norm whenever she was near Dana. For a few wobbly moments she thought she might pass out even though she was sitting down. She forced herself to continue. "Thanks for coming with me today. I like being with you."

"I like being with you, too," Dana said.

"I feel the need to say something about kissing you. I still..."

"Don't." Dana held her hand up. "Don't. It's sweet of you to be so concerned about how I feel, but I'm not that delicate and I'm not upset about you kissing me. Correct me if I'm wrong, but I do believe you sort of asked me and I do believe I sort of said yes."

"I hardly remember anything except that kiss."

"You do understand I don't want to get involved, don't you? It's not about you."

"That's what you told me." Ridley stared straight ahead at the garden and they said nothing for a minute or two. "I remember telling you that I'd never been in love. I've had a lot of dates and short-term relationships, but I never met anyone I wanted to be with for a long time — anyone I felt deeply about." Fortunately, Ridley was spared from pouring out the contents of her heart by her mother's voice calling them in for dinner. She realized that she'd been offered a reprieve and took advantage of it by springing to her feet. "We have to go in now. It's time to eat."

"Good." Dana stood up. "I'm hungry."

"So am I." Ridley was relieved to end their conversation. She'd been heading in the wrong direction and she wasn't sure it was wise to reveal her innermost feelings to Dana at this point. It would be a mistake and she'd made enough of them already.

AFTER DINNER, VICKI served homemade apple pie and coffee and as soon as they were finished with dessert, Ridley got up from the table and told her mother that she would clear the dishes and clean up the kitchen. Dana offered to help, but Ridley insisted on doing it alone. "You stay here and visit with my mother."

"Why don't we sit in the living room while Ridley takes care of things?" Vicki suggested. "Would you care for another cup of coffee?"

"No thanks. I'm stuffed and I don't think I could eat or drink another thing." Dana stood when Vicki did and followed her into the living room.

"Dinner was delicious," Dana said once they were seated across from each other. Vicki's home was warm and inviting and Dana was surprised by how comfortable she felt there. She was even more surprised by how easy it was to talk to Ridley's mother.

"Thank you. That's a compliment coming from a chef."

"I make a lot of fancy dishes at the restaurant, but in my heart, I've always preferred old-fashioned comfort food. I grew up having Sunday dinners like roast chicken and roast beef and my mother was an excellent cook — is an excellent cook I should say."

"I grew up the same way, but now there's no one to make Sunday dinner for unless Ridley or my sister come over. That's why I was so happy when Ridley said she'd invited you to come today. It means a lot to me to have you girls here."

"I enjoyed being here," Dana said.

"Good. Then maybe you'll come again, sometime?"

"Sure. I'd like that."

They chatted about mundane things a while and then, during a break in the conversation, Vicki leaned forward and scanned with her eyes as if to make sure Ridley was no where around. "Dana, please tell me if you feel this is none of my business, but there's something I want to know and I don't know how to ask you except to come right out with it. Are you and Ridley seeing each other? Dating in other words?"

"No, we're not. We're just friends."

"Are you a..." Vicki hesitated. "This is terribly awkward."

"Yes, I'm a lesbian." This was a first. Dana couldn't remember ever having been asked about her sexual orientation by a friend's mother. Still, she felt at ease talking to Vicki and she sensed nothing coming from her but sincere interest. In fact, she got the distinct impression that Vicki needed to talk to someone about her daughter.

"Thanks for making that easier. I hope I wasn't intrusive. It's just that Ridley seems quite taken with you. I saw something in the way she looked at you and I assumed that meant — well, it seems I assumed incorrectly. It's just that I had hoped..." Vicki took a sip of her coffee. "You see, I want to see my daughter happy and sometimes I worry about her."

"Why do you worry about her?" Dana asked. She could see that Vicki cared very much for her daughter, but more than that, she wanted to know the answer.

"She's sensitive and she cares deeply about things. She's always had a beautiful heart and an even more beautiful soul. Some of the women she's dated have overlooked that fact about her. I know she would never give her heart away easily but sometimes I fear she'll never give it to anyone. I would hate to see that happen to someone like my Ridley, someone that extraordinary. I know you're thinking that I'm her mother and I'm terribly biased and I would have to agree with you that I am, but I love her more than anything in this world."

Vicki's candid and loving assessment of her daughter touched Dana deeply and she didn't doubt one thing Vicki had said about Ridley. "I wouldn't worry if I were you. She won't end up alone." Although she didn't go on to explain her reasons, she instinctively knew that Ridley wouldn't have to be alone unless she made that choice. She had way too much to offer. Besides being attractive, desirable and interesting, she was kind and sensitive and had a quality about her that made her almost irresistible. She was someone who could capture your heart and soul.

"I hope you're right," Vicki said.

"I can't imagine that happening. Not in her case."

"I hope you didn't mind me asking. It's difficult when your daughter's a lesbian. I never quite know if someone is a friend or a love interest unless she tells me. When she said she wanted to bring you here, I guess I thought..." Vicki leaned forward in her chair. "Never mind what I thought. Can I ask you another personal question?"

"Go ahead," Dana said with amusement. It amazed her that Ridley's mother was brave enough to get this personal in the first place, especially with a relative stranger.

"Do your parents know you're gay?"

"I'm ashamed to admit it, but I haven't told them." Dana shrugged her shoulders. "I know I should. I'm getting tired of keeping my personal life a secret."

"Don't they wonder why you don't date men or have any interest in them?" Vicki asked. "Don't they ever ask you any questions about your personal life?"

"They do, but I tell them I'm too busy to have a social life. So far, that's been working." Dana stopped to think about what she would say next and decided she might as well be honest. "I've wanted to tell them and I almost did a few times, but I couldn't get the words out. I feel especially bad that I haven't told my sister, because we've always been close." Dana had never told anyone other than Tracy how she felt about this, but Vicki made her feel open and willing to share her thoughts and feelings, just like her daughter did.

"I imagine that wouldn't be an easy thing to do, but speaking from my own experience, I felt relieved when Ridley told me. Something was driving a wedge between us and I suspected she might be gay, but I didn't know how to ask her."

"I don't like deceiving my family, but I'm afraid to tell them."

"I really think it's better to know the truth," Vicki said.

"How did you feel when Ridley told you?"

"It wasn't exactly what I'd hoped to hear, but once it was out in the open, we were able to be close again like we always were. It was impossible for us to have an honest relationship when she had to hide something that important from me. Did she tell you about her father's death? She never told him and she suffered dearly for it."

"She did tell me about that," Dana said.

"She'll have to carry that around with her for the rest of her life."

"By the way, I'm sorry about your husband."

"Thank you." Vicki said. "My Jeremy was a wonderful man and I miss him every day."

"I'm sure you do." Dana paused, feeling at a loss for words. "I'm afraid my family will turn away from me." God, where did that come from? She'd just revealed to Ridley's mother the one thing that terrified her the most, the one thing that had stopped her from telling them.

"That's what everyone fears, isn't it? In reality, someone might turn away from you for a time, but if you don't tell them who you really are, you deny your loved ones the chance to be there for you and to share your life. You do realize some of your family may already know or at least suspect it and that maybe they've been afraid to ask you?"

"I have entertained that possibility," Dana said.

"You might be surprised to find out how much they've already figured out on their own and keep in mind that once you tell them, the ball is in their court, so to speak. You can't control how they react or how they feel about it."

"I understand that, but those reactions and feelings are what scare me." How strange that Ridley's mother had brought up the very thing that had been preying on her mind as of late. It had begun nagging her right after she and Ridley talked that night on the beach and she knew she had to tell them and soon.

"Maybe I've given you something to think about and I thank you for being so honest with me. I hope you didn't find my questions shocking."

"Not shocking, exactly. I'm just not used to being asked about that," Dana said.

"And I'm not used to asking. We started talking and it just seemed to come pouring out." Vicki stood up. "If you don't mind, I think I'll go see if Ridley needs help. You stay here and when I return I'd love to hear about your restaurant. I've got a lot of questions I'd like to ask you, much less threatening ones this time."

Dana smiled. "I'll be right here. Take your time."

VICKI HELPED HER daughter put the pots and pans away and

wipe the counter tops clean. They'd performed this task as a team many times and they worked quickly and quietly until they were through. In no time, all vestiges of their dinner together had vanished.

Vicki stood next to Ridley near the sink. "I like Dana. She's a nice girl."

Ridley stopped what she was doing and turned to her mother. "I know Mom. She's beautiful isn't she? And she's so nice. I like her so much."

"Honey," Vicki said as she placed her hand on her daughter's shoulder. "I don't want you to think I'm prying into your personal affairs, but it seems to me that she means a lot more to you than just a friend. Is that true?"

"Mom..." Ridley felt her eyes become wet with tears. "How do you always know?"

"I know you so well and I can't say as I blame you. Anyone can see how extraordinary she is." Vicki pulled Ridley closer. "Does she share your feelings?"

Ridley shook her head. "I think she's in love with someone else."

"I'm sorry to hear that." Vicki tightened her arm around Ridley's shoulder and held her to her side. "If it's meant to be it will be and if it doesn't turn out to be Dana it'll be someone else, I promise you. It's only a matter of time."

"I don't want it to be someone else. I want it to be her."

Vicki held Ridley's chin and turned her head so their eyes met. "Here's something I don't think I ever told you. I wasn't crazy about your father at first, but the more I got to know him the more I liked him and eventually my feelings changed. Or, maybe I should say they changed after the first time he kissed me." Her laugh was soft and she brushed a tear from Ridley's cheek. "You never were one to hold back your tears, my sweet girl." She let Ridley go and put a little space between them. "I know you wouldn't want to be with someone who didn't want to be with you, now would you?"

"No, I wouldn't, Mom."

"That's the right answer. Now, let's get back to our guest, shall we?"

"WE'RE ALL DONE," Vicki said as she and Ridley returned to the living room. "I hope we didn't leave you out here all by yourself for too long?"

"Not at all," Dana answered. "I was just enjoying this lovely room and thinking that I'd be delighted if you'd be my guest at my restaurant. You can come for dinner or brunch, your choice, and bring Ridley and your sister if you'd like." Dana glanced at Ridley. "We're booked far in advance on the weekends, so a week day would be better and a lot less crowded."

"I'd love to do that," Vicki replied. "We'll come soon, won't we sweetheart?"

"Sure we will, Mom." Ridley made an effort to pull herself together. If she couldn't control her emotions any better than she had today, it was going to be impossible to carry on any kind of relationship with Dana, either friendship or otherwise. Her normally solid foundation had begun to crumble and for the first time in her life, she found herself teetering on shaky ground.

"By the way, Ridley," Vicki said. "I need you to do something for me. Could you drive down to the shore house sometime soon and take care of a few things? I've got a lot going on and I don't know when I can get down there."

"I can go next weekend. What do you need me to do?"

"I wrote it all down for you." Vicki took a piece of paper out of her pocket and handed it to Ridley. "I won't have the plumber drain the pipes and shut the house down for the winter until after Thanksgiving, but I want you to cover the deck furniture and do a few other things before it gets too cold. Are you sure you don't mind?"

"No. I wanted to go down again, anyway."

"Take a friend with you if you'd like to." Vicki glanced at Dana and then back at her daughter. "You could spend the weekend. It's so nice down there in the fall."

"Maybe I will." Ridley knew her mother was suggesting that she should ask Dana to go with her and she thought it was very sweet of her. She stood up to go. "I think we'll head home now before it gets too late."

"Give me a call when you get back to let me know you made it home safely, will you? And you both have a good week."

"YOUR MOTHER'S A special lady," Dana said as soon as they turned out of the driveway.

"She is, isn't she."

"You know something? Being with you and her today made me think about how much I miss doing things with my family. I don't get to see them often enough now that I live far away and I miss my sister most of all. We talk on the phone a couple of times a week, but it's not the same as seeing her and being able to do things with her."

"That must be tough." Purely on impulse, Ridley steadied herself with a deep breath and asked, "Would you consider going with me next weekend? I know you love it there and it would be great if you came with me. I hate to go alone." Those words weren't quite true because Ridley had never minded going there alone, but the prospect of being with Dana made her say anything she could come up with to convince her to go.

"I don't know. When would you go down?"

"We wouldn't have to go until Sunday morning if that works better for you."

"That would be better. You'd drive?" Dana asked.

"Yeah, I'll drive. What do you say?"

Dana studied Ridley's face before she replied. "I guess I could go. Tracy can do brunch and I don't think she'd mind. She's been bugging me to get out and do things."

"Fantastic." Ridley's smile almost hurt. "Why don't we leave early? How about if I pick you up around nine o'clock?"

"That will work. When are you planning on coming back?"

"I'll take a personal day on Monday since you're off. That way we can stay overnight and come back after dinner on Monday." Ridley couldn't think of a more valid reason to use up one of her personal days. The teacher's union intended them to be used for personal emergencies and in Ridley's mind, having an opportunity to be alone with Dana De Marco for two whole days definitely qualified as a personal emergency.

"Okay," Dana answered.

Except for polite conversation, they were mostly quiet as they drove home. Ridley kept a tight rein on her feelings and everything she wanted to say remained unsaid as they pulled up in front of Dana's building. Ridley released her seat belt and turned in her seat. "I guess I'll see you next Sunday, then?"

"Yeah, see you next Sunday." Dana gathered her things and opened the door, but before she stepped out onto the sidewalk, she turned. "Thanks for taking me to your Mom's house for dinner. I had a good time and..." Dark eyes gazed at Ridley as if they held something inside.

"What is it? What do you want to say?"

"Nothing, it's..." Dana averted her eyes for a second and then she faced Ridley again. "It's just that I like your mother and I like you — I like you both a lot."

Ridley stared into Dana's captivating eyes. "Believe me I like you just as much."

After a moment, Dana cleared her throat. "All right, so have a nice week and don't work too hard keeping those students of yours in line."

"Don't worry, I won't. Don't work too hard yourself and say hello to Tracy for me." Ridley watched as Dana walked away, taking a part of her with her. Was it crazy to feel so much for someone she'd known such a short time? Regardless of the answer, she couldn't do anything to change it. She questioned whether she should have invited Dana to go with her to the shore next weekend, but she only questioned it briefly because it raised a far more disturbing question. How would she make it through the rest of the week until she saw her again?

Chapter
Fifteen

THE FOLLOWING SUNDAY, around one o'clock in the afternoon, Ridley and Dana sat in the kitchen at the shore house eating sandwiches they'd picked up at a local Deli. "Thanks a lot for helping me with my mother's list of chores," Ridley said. "I hope I didn't wear you out by making you work so hard."

Dana shook her head. "I didn't mind helping you and it wasn't that much work." She picked up the last bite of her sandwich, popped it into her mouth and washed it down with the rest of her iced tea. "Are we done or do we have more to do?"

"No, that's everything. She'll come down once more before she shuts the house down for the winter and then we'll open it up again in the spring."

"No one comes here in the winter?"

"Not anymore. We used to years ago, but it's expensive to heat the house and we don't come down enough to make it worth the money. When my father and grandparents were alive, we used to come here for the holidays, but now my Mom prefers to be home with my aunt. Besides, it's cold and dead here during the winter."

"I guess it would be, although I can't say I've ever seen the shore in the winter." Dana got up, dumped her ice cubes in the sink and set her glass on the counter. She did the same with Ridley's glass and then she washed her hands in the sink. "What do you want to do now?"

"This might sound boring, but would you like to see some family pictures?"

"I'd love to," Dana replied. "I like looking at photos and they're not boring if there's a story to go along with them."

"Let me wash my hands and we'll go into the living room."

Once in the living room, Ridley reached for a large photo album on the top shelf of one of the bookcases and sat on the sofa next to Dana. Tenderly, she brushed a fine layer of dust from the heavy album cover and pulled it open.

Dana covered a few of the photos on the first page with her hand. "Wait, before you start, is there a naked baby picture of you? Mother's have a thing about cute baby butts."

"Can you blame them? They are cute. I don't remember any, but I haven't seen these for a while so you might get lucky." Ridley's upper thigh pressed against Dana's and she felt the heat of it penetrate the fabric of her jeans. "This album has a lot of my baby pictures in it, but I also chose it because it has some nice pictures of my parents when they were younger and some of my grandparents."

"You just wanted me to see how cute you were."

"That might be part of it." Ridley said. "I'll bet you were cute when you were little, and I'll bet you were sweet."

"You'd win that bet."

Ridley explained the story behind each photo as she told the stories of her childhood. "This was my grandmother. Wasn't she pretty? She was such a nice lady and look at my grandfather. He was quite the dapper gentleman." Ridley brushed the tips of her fingers over their faces.

"I love this one." Dana pointed to a picture of Ridley as a baby. "Is that your father?"

"Yes, that's him." In the picture, he was holding Ridley's hands above her head as she tried to walk. "My mother said I had just started walking the day before."

"Look at your pudgy bottom and those short bowed legs."

"I'm wearing a diaper. What do you expect?"

"It's a wonder babies can walk at all in those," Dana said.

They both laughed out loud at the same time when they turned the next page. There stood Ridley in her small plastic kiddy pool, naked as the day she'd entered the world.

"See, I knew I'd get to see you naked." Dana bent forward with laughter.

"I'm so happy I made your day," Ridley said between breaths. After they stopped laughing, she showed Dana the rest of the pictures and when she reached the last page, she closed the album soundly. "That's enough of that. I don't want to put you in a coma. Next time, I'll show you some pictures of me when I was eleven and twelve years old. I call that my gawky period."

"Most of us were gawky at that age. You certainly didn't stay that way."

Ridley's eyes appraised Dana. "Neither did you."

"I can see why you grew into such an attractive woman. You look like your mother and she was striking. She still is. And your father was handsome. Sometimes two good-looking people produce a homely child but not in your case."

"Do you really think so?" Ridley's felt the heat creeping up her neck.

"Yes, I think you're very attractive. And I can see I'm making you blush."

"I can feel it." Ridley fanned her face. "Since I'm already blushing, I might as well confess that I think you're extremely attractive in every way."

"We sound like some kind of mutual admiration society."

"We do, don't we?" Ridley fell into Dana's eyes and when she felt the urge to let her eyes drop to Dana's mouth, she forced herself to look off in another direction. "What do you feel like doing for dinner?"

"I'd like to have some seafood. Is my favorite place still open?"

"It should be. Why don't we drive there and see if it is and if not, I know a couple of other places we can go to that are open all year. Would you mind if I go up and take a short nap before we get ready to go out? No more than an hour or so?"

"I think I'll do the same. That work made me tired." Dana stood and stretched.

"I'll meet you back here in the living room in a couple of hours."

"I'll be here," Dana said.

After Dana left to go to her room, Ridley climbed the stairs to the master bedroom. She drew the blinds and kicked off her shoes and as soon as she laid her head on the pillow, she fell fast asleep.

AN HOUR AND a half later, Ridley stepped out of a hot shower and got dressed. The house was filled with silence when she tiptoed down the stairs. Half-way down, she saw Dana curled up in a chair by the window with a book in her hands. She wore faded jeans and a soft burgundy sweater. Since Dana seemed to be unaware that she was on the stairs, Ridley paused to savor the sight of her for a few stolen minutes.

Dana must have sensed she was being watched because she looked up. "Hi there, were you able to sleep at all?"

Ridley came down the rest of the stairs. "Yes, much to my surprise. I'm not one for taking naps, but I must have been tired." Tucked away in Dana's eyes, Ridley saw something she'd never seen there before and it took her breath away. Her throat felt constricted as she tried to speak. "Did you get any sleep?"

"I slept for about an hour and then I took a shower and got dressed. Now I feel rested and ready for an evening out. I came in here because it's so cozy and peaceful."

"It means a lot to me that you like it here," Ridley said.

"I feel good in this house and you look nice, by the way. That sweater's a good color for you and I'm glad you wore jeans. I figured you would."

"We don't have to dress up around here." Ridley continued to stare. She didn't know what to say next because anything that came to mind seemed unimportant and what she wanted to say had no place in their relationship. In the end, she said the only thing that felt safe. "Are you ready to go? I just realized how hungry I am."

Dana put her book down and got up. "So am I. Let's go."

AFTER DINNER, RIDLEY drove south to the bay side of the island in the town of Beach Haven. The cloudless night sky was a dark blackish-blue and the night air carried autumn's sting upon its back. Above their heads, a bright white moon illuminated the entire bay. Ridley drove to an open area near the docks and parked facing the water.

"Dinner was great. I love that place." Dana released her seat belt and turned in her seat to face Ridley. "I can't believe I've been to the shore twice since I moved back to Philly."

Ridley just smiled. Nothing made her happier than to make Dana happy and so far, the evening couldn't have turned out better. If only she could make this night last forever. She held that wish in her mind knowing full well this night would slip away like every other night before it and just as quickly. Her senses were honed to a sharpness she'd never experienced and she was all vibrant with feeling and devoid of discretion. In this moment, her world consisted of the two of them and nothing else mattered.

"It's so beautiful here," Dana breathed.

"This is my favorite view of the bay." Ridley spoke with a hushed voice as if they were in a sacred place. The windshield made it appear as if one long unbroken filament of light stretched all the way from the moon to the bay and when it touched the water it unraveled and spread over the waves like a ribbon of white light. Ridley's eyes remained engrossed by the strand of light, but inside she felt like screaming from the sexual tension that had seized control of her. It had become hard to pull in each breath and push it back out and the heat and energy emanating from Dana's body threatened to drive her insane. No longer able to tolerate it, she freed herself from the confines of her seat belt and shifted closer to Dana.

Dana fixed her eyes straight ahead and kept her hands securely in her lap as if she felt the tension and knew what Ridley was feeling. "Ridley, I..."

The way Dana clutched her hands together as if she was holding on for dear life was more than Ridley could bear. She reached out, separated Dana's left hand from her right and took it in her own. She was astonished when Dana didn't pull away and even more amazed when Dana rubbed her thumb across the back of her hand.

"It feels so good," Dana whispered with her eyes now focused on their joined hands. "Being here with you and holding your hand like this."

"Do you remember when you held my hand that night on the beach?"

"I remember." Dana lifted her dark eyes and captured Ridley's.

"You were so kind, so gentle," Ridley said.

Dana said nothing. She stared at the bay and took a deep breath.

"Do you remember kissing me?" Ridley hardly recognized her own voice.

Dana offered no reply. She shifted in her seat and their eyes met again. Slowly, she removed her hand from Ridley's grasp and returned it to her lap.

"I haven't upset you, have I?" Ridley asked. "That's the last thing I'd want to do. I respect you and care about your feelings and I want you to know that you're perfectly safe with me."

"I know what you're saying, but I feel anything but safe." Dana flashed a thin smile. "It's sweet of you to be concerned about my feelings and I'm not upset about anything. In fact, I feel better than I've felt in a very long time. It's a beautiful night and I love being here with you more than I can say."

"Do you know how beautiful you are tonight?" Ridley's eyes searched Dana's face for anything that might tell her she stood a chance. She wanted to be a part of Dana's life and she wanted to mean something to her. This time she let her eyes openly stare at Dana's mouth and she wanted to kiss her so bad she ached from it. Ridley stretched her hand out and rested it on Dana's shoulder. "I'm finding it hard to keep my hands off you."

Dana lifted Ridley's hand from her shoulder and brought it to her lips. "I remember kissing you," she murmured, her breath caressing the back of Ridley's hand, her lips caressing as they moved. "God help me, I've thought about that kiss every single day."

Ridley failed to stop the moan that escaped from her. "So have I and I might go insane if I don't kiss you again."

With her eyes closed, Dana gently sucked the tip of one of Ridley's fingers into the warmth of her mouth. Then she let it go. "I want you to kiss me." She opened her eyes and turned toward Ridley. "Please kiss me."

Another moan escaped from Ridley as she leaned forward and cupped Dana's cheek in the palm of her hand. With deliberate slowness, she brought her mouth to Dana's. At first she kissed her tenderly, just to feel her mouth and experience the exquisite softness of her lips, but soon the kiss grew hungry and their mouths opened to each other. After that, there was only heat and the smoothness of warm silk.

After a few impassioned kisses, Dana gasped and tore her mouth away. With her forehead pressed against Ridley's, she struggled to breathe.

"Do you want me to stop?"

"No, I don't want you to stop," Dana whispered as she tugged at the lapels of Ridley's jacket. "I should want you to stop, but I'm beyond caring at this point. I only know I can't get close enough to you, not in here."

"We need to go back to the house," Ridley whispered.

"Why don't we?" Dana touched Ridley's cheek. "Let's go now."

"I'll go as fast as I can without breaking any laws." Ridley threw her vehicle into gear and turned around, her tires squealing as she headed back to the main road.

Dana let her head fall back on the headrest as she placed her hand on Ridley's thigh. She turned to watch Ridley drive. "You're awfully cute. The first time I saw you I thought you were so cute and sexy. You're incredibly sexy."

Ridley smiled, but kept her eyes on the road.

"Does it bother you if I look at you while you drive?" Dana asked.

"That's not bothering me, but your hand on my thigh is proving to be a problem." Dana's hand felt hot enough to burn a hole through her jeans and turn her insides into molten lava. Such a simple touch and yet it aroused her more than she'd ever been aroused. She placed her hand on top of Dana's and pressed their hands firmly against her thigh muscle. "Your hand is so hot."

"I thought the heat was coming from you." Dana spread her hand out and inched it a little higher up. "You feel so good."

Wetness seeped into Ridley's underwear and she shifted in her seat. She glanced at Dana and said the only thing on her mind. "I want to make love to you."

Dana squeezed Ridley's thigh. "I know you do. It's what I want, too."

In the back of her mind, Ridley questioned why Dana had changed toward her, but she didn't want to talk about the whys. She didn't want to ask questions or listen to warnings or spoil this perfect moment. She had cast aside the realm of caution the instant she'd touched Dana and she was out of the reach of reason. No longer did she possess the strength required to tame the wild craving that had tortured her for weeks. It was time to surrender, time to let actions and decisions be dictated solely by need and desire.

Tomorrow and for all the tomorrows to come, she would have to deal with the consequences of the choices she made tonight. But, tomorrow seemed like a remote and intangible threat whereas tonight the urgency to quench her desire for Dana was all she cared about. Just for tonight, just for one precious breathtaking night, she would have Dana and that was more important to her than anything.

Chapter
Sixteen

AS SOON AS they entered the house and closed the door behind them, Ridley pulled her jacket off and helped Dana out of hers. With uncharacteristic impatience, she flung both jackets onto the back of a chair, wrapped her arms around Dana from behind and buried her face in Dana's hair. "You smell so good." She kissed the sweet spot just under Dana's left ear and whispered, "God, Dana. I want you more than anything."

Dana turned and wrapped her arms tightly around Ridley's waist. She pressed the length of her body against Ridley's. "This is going to be so good."

Ridley held Dana in her arms and savored the feel of her soft breasts as they pressed against hers. She kissed her deeply and when it was over, she said, "Come upstairs with me. I want to touch you and make love to you all night."

"Yes..." Dana closed her eyes. "I want that, too."

Ridley held the palm of her hand against Dana's cheek and met her eyes. "You know it's okay if you want to change your mind, don't you?" She kissed Dana's forehead. "I don't want you to do anything you'll regret later and it's not too late to say no."

Dana shook her head. "It's too late for me and I don't want to change my mind. I don't want to change a single thing about this night. I just want to be with you."

"That's what I want." Ridley took Dana's hand in hers and led her up the stairs and into the master suite. She'd left a small lamp on before they went out to dinner and it cast a mellow glow into the room. "Do you want me to turn the light off?"

"No, leave it on. I want to be able to see you." Dana stood in front of Ridley and rested the palms of her hands on Ridley's chest just above her breasts. "Your heart is pounding."

"I know. I'm excited and nervous."

"Here, feel mine." Dana reached for Ridley's hand and held it over her heart. "It feels like it's going to burst right out of my chest."

"I see what you mean," Ridley said. "I've wanted you so much and I've dreamed of being with you since I met you. I love your smile and those adorable dimples and your mouth..." Ridley moved her hand and traced Dana's lips with her fingers. "I can't look at it without wanting to kiss you."

"In that case, I think you should kiss me."

Ridley's body trembled as she kissed Dana again and again. She held her close with one hand on her back and when her desire became more than she could bear, she reached under Dana's sweater to cup her breast.

Dana stepped back and pulled her sweater off in one smooth motion.

"I want to see you." Ridley reached behind Dana and unhooked her bra. Cupping both of her breasts in her hands, she leaned down to kiss first one and then the other. "They're perfect," she said just before she sucked a taut nipple into her mouth.

"God, your mouth is so soft." Dana pulled Ridley up again and captured her mouth. As they explored each other's mouths, Dana's hands traveled up the smooth skin of Ridley's back and unfastened her bra. She pulled Ridley's bra and sweater off together. "Mmm...nice. Now I want to see the rest of you." She wrestled with Ridley's jeans.

Ridley took Dana's hands in hers and held them. "Let me do that." She let go of Dana and removed her jeans along with the rest of her clothing until she stood naked before Dana. "Now you," she said, opening Dana's jeans and sliding the zipper down.

"You're so beautiful," Ridley said when Dana was finally undressed. "I've tried to imagine how you would look, but I never would have imagined this. You're better than even my wildest dreams." She stared at Dana's body while she ran her hands over Dana's shoulders and down her arms. "I need to touch you."

"Wait. Let me look at you." Dana studied Ridley's athletic body. "You look just the way I thought you would." She took Ridley's hand in hers and brought it to her lips for a kiss before she directed it between her legs. "You can touch me now."

Ridley almost fainted at the first feel of Dana's most intimate places. There would only ever be one first time and it was magical. She led Dana to the bed and lay down with her. Never had she experienced anything as exquisite as this first exploration of Dana's body and she closed her eyes as she continued to caress her. It was all perfect, the way they moved together, the feel of Dana and the sounds she made as Ridley made love to her.

"I'm so close," Dana murmured.

Although Ridley would never have thought it possible, Dana became even more beautiful as she brought her to orgasm. She held her until the tremors subsided. "You're incredible. You take my breath away." Ridley's eyes held onto Dana's as she brushed a stray wisp of hair away from her slightly damp forehead.

Dana captured the hand Ridley had used to pleasure her and brought it to her lips. "That was amazing." Ridley watched as Dana kissed her hand and then she brought their hands to her own lips.

"Mmm, you are completely yummy."

Dana rolled Ridley onto her back and lay on her side next to her. "Now it's my turn." As her eyes caressed the planes of Ridley's body, her hands touched in turn. "Your breasts are perfect," she said as she cupped one in her hand as if to feel its weight. The nipple flushed a dark pink and stiffened as Dana rolled it between her thumb and index finger and they moaned together as she captured the erect nipple in her mouth.

"Please don't stop."

"I have no intention of stopping," Dana said as she positioned herself so she was lying on top of Ridley. She wedged her thigh in between Ridley's legs and began to slide against her wetness as she rubbed her own wet center against Ridley.

"I need you so much." Ridley spread her legs and lifted her hips. "Please, Dana."

"No, not like this. I want to know what you taste like." Dana forged a path down Ridley's body with her mouth until she reached the silky skin at the very top of Ridley's thigh. Using her fingers, she opened Ridley and took in the sight of her and after a few moments, she lifted her head and looked up at Ridley.

Ridley met her eyes. "Don't make me wait any longer."

Dana covered Ridley with her mouth and began to take her the rest of the way.

It wasn't the first time anyone had made love to Ridley this way, but with Dana it felt like a totally new experience. She'd never felt this way about anyone she'd been with and she had no concept of how much her feelings could heighten her sensations and deepen the bond between them. She felt her soul slip away, her surrender absolute.

When it was over, Dana held Ridley close and showered her with the lightest of kisses wherever her mouth would reach. "I love the way you taste...your smell...how you feel. I'm afraid I'll become addicted to you."

"I should be so lucky." Ridley sighed and closed her eyes.

"Are you tired?" Dana asked her.

"No, I'm just..." Ridley opened her eyes. "I've waited so long for this."

"You can rest for a while," Dana said. "I'm right here."

"I don't need to rest. I need you. I've wanted you for so long."

"Well, here I am," Dana whispered against Ridley's lips.

"And I'm dying to taste you." Ridley kissed Dana's mouth and then the rest of her body on her way down. Driven by Dana's soft moans, Ridley wasted no time taking her with her mouth. The first taste and feel of her was incredible and as she stroked her, she filled her completely. From that point on, there was nothing but movement and soft sounds.

After it was over, Ridley rested her head on Dana's abdomen and breathed in the same rhythm as her until they both recovered. After a while, she moved up on the bed to lie beside Dana and gather her into her arms.

Dana pressed her fingers to Ridley's lips. "Making love with you has been..." She tugged on Ridley's lower lip and then let it go. "I've never experienced anything that even came close to what we just did. I've never felt this open or this passionate."

"It's the same for me." Ridley smiled. "I knew it. I just knew it."

"Knew what?" Dana reflected Ridley's smile.

"That you would be the sweetest thing I'd ever touched or tasted."

"No, it's you. You're the sweetest thing."

Although she felt the need to sleep, Ridley fought to stay awake. Being able to hold Dana and touch her was so precious that she couldn't bear to miss a single moment. Even if this turned out to be their only night together, she would have the memory of it to keep in her heart forever. She moved as close to Dana as she could get and still qualify as a separate entity so she could feel her breathe and share her heartbeat. Maybe, if she committed to memory every detail of this night and stored away every sensation for safe-keeping, she'd never have to lose her and never have to be without her.

If some tragic twist of fate were to end her life at this precise moment, she'd have no regrets, for her life would have been complete. It would have lacked for nothing. She knew, just as she knew the sun would rise every morning and set every evening that she'd given her heart and soul away to the woman she held cradled in her arms.

AS DAYLIGHT SEEPED into the room, Ridley awoke on her side curled against Dana's back. Gently, she kissed Dana's neck and shoulder before she slid her arm underneath Dana's and cupped her breast from behind. The nipple hardened in her palm and as she rubbed it, Dana stirred. "Are you awake?" Ridley asked.

Dana rewarded Ridley with a low moan and pushed her backside against Ridley's belly. "I am now. That feels so good."

"Don't move. I have plans for you." Ridley shimmied even closer, her nipples achingly tight as they rubbed against the smooth skin of Dana's back. Already lost in a swirling sea of desire, she ran her hand over the curve of Dana's hip, down over the soft swell of her buttocks and into the crevice between her legs until she reached the wetness she knew she'd find there. "I want you so much," she said as she touched her.

Dana turned around. "You sure know how to wake a girl up." Dana's eyes appeared to glaze over as Ridley touched her and it didn't take long before she reached her climax. Afterward, she held Ridley's face in her hands. "What you do to me. It's too much."

"No, you're wrong. It's not too much — it's not nearly enough."

"Is that so?" Dana said. "Let me see what I can do about that." She kissed Ridley's mouth and breasts and belly without lingering for any length of time in any one place until she was in position to pleasure her with her mouth.

Ridley clutched the sheets and came almost immediately. She wanted to hang on and make the exquisite sensations Dana was creating with her mouth last as long as possible, but her body ignored her wishes. It was so desperate for release, it cared about nothing more. Afterward, as they lay in each other's arms, Ridley stared at the ceiling and felt her eyes fill as she wondered if this would be the only time she would ever make love with Dana.

"How do you feel?" Dana asked after a while.

"Never better. And you?"

"I feel the same, but I could use something to eat and some coffee."

"So could I, especially the coffee part. Let's take a quick shower and get dressed and I'll take you out and treat you to a nice breakfast." Ridley reluctantly separated herself from Dana and got out of bed. "You know I'd much rather stay here with you all day, don't you?" she said from the side of the bed.

"Yes, but I'm really hungry." Dana stretched and opened her mouth wide in a lazy yawn. She watched Ridley as she turned and walked to the bathroom. "Hey! You've got a cute butt," she called out as Ridley disappeared through the bathroom door.

Ridley peered back into the room. "Gee, thanks."

"Don't mention it," Dana said just before another yawn.

As soon as the water was hot enough, Ridley stepped into the revitalizing spray. She'd just started to soap her body when she saw a ghostly image shimmering on the other side of the shower door. "I thought you were going to shower downstairs," Ridley said, opening the door just enough to peek out.

"I was just watching you through the door." Dana opened the door a little bit more. "And I thought you might want me to wash your back."

"I might want you to wash more than that. Come in and shut the door before the floor gets any wetter." Ridley pulled Dana into her arms. "Don't make me promise not to touch you. That's a promise I can't keep. Not this morning."

"That's not a promise I want you to keep." Dana held Ridley's face in her hands and kissed her wet mouth hungrily. "Your mouth is so warm."

Ridley soaped Dana's body all over with her hands. "I can't stop wanting you. I've never wanted anyone this much. I don't even want to do anything else but this and if I had my way, I'd never leave the bed or let you out of my arms for God knows how long." Ridley guided Dana backward until she was pressed against the tiles.

Dana gasped as Ridley touched her. "Here we go again."

Chapter
Seventeen

ABOUT AN HOUR or so later, they arrived at a small family restaurant in Surf City, a homey little place with gingham curtains and matching tablecloths. They had the place to themselves save for a man and woman who were seated at a table in the back and two men seated next to each other at the small counter.

Ridley selected a table in the corner on the opposite side of the room from the man and woman. They both ordered juice and coffee with eggs, bacon, home fries and toast. As they ate, they shared a smile now and then, but said very little to each other.

Close to fourteen hours of sex had done little to extinguish the fire that still burned hot in Ridley. She still wanted to touch Dana all the time and she still wanted to make love to her. As they lingered over a third cup of coffee, she leaned closer to Dana and said, "You look radiant this morning and so beautiful."

"Do I? Thanks." Dana's gentle eyes were nothing but kind. "I feel wonderful and more relaxed than I have in a long time. I guess it's the fresh air, among other things."

Ridley covered Dana's hand with her own. "I've never felt better myself."

Dana turned her hand palm up and entwined her fingers with Ridley's. "I love the color of your eyes. The shade varies from emerald green in the bright sunlight to a pale olive green when it's gray or cloudy. When you look at them up close, they have tiny specks of gold in them, like some kind of precious gemstone."

"I didn't realize you'd noticed them."

"I noticed them the first time I saw you. It would be hard not to because they're so striking, especially with the color of your hair." Dana must have been worried that the other people in the restaurant would see them because she slid her hand out from under Ridley's. "It might be a better idea if we talked about something safer."

"There is something I'd like to talk to you about, something I think we really should talk about but I don't know if it comes under the heading of safer."

"What is it?" Dana asked with concern.

Ridley leaned closer. "That night we kissed for the first time you told me that you'd been involved with someone, that you'd given your heart to her. It's obvious to me that she broke your heart and I'm guessing that's the reason you don't want to become involved with me. Am I right about that?"

"Yes." Dana's expression changed from concern to sadness. "Her name is Sarah."

"Do you mind if I ask you how you met her?"

"No, I don't mind." Dana folded her hands in front of her. "I met her in Chicago. She was a chef and we worked together in the same restaurant. We started out as friends and later on, one thing led to another and we became lovers. I was the first woman she'd ever been with." Dana focused on her hands as she went on with her story. "After we'd been together for six months, someone offered her a job as a pastry chef at an elegant resort in the mountains of Northwestern Pennsylvania. She asked me to go with her. It had top notch restaurants and I thought it would be good for me to learn the techniques of spa cooking." Dana shrugged her shoulders. "So I applied for a position and got hired as a sous-chef in one of their restaurants and we went."

"Did you like it?" Ridley asked a less dangerous question than the one she really wanted to ask. She skirted around the real issues because she didn't want to make Dana shut down or turn away from her. More than that, she was afraid to hear something she didn't want to hear. When it came to Dana she was already too far gone and she couldn't bear to hear the rejection she feared was waiting to pounce on her from the shadows behind her happiness.

"Very much so. I became a better, more health conscious chef and more eclectic in my style. Spa style cooking is lighter, healthier and very artistic. I apply a lot of the skills I acquired in my restaurant dishes."

Setting her fears aside, Ridley asked a question that addressed what she really yearned to find out. "So what happened with you and this woman?"

"We lived there and we worked and we were lovers, until..." Dana leaned on the table and looked down, her face somber. "Let's just say she decided she wanted something else."

"I'm sorry. You don't have to tell me any more about it if you don't want to."

"I don't want to talk about her, not with you." Dana lifted her eyes to meet Ridley's. "You aren't really that interested in our breakup, are you? What is it you really want to know?"

Ridley swallowed hard. "I want to know what made you change your mind about being with me and why you wanted to come here this weekend. I guess I want to know why you decided to make love with me."

Dana sat up straight and scraped her chair nearer to Ridley's so no one else could hear what she had to say. "You must know I'm hopelessly attracted to you. You're adorable and sweet and very,

very hard to resist. I am made of flesh and blood, not stone."

"That I know." Ridley took in a deep breath and let it out. "And you must know that I'm hopelessly attracted to you, but I also haven't forgotten what you told me about not wanting to get involved. So, I suppose what I'm saying is, I hope you're not sorry about what happened last night and I hope you won't run away from me because of it."

"No, I won't. Please don't think that."

"I guess I need to know if I stand a chance with you." Ridley had finally voiced what was eating at her the most, the one thing she wanted to know more than anything else.

"I don't know right now. I'm sorry, I...I just don't know."

"At least you're honest. I'd like to think I'm mature enough to enjoy being with you on your terms, while it lasts. I want to be able to do that and I want to be careful not to ask you for more than you can give." These statements were out and out lies and it hurt Ridley to say them. When it came to Dana she wanted it all and she believed that Dana would run the other way if she told her that in so many words. "I just want to be with you whenever I can for as long as I can."

"Is that good enough for you?" Dana asked.

"It's good enough for now. It has to be." Ridley didn't dare say more. Every word coming out of Dana's beautiful mouth sounded like goodbye and she could hardly bear it. As if there were a crystal ball on the table, she could almost see the heartache she'd have to suffer down the road, but now that she had gone down that road there was no turning back.

"I'm not sure I can promise you more."

"I understand and I won't ask you to." Nothing remained to be said and when the silence began to stretch into awkwardness, Ridley asked, "Do you want another cup of coffee?"

"No, I'm finished. I don't want anything else."

"Why don't we go for a ride? I'll show you some of my favorite places and take you to the other end of the island to see the National seashore. It's pretty there and we can take a walk on the beach if you'd like to."

"I'd like that." Dana downed the last of her coffee.

"I HAD A wonderful time," Dana said after they got back to the house in the late afternoon. "I wouldn't mind looking at the ocean for the rest of my life."

"I feel the same way." Ridley enfolded Dana in her arms. "It's been hours since I've kissed you. I almost kissed you on the beach, but those other people showed up. "

"Nothing's stopping you now." Dana pressed her lips to Ridley's.

The kiss left Ridley panting and barely able to speak. "Let's go upstairs and leave a little later. We've got time and it won't take us long to get home. Please?"

"I guess we can stay another hour or two." Dana took Ridley's hand. "I just need to be with you a little longer."

A couple of hours later, after another heated lovemaking session, Ridley held Dana in her arms. Like a fool, she thought if she held Dana tight enough she would never have to leave her and this happiness she'd been granted would never have to end.

"I was right," Dana said with her cheek nestled against Ridley's soft breast. "You are every bit as sexy as I thought you would be."

"All day I wanted this. I couldn't wait to be alone with you." Ridley's words were as tender as a caress. "I don't want this to end and I don't want to leave, but I suppose we should get ready to go home."

"Can't we stay here forever?"

"I'd give anything if we could. However..." Ridley pushed the covers down and got out of bed. How could she feel so sad in the midst of such joy? She started to gather her clothing. Being here with Dana had meant everything to her and the last thing she wanted to do was to go home. She couldn't help but be filled with a sense of foreboding about her future with Dana.

"I guess you're right." Dana got out of bed and stood next to Ridley. "Do I have time for a shower before we head back? It won't take me long to get ready."

"Let's both take one, but not with each other. We'll never get out of here if we get into that shower together." Ridley's eyes surveyed Dana's naked body. "We could, uh, we could..."

"We could what?"

"I'm sorry. I can't seem to speak clearly when I'm standing this close to you with nothing on. I was trying to say we could stop somewhere and get something to eat before we get home. I know a good diner in New Jersey and it's on the way."

"That's fine with me. I'll go to my room and shower and get my things together. It shouldn't take me any longer than half an hour."

"Perfect. I'll meet you downstairs."

DURING THE RETURN trip, Ridley held Dana's hand almost the entire way. Dana had never known anyone as affectionate and tender as Ridley and she liked the physical contact very much. She was warmed by Ridley's contented smile and she liked the way her hair curled around her ears and the way she looked at her as she drove.

Before they got to the Benjamin Franklin Bridge, they stopped to eat at the diner Ridley had mentioned and before long they were pulling up in front of Café De Marco. Ridley stopped to let Dana out and turned in her seat. "Well, here we are."

"Yeah, here we are." Dana repeated Ridley's words. She was happy to be home and at the same time she felt sad that the weekend had come to an end. Tracy had encouraged her to enjoy Ridley and she had, so why didn't she feel better about it? The sex with Ridley had been the best she'd ever had, although she would never claim to be the most experienced lesbian in the world when it came to sex, but just the same, it was only sex, right? It just meant they were strongly attracted to each other, but it didn't mean they had to get serious about each other.

"When will I see you again?"

"I'm not sure. It's going to be a busy week." Dana stalled for time because she didn't know what to do. Her old anxieties rose up and warned her that she might be rushing into something she wasn't prepared to handle. They told her to put some distance between her and Ridley and to be careful before she made any promises she couldn't keep.

"I'm going to miss you," Ridley said. "Would it be all right if I called you later this week just to talk and see how you're doing?"

"Of course you can call me," Dana said. The disappointment in Ridley's voice and the hurt in her eyes made Dana ignore her inner voices. No one deserved to be treated with indifference, least of all someone as nice as Ridley. Despite her fears, she couldn't bring herself to shut Ridley out of her life. They'd made love to each other and had shared the deepest kind of intimacy and she couldn't bear to leave Ridley with the impression that it had meant so little to her. "Why don't you come over this Sunday after brunch, say around three-thirty? We can spend the rest of the day and evening together."

Ridley's face brightened. "That sounds like fun. I'll look forward to it."

Dana felt better when she saw the heaviness lift from Ridley's eyes and the pain vanish from her features. "I don't know what we'll do. Maybe I'll rent a movie or something."

"I don't think we'll have a problem finding something to do."

"No, I guess we won't," Dana said. "Ridley?"

"What is it?" Ridley put her hand on Dana's shoulder.

"I don't know how to thank you for this weekend. It was wonderful and I want you to know it meant a great deal to me. I enjoyed being with you and talking to you and..." Dana hesitated but then continued on in spite of her fears. "I enjoyed being close to you."

"I'm glad you feel that way because I loved making love to you."

Ridley cupped Dana's cheek and rubbed her cheek bone with her thumb. "And I loved everything we did together." She gave Dana a long, lingering kiss.

"I'd better get inside," Dana said when the kiss ended. "You have a good week. Call me in a few days and I'll see you this Sunday." Dana got out, grabbed her bag and walked away. Before she turned to go around the rear of the house, she turned and waved goodbye.

Chapter
Eighteen

THE REST OF the week was busy for Ridley and it passed by quickly. She had talked to Dana on the phone twice, once on Wednesday just to see how her week was going and then again on Friday, just to hear her voice. With each day, her desire for Dana grew more pressing and by the end of the week, she had trouble keeping her mind on anything else. On Friday she went out with friends from her previous school which provided her with some relief, but on Saturday, she had nothing to do all day but to dwell on how much she missed Dana and wanted to be with her.

Sunday morning she made herself eat breakfast, read the paper, clean her room and do the laundry. Performing mindless chores helped the time go by, but it had little or no effect on the persistent desire that plagued her. Later in the afternoon, she showered and got dressed and by the time she stood in front of the door to the kitchen at Café De Marco, her heart was pounding in her ears. As she knocked, she opened the door and poked her head inside. She waved to Jimmy and walked up to greet Tracy. "Hi. Dana's expecting me. Is she around?"

Tracy wiped her hands. "Dana already went upstairs. She told me to tell you to go right up when you got here. Are you hungry? We have some stuff left over."

"No thanks. I had a big breakfast," Ridley said although she'd had to force down the toast she made to go with her coffee. All week her appetite had been lousy and according to her scale at home, she'd dropped five pounds in the last few weeks. She didn't need food, she needed Dana and her constant state of arousal seemed to be the only bodily preoccupation she had any awareness of or need to satisfy. "Did you have a lot of people today?" she asked Tracy.

"Yeah, we did earlier but we slowed down so Dana went upstairs. Our last customers are almost done. Why don't you help yourself to some coffee?"

"Honestly, I couldn't eat or drink a thing. I'm just going to head up to Dana's apartment and get out of your way so you can get on with your work. I'll talk to you later." Ridley backed out the door as she said goodbye. Since she'd met Dana, her life seemed to be all about waiting and she had waited all week. She needed her like she needed water and air and she couldn't wait one more minute. Her pent up energy sent her bolting up the stairs to Dana's apartment.

Dana answered the door wearing nothing but goose bumps and a towel. "Brrrr, get in here. It's chilly out there." She grabbed Ridley by her jacket sleeve, pulled her inside and shoved the door shut. "Sorry, I'm not ready yet. I just got out of the shower. We were really busy earlier and..." Dana stared into Ridley's eyes and let go of her sleeve, but she didn't move. "I'll go get dressed."

Ridley grabbed her by the waist and held her firmly. "No, don't. I've ached for you all week and I want you so much right now, I can't think straight. I don't want anything else." She pulled Dana toward her and in doing so, she caused Dana's towel to come loose and fall to the floor. Ridley kicked it aside. "Leave it."

"You've got it bad. Why don't I see if I can relieve some of your suffering?" Dana spoke with her lips moving against Ridley's mouth, her breath mingling with Ridley's.

"Please. Only you can," Ridley whispered.

Dana tugged at the buttons on Ridley's shirt. "It was very thoughtful of you not to wear a bra," she said as she got the shirt open and covered Ridley's breasts with her hands.

Ridley moaned from deep inside. "I need you so bad."

Dana covered a nipple with her mouth and sucked on it.

"Good God." The sensations produced by Dana's mouth made Ridley feel faint. She moved until her back was against the wall for support, unbuttoned her jeans, tugged the zipper down and brought Dana's hand to her lower abdomen. "Touch me, please"

Dana ran her hand down Ridley's abdomen and into her panties. As if she wanted to tease just a little to prolong the anticipation, she stopped when her fingertips reached Ridley's damp curls. "Tell me what you want."

"You know what I want." Ridley put her hand on Dana's and urged her on.

Dana reached into Ridley's wetness and entered her. "Is this what you need?"

Ridley threw her head back against the wall, clamped her eyes shut and became rigid as the waves of her climax gripped her body like a series of electrical shocks. As she rode it out, she clung to Dana and after it subsided she fell into her arms. After a minute or two, she stood up. "God, I'm sorry. I never even said hello or kissed you."

"You'll have to make up for that, but first I think we should lie down." With her arm around Ridley's waist, Dana walked her into the bedroom. "Why don't you take your clothes off? It would make things a lot easier."

Ridley removed her clothing under Dana's watchful eyes and as soon as she was naked, she gathered Dana into her arms and kissed her. "I could kiss you forever."

"Forever?" Dana repeated with a sparkle in her eyes. "What's gotten into you?"

"I have no idea. All I know is that I've never been like this, not ever." She kissed Dana on her neck just below her ear. "It's not a problem, is it?"

"Not for me. I like it."

"I'm glad to hear you say that because I still haven't done what I've wanted to do all week." Ridley urged Dana to the bed and helped her lie back with her legs hanging off the edge. She parted Dana's legs and knelt on the floor between them. Prompted by Dana's urging, Ridley ran a hand up the inside of her thigh and entered her. Since Monday, she'd wanted to make love to Dana in this way again. In fact, she'd found it difficult to keep her mind on anything else and now that they were together, she knew she'd never get tired of this.

After Dana screamed her release into the room, Ridley climbed up on the bed, took Dana in her arms and kissed her. "You're so beautiful. I love how you look, how you feel, how you taste. I love..." Her hand found Dana and she began to touch her again.

Dana reached to touch Ridley. "And I love how wet you get when you're really hot for me and how you feel inside. It's just like...God, this feels so good. I..."

Their words and their touching transported them to a place where they lost all awareness aside from the feel of each other's bodies and the quest for mutual gratification. Ridley was the first to let go and Dana followed right behind her.

Afterward, with her cheek against Dana's, Ridley whispered, "Being with you is wonderful. Everything about you is wonderful."

"And you are the sexiest thing alive. I've never..."

Ridley propped herself up on her elbow and looked into Dana's eyes. "You make me sexy." Although Dana hadn't finished her thought, Ridley knew what she'd wanted to say. "I haven't either. You must know how special this is. Everything until now has been like child's play and I can't believe I still want you this much. Do you think I've gone mad?"

"I doubt it. If you have, then we're both raving lunatics."

Ridley exaggerated a sigh of relief. "That's a relief. I was afraid I might be the only one who had completely lost my mind."

"Well, you're not." Dana kissed her. "This is a nice way to spend a chilly Sunday afternoon, don't you think? We can make love all day if you want to."

"If I want to?" Ridley gathered Dana into her arms. "Believe me, I want to."

HOURS LATER, DANA disentangled herself from Ridley's embrace and got out of bed. "Are you hungry? Because I'm so hungry I could eat a horse or a house or maybe a cardboard box." She pulled her jeans and tee shirt on over her naked body and stuck her bare feet into a pair of moccasins. Then she went over and nudged Ridley. "Get up and put some clothes on. We'll go downstairs and I'll make us something to eat."

Ridley stretched her arms over her head. "Don't you have any food up here?"

"I'm afraid not. I'm always eating downstairs and it doesn't make sense to stock up on groceries in both places. Quit asking questions and come on."

"I see your point. Okay, downstairs it is. Just give me a minute." Ridley went into the bathroom and when she came out she stepped naked into her jeans and put her shirt back on. "No one's down there, right?"

"Are you kidding? Everyone went home a long time ago and Tracy told me earlier that she'd be spending the night with Erika, so we have the place to ourselves. Unless..."

"Unless what?" Ridley asked.

Dana walked over to Ridley and stood in front of her. "Unless there's someone or something lurking in the shadows down there that I don't know about."

"Stop trying to scare me, silly." Ridley grabbed her, picked her up off the floor and spun her around. "So, what you're saying is we'll have to keep an eye out for attack-trained chickens or killer cucumbers or karate trained carrots or..."

"Or the boogie man."

"He's not here. He's in the closet of my old room at home."

"So you think we're safe then?"

Ridley laughed. "Yeah, we're safe. Let's go before you starve to death."

In a matter of minutes, Dana whipped up two cheese and mushroom omelets along with toasted bagels and cream cheese. They ate at the kitchen counter and drank hot tea without saying a word to each other until they had consumed every morsel.

Ridley pushed her empty plate away. "That was good. I didn't realize how hungry I was—for food I mean. I haven't eaten since this morning and that wasn't much. I was too nervous to eat before I came over here."

"Couldn't wait to see me, huh?"

"I couldn't wait to see you and touch you."

"Have you touched me enough?" Dana asked.

"No, but I think we could both use a break."

"I agree, so let's talk a little. How was your week?"

"Busy as usual and filled with teenage drama. One of my ninth graders told me she was pregnant. It's a shame because she's smart and has potential. I convinced her to talk to Erin Lafferty about her options, but she made it clear she planned to have the baby and keep it. Of course she expects her mother to raise it."

"Did she go see Erin?"

"Yes, the next day. I really like Erin. We've gotten friendly and sometimes I go up and eat lunch with her or she comes down to the gym to see me."

"She does, huh?" Dana chewed on the inside of her cheek. "Uh, about this Erin Lafferty...is she attractive?"

Ridley didn't answer right away. What did she see hiding in Dana's face? Was it jealousy? "Yeah, she's attractive. As a matter of fact, she's quite cute. She came home with me after work on Friday and we hung out and talked for a while and then later on, we went out to eat at South Street Souvlaki. They have great Greek food. Have you been there?"

"Hmm...whose idea was that?"

"Mine. I invited her because I wanted to get to know her better and it's hard to talk at work. She's constantly busy and so am I."

Dana chewed on the opposite cheek. "You went out to dinner with her and you didn't bring her to my restaurant? I'm just a few blocks from South Street Souvlaki."

Ridley reached over and flicked a small crumb away from the side of Dana's mouth with her thumb. "That's right. I wouldn't want to make a pest of myself and I wouldn't want you to think I was stalking you. Besides, your restaurant's expensive."

"Did you consider your evening with her a date?"

"No, Dana, I didn't. We're becoming friends and we just wanted to talk." Ridley raised her eye brows. "If I didn't know better, I'd say you were jealous."

"I am a little, but I know I don't have any right to be."

"That's true, but aside from that, you don't have to be." Ridley covered Dana's hand with hers. She longed to tell Dana that she didn't want anyone else and she could have reassured her that even though Erin was attractive, she wasn't attracted to her, but she didn't. Dana had set the limits for their relationship and she would have to deal with the consequences. "I found out she's one of us. I had suspected she was because of something she'd said and while we were talking, we just came out and told each other."

"Great. Does Laurie know her?"

"Not that well, but I told Laurie about her and Laurie thinks Erin should join our group of friends. We're all going out together sometime soon or Laurie's going to have us over to her house for dinner some weekend."

"Swell. Does she have a girlfriend?"

"I asked her that and she said she's currently single."

"So, that means she's available?" Dana asked.

"Yes, that's what that usually means," Ridley replied.

Dana picked up their plates and carried them to the sink. "Help me clean up." She threw a dishtowel at Ridley. "Here, you can dry."

Ridley thought Dana had thrown the dishtowel a little harder than she had to, so she dropped the subject of Erin. However, it did please her that she'd gotten a rise out of Dana. "Did you mean it when you invited me to bring my mother here for dinner?" Ridley dried the dishes as Dana handed them to her and stacked them on the counter. "She has to come into the city this Tuesday and she wants to meet me for dinner. Would it be all right if we came then?"

"Of course it would. I'll write you in the book for six o'clock. Is that okay?"

"That's when she wanted to meet me."

"Remember, though, I told her it would be my treat. You can bring some wine if you want it, but you're not paying for dinner. Does your mother have any favorite foods?"

"She loves duck," Ridley answered immediately. She paused to think of more, but ended up saying, "I can't think of much she wouldn't like on your menu."

"I'll make something special. I know just the thing."

"Don't go to any trouble. Anything you make will be fine."

"It's no trouble. It'll make me happy to do something nice for her and for you."

"Thanks," Ridley said.

"You're welcome." Dana handed Ridley the omelet pan and washed the silverware and utensils. She drained the water out of the sink and dried her hands prior to giving Ridley her undivided attention. "So what do you want to do now?"

"What a question." Ridley moved close enough to feel the heat radiating from Dana's body and get her nose tickled by Dana's rapid breathing. With her arms wrapped around Dana she walked her backward, until they reached the counter. In a display of strength, she picked Dana up, set her down on the stainless steel top and situated herself between Dana's knees. As they kissed, she held onto Dana's thighs.

"What are you up to now?" Dana asked between kisses.

"I'm thinking about having something sweet for dessert." Ridley opened Dana's jeans and slid the zipper down. "Lift your hips so I can pull these off."

"Here?"

"Why not? You do serve dessert, don't you?"

Dana kicked her moccasins off and lifted her hips. "Ooh, that's cold on my butt," she said as she settled her bare behind back on the counter.

"You'll warm it up soon enough." Ridley kissed her again, this time more urgently.

Dana broke away from the kiss. "Wait. Hold on a second. Before you get carried away I want you to promise me you'll never tell anyone I had my naked butt on this counter." Dana put her hands on Ridley's shoulders and kept her at a distance. "I'm begging you. I'll never hear the end of it if you do."

"I can just imagine," Ridley said, unable to hold back a mischievous smile.

"I don't think you can. I know them and it would be awful." Dana still held onto her so she couldn't move closer. "Promise me right now or I'll put my jeans back on."

"All right, I promise. I wouldn't want you to go through that. I'll keep quiet if you let me have my way with you, but I'm also thinking this will come in handy if I ever need to blackmail you." Ridley ran her hands under Dana's tee shirt and reached for her breasts.

Dana jerked as Ridley touched them. "Oh...they've never been this sensitive."

Ridley lifted Dana's shirt enough to expose her breasts and with one arm around Dana's back to support her, she leaned in and took a swollen nipple into her mouth.

Dana groaned as Ridley brought her nipple to a stiff peak and pushed her hips firmly against Ridley's abdomen. "I'm getting your jeans all wet."

Ridley let go of Dana's breast and lifted her head. "Don't worry about it. They're already plenty wet inside." She brought her mouth to Dana's nipples a second time, but she didn't linger there for long because she couldn't wait any longer for what she really wanted. She bent her head and found Dana wet and open and more than ready.

"I almost fainted that time," Dana said minutes later.

"If you had, I'd have held you up. I'd never let you fall."

"That's comforting. Now help me get down from here," Dana hung onto Ridley's shoulders as she slid to the floor and then she held on to her arm as she pulled her jeans on and stepped into her shoes. After she pulled her tee shirt over her head, she put her arms around Ridley and kissed her soundly. "Let's go back upstairs before you find some other crazy place to attack me."

"I love making love to you," Ridley said as she pulled Dana closer.

"I have noticed that and now that we've had something to eat, I'd like to do to you what you just did to me—only in bed." Dana gave Ridley a light spank on the butt.

"Let's go," Ridley said. "We're wasting time."

Chapter
Nineteen

ON MONDAY AFTERNOON, the phone rang and Dana ran to answer it before the answering machine picked up the call. She expected it would be her sister since Donna had called on Sunday evening while Dana was in bed with Ridley and had left a message that she would call back the next afternoon. "Hello," Dana said.

"Dana? Is that you?"

The caller was not her sister and at first, Dana couldn't recognize the voice. "Yes, this is Dana. Who's this?" Dana's heart began to race as her memory banks re-deposited the identity of the voice's owner into her consciousness.

"Dana? Is that really you?"

"Sarah?" Yes, it was her all right. No doubt about it. Dana's hands shook so violently, she almost dropped the phone. "I never expected I'd pick up the phone and hear your voice." For a long time after they broke up she'd prayed for this call until eventually, she was forced to accept that it would never come and now here she was listening to Sarah's sugary voice on the other end of the line.

"I didn't mean to shock you," Sarah said. "Did I call at a bad time?"

"Uh...you just took me by surprise, that's all. I wasn't..."

"I'm sure you weren't. I'm sorry about that."

Dana ignored the apology. "So, how did you get my number?"

"I called your mother. She's the one who told me you moved to Philadelphia."

"I did. Where are you calling from? Where do you live?"

"Here in Chicago. Your mother said you opened your own restaurant. That's what we were going to do, remember?"

"I remember. Funny you should remind me of that because I could have sworn you were the one who forgot." A surge of anger scraped its way through Dana's gut and burned its way into her throat. She swallowed it back down.

"I..." Sarah said nothing for a few seconds. When she did speak, her voice sounded high and a bit cheerful. "So, how are you doing?"

"I'm doing great, thank you very much." Dana noticed that Sarah didn't respond to her remark or try to explain herself. Even if she did, it wouldn't have made a difference.

"I'm happy for you — for opening the restaurant."

"Gee, thanks. So, how's what's his name?" Dana asked, tired of

trying to keep the anger from oozing into her tone. Sarcasm wasn't
usually her style but everything she said to Sarah sounded sarcastic
to her own ears. What's more, she didn't care.

"You mean Kevin? He's okay, I guess."

"You guess?"

"We split up. He decided taking care of me and the baby was too
much for him."

"Too bad," Dana said with sharpness in her crisp words. What
did she care? As a matter of fact, it pissed her off to hear about
Kevin. Why had she even asked about Kevin, she wondered? This
was no time to be polite. "I almost forgot you had a baby. What did
you have?"

"A girl. Her name's Tori."

"Congratulations." Dana forced that out through clenched teeth.
She waited through the silence that followed and then spoke first.
"Look, Sarah. I'm sure you didn't call just to engage in this chit-chat.
What do want?"

"I've missed you," Sarah said.

"Are you serious?" Dana almost laughed out loud at Sarah's
ridiculous declaration. Her voice had sounded sheepish when she
said it and Dana didn't believe her. "You missed me? You could have
fooled me."

"I know. I should have called you way before this. I've thought
about you a lot, you know? And I thought maybe I could see you
again and we could...we could talk."

"I don't know about that."

"Maybe you can't forgive me," Sarah offered.

"I don't know about that either."

Sarah continued on in spite of Dana's responses. "I regret what
happened between us and I'm sorry about what I did to you. It
bothers me and I'd like to make it up to you." Sarah waited a few
seconds as if she expected Dana to jump in during the silence and let
her off the hook. "We all make mistakes, don't we?"

"You were in our bed having sex with a man. That's quite a
mistake."

"I know. It was rotten of me," Sarah whined.

"Rotten? That's it? You destroyed my hopes and dreams."

"I don't want to upset you. We should talk about this, in
person."

"This is..." A deluge of emotions coursed through Dana and
much to her chagrin, her voice broke and she thought she might
cry. That was the last thing she wanted to do. With a steady voice,
she said, "I'd have to think about that. I'm not sure I want to see
you."

"Geez, Dana, I'm sorry I hurt you, you know, but I was only

doing what I thought was right for myself at the time. I was stupid and I..."

"I know. That's what I used to tell myself."

"Would you come here to see me? I'm lonely and miserable and we used to have something good once, you know? We did, Dana, didn't we?"

"We did, but..." Dana took a deep breath and managed to salvage her dignity a second time. "I'm not sure I can get away. Let me think about it."

"Okay. Will you let me know?"

"Yes. Give me your number and I'll call you back."

Sarah recited her number and had Dana repeat it. "So, I'll wait to hear from you. Call me tonight or tomorrow and please consider coming. We should talk and maybe you don't believe me, but I do miss you."

"Goodbye, Sarah." Dana hung up and stared at the phone.

AS SOON AS she was able to move her legs, Dana sprinted out of her apartment and up the back stairs to Tracy's apartment. She banged on the door.

Tracy flung the door open. "Christ, Dana, is the house on fire or something?"

"Thank God you're home." Dana was on the verge of tears and didn't bother to hide it. She pushed past Tracy and stormed into her apartment. "I need to talk to you."

"What the hell happened?" Tracy caught up with Dana who was already in the living room. "So, sit down and tell me what's going on."

"She called me." Dana sat on the sofa.

"She who?" Tracy remained standing.

"Sarah, that's who. She just called me."

"Well, well, well. Will wonders never cease? What did she want?" Tracy's words were clipped and she made a face as if she'd just found a couple of six month old bananas on top of her refrigerator.

"She got my number from my mother and she wants to patch things up. She's sorry and she wants to see me."

"She should be sorry. Did she have anything to say for herself?"

"We didn't talk that much about it on the phone." Dana sniffed and pulled a tissue out of her pocket. "She's living in Chicago."

"Goodie." Tracy's face scrunched up even more. "So, what happens next?"

"I'm not sure." Dana dried her eyes. "Do you have time to talk?"

Tracy's face softened just a bit. "Of course I do, honey. I always have time for you." She sat in a chair next to the sofa.

"I can't believe she called after all this time. I'm not sure how I feel about it and I don't know what to do. I don't want to hurt Ridley. She doesn't deserve that."

"Why are you so concerned about Ridley's feelings? I know you've been seeing each other, but aren't you just friends?"

"Not exactly," Dana said.

"What does 'not exactly' mean?" Tracy's mouth fell open and her eyes widened as if she'd just had a revelation. "Why do I get the feeling something important has happened and I don't know anything about it? You're not keeping secrets from me are you?"

"Well..." Dana answered. "Something has happened."

"I hope it's what I think it is." Tracy's face lit up.

"It is what you think it is."

"You'd better fill me in and I want to know everything. You know I have to know what's going on in my best friend's personal life."

"Remember you said something along the lines of what harm would there be in having fun with Ridley and getting to know her? You said why don't you go for it?"

"Sure, I remember. So?"

"I thought about what you said." Dana paused.

"You did?" Tracy waited. "And?"

"And I have needs and she wanted me. She wanted me so much and that's awfully hard to resist, especially when it's someone as sexy as she is."

"Whoa. I can fill in the rest." Tracy held her hand up. "So you figured, what the hell, right? Why not enjoy some casual sex with a super adorable lesbian? Have you actually done it? Have you had sex with her?"

Dana felt her cheeks start to get warm. "I couldn't help myself. When we were at the shore I wanted to kiss her so bad I couldn't stand it for one more second. She told me she wanted to kiss me, so I kissed her. And then one thing led to another and we ended up in bed."

"That explains a lot. When you got back, you were glowing. You didn't tell me what had happened, but I knew something had. I figured you'd tell me when you were ready to." Tracy hesitated and then asked, "How was it if you don't mind me asking?"

"It was wonderful. She was wonderful. Whenever we're near each other, we can't stop touching." A surge of heat set Dana's body on fire as she recalled the intimacy she'd shared with Ridley only yesterday.

"Look at you." Tracy fanned herself. "You're making me hot."

"It was hot all right and I enjoyed it. I also liked being with her, but beyond that, I haven't thought much about my feelings. She's kind, she's considerate, she's..."

"Yeah, yeah, she's all that. But do you know how she feels about you?"

"Not really." Dana thought for a moment. "She's told me she thinks I'm beautiful and the way she looks at me...sometimes I think..."

"Go on. Sometimes you think what?"

With her hand, Dana waved away whatever she'd been about to say. "Never mind, I don't know what I think. I do know one thing, though. I wouldn't want to hurt her and I hope I didn't do the wrong thing by giving in to my attraction for her. Maybe I should have left her alone."

"Here's my advice to you and I can't believe these words are coming out of my mouth. Why don't you go to Chicago and talk to Sarah? As you know, I've never been crazy about her and as you also know, I really like Ridley. That woman has turned the lights back on in your eyes." Tracy paused as though to give Dana time to digest her words. "You'll never get on with your life unless you confront Sarah and find out if you still feel anything for her."

"I think you're right. I'll always wonder if I don't."

"Exactly, so why don't we come up with a plan?"

Dana devised a plan in her head right then and there and presented it to Tracy. "Would it be all right with you if I left early on Wednesday morning, if I can get a flight? Would you be able to drive me to the airport?"

"Yes to both. Will you visit your family while you're there?"

"I can't go to Chicago and not spend a few days with my family. I haven't seen them in months and I miss them. Do you think you can manage without me for a few days?"

"Sure. We've got the hang of it by now and I like being in charge. You do what you need to do and don't worry about a thing. You'll pay me back later."

Dana gave Tracy a big hug. "You're the best friend a person could ever have."

Tracy broke out of the hug and held Dana's arms. "Just don't come back and tell me you're moving or closing the restaurant. I love this job and I love living here and I love you. I don't want to lose any of it. You're the best boss and the greatest friend I'll ever have."

"That's not going to happen. I could never give this up and any decisions I make will be based on what's best for this restaurant and you. You can count on that."

"What about Ridley? She's obviously crazy about you. You should talk to her before you go. She's a nice person and I think you owe her that much."

"I agree. She's bringing her mother here for dinner tomorrow. I don't want to tell her on the phone, so I'll try to get her alone and talk to her. Hopefully, she'll understand."

Chapter
Twenty

ON TUESDAY EVENING, Ridley drove to Café De Marco to meet her mother for dinner. The streets were crowded and she had to park a few blocks away on a side street and walk to the restaurant. In spite of her parking problems, she was surprised to find she was only ten minutes late. From across the street, she spotted her mother waiting out front and hurried to join her.

"Sorry I'm late, Mom. I couldn't find a parking space and I had to circle around several blocks until someone pulled out of one. Why didn't you go inside and wait?"

"That's all right, sweetheart. I just got here myself. I had the same problem finding a place to park and I ended up on 11th Street."

"You should have come over to my apartment and left your car there like I told you to. We could have come together and I would have driven you back for your car later on."

"I know and I would have, but I'd like to leave right after dinner," her mother explained. "I have an early morning appointment with the dentist tomorrow and a bunch of errands to run and I don't want to get home late. Besides, I don't want you to have to leave on my account. Maybe you'd like to spend some time with Dana?"

"She'll be too busy to visit with me and I have to work tomorrow, so I'll probably leave right after we eat, anyway." Ridley pointed to the front door of Café De Marco. "Let's go in."

Vicki inspected the restaurant façade. "This is a lovely place." She took hold of Ridley's arm and walked through the door with her. "Now, I really am excited."

The hostess was expecting them and she took them to their table without delay. She also relayed a message from Dana that they should make themselves comfortable and she would join them as soon as she could.

"It's so warm and inviting in here and this is a nice table," Ridley's mother remarked. "I'm sorry to see there aren't more people, though. Is that usual?"

"Tuesdays and Wednesdays are slow, but it picks up on Thursday and she's booked solid on Fridays and Saturdays. Sunday brunch is always crowded." Ridley touched her mother's arm and changed the subject. "Why don't you tell me about your weekend while we're waiting?"

Ridley and her mother took the time to catch up on things until Dana came out of the kitchen and hurried to their table. Dana appeared stressed as she flopped into the seat next to Ridley's. Her face was strained and her eyes were full of tension. Even so, she was as beautiful as ever and just the sight of her made Ridley want her more than ever.

"I'm so glad you're both here," Dana said.

"Look at you," Vicki said. "Aren't you the cutest thing in that chef's outfit?"

"Thanks, Vicki." Dana seemed pleased with the compliment.

"I've been looking forward to this," Vicki told Dana.

"We both have," Ridley said. She couldn't stop staring at Dana. The sight of her brought it all rushing back, everything they'd done together and everything she'd felt.

"Your restaurant's lovely," Vicki said. "It reminds me of a Trattoria in Tuscany my husband and I used to visit when we traveled to Italy." Vicki's face darkened and she lowered her eyes. "It was one of my husband Jeremy's favorite places."

"That's exactly the look I was going for," Dana said.

"And you've captured it." Vicki raised her eyes. "You're fortunate to have all of this at such a young age. Your parents must be very proud of you."

"They are, but my father helped me a lot so he claims all the bragging rights."

"Ridley's father was proud of her. She was his pride and joy. He cried when she was born and the first time he held her in his arms he stared at her for over an hour. The nurses practically had to pry her out of his hands." Vicki glanced at her daughter, a fleeting glance but one laden with a shared sorrow. "Well, girls..." Vicki cleared her throat and took a sip of water. "This is a special evening, so let's not dwell on sad things, shall we?"

"Ridley told me you liked duck, so I have a special tonight just for you," Dana said after a polite moment of silence. "It's a raspberry vinegar glazed duck and we're serving it with roasted root vegetables and a wild rice pilaf. Of course, if you don't feel like having duck, we have other specials or you can order from the menu."

"The duck sounds divine," Vicki said. "I'll have that."

"Good. We also have a special salad of mixed greens with roasted beets, oranges and honey glazed walnuts. It comes with a light citrus and honey dressing."

"I'll have that, too," Vicki said. "It will go well with the duck."

Ridley observed her mother and Dana as they talked. Although it wasn't crucial, it had often occurred to her that if she were to find that certain someone to share her life with it would be all the better if it were someone her mother was fond of and someone who'd want to be a part of her family. If only Dana could be that someone. Her thoughts were interrupted by Dana's next question which was directed at her.

"What are you going to have, Ridley?"

"I want everything my mother is having." Dana's dark eyes stoked the flames of Ridley's arousal and she felt as though she was on fire. Her heart raced and her mouth felt dry, but she tried not to let it show because she was with her mother. Did Dana have the same feelings, she wondered? Was she craving her kiss and dying to touch her?

"Let me put your orders in and I'll come back and spend some time with you. We're not that busy tonight." Dana stood up, but before she left, she said, "I forgot to ask you what you wanted to drink. Did you bring any wine?"

"No. Mom's a little tired and she has to drive home alone. And I need my wits about me this evening. We'd both like some ice water and I'd like a glass of iced tea if you have any. Mom, do you want iced tea?"

"Yes, I'll have some," Vicki answered.

"I'll have the waiter bring that right away," Dana said.

"Ridley, I can see why you're so taken with her," Vicki said as soon as Dana was out of earshot. "I'm quite fond of her myself."

"I'm glad you like her. She means a great deal to me."

"It's easy to see that, sweetheart."

"DANA, I'VE NEVER had better duck," Vicki said after they finished eating dinner. "The vegetables and rice were perfect with it and I loved the salad." Ridley certainly didn't exaggerate when she raved about your restaurant. Next time, I'll save room for dessert." Vicki finished the last of her hazelnut crème coffee and got up. "I think I'll be on my way. I have to get home."

Dana rose to her feet. "Thank you so much for coming."

"Thank you for a wonderful evening. I'd love it if you'd come to see me again," Vicki said. "Maybe next time I'll take you both out to dinner."

"That would be nice," Dana said. It saddened her to think there probably wouldn't be a next time after what she was about to tell Ridley.

"Let me walk you to your car." Ridley stood up.

"You don't have to." Vicki hugged Ridley and kissed her on the cheek. "Call me in a day or two, will you? And give your aunt a call. She loves to hear from you."

"I will, Mom. Be careful driving home."

"I always am. Goodbye, you two." Vicki grabbed her purse and headed for the door. Just before she exited the dining room, she turned and waved.

"Your mother's nice. Thanks for bringing her."

"She enjoyed it." Ridley sat at the table again and fiddled with her napkin. "Can you sit with me a minute? I want to talk to you."

Dana's heart raced as she slid into the chair next to Ridley's. "I have something I need to talk to you about." She dreaded telling Ridley about going to see Sarah. She knew she was faced with a true dilemma — when she told Ridley the truth she would hurt her and if she didn't tell her, she would hurt her even more. This would take courage and she couldn't find any.

Ridley pulled her chair closer. "I'm dying to touch you. I've missed you so much." Dana had her hand on the table and Ridley covered it with her own.

Dana turned her hand over and gave Ridley's hand a quick squeeze. Then she pulled her hand away and began to fiddle with the buttons on her chef's jacket. With her gaze fixed on the table in front of her, she undid the top button and re-fastened it three or four times before she realized what she was doing.

"You look nervous, Dana. You said you needed to talk to me. What's going on?"

Dana didn't answer. Ridley's question had provided her with the opening she should have taken, but she lost her nerve as soon as she turned her head and saw the concern in Ridley's eyes. That and the compassion on Ridley's face made her feel as if she were about to do the cruelest thing she'd ever done to anyone.

Ridley pressed the issue. "You were fine during dinner and now something's wrong. Did I upset you? Maybe I shouldn't have touched you in here."

"No, that's not it. I'm just nervous." Dana's inner voice told her to quit stalling. "I have to tell you something and I'm having a hard time getting it out."

"What is it?" The concern in Ridley's eyes turned in to anxiety.

Dana paused to take a deep breath. "I have to go away tomorrow morning. I'm flying to Chicago to see my family and while I'm there I'm..."

"Go on," Ridley urged.

"I'm going to see the woman I was involved with before I moved here, the one I told you about at the shore. She called me and she wants to see me."

"Why are you going to see her now, after what we...?" Ridley's voice sounded frail and her face clouded over. "She wants you back, doesn't she?"

"I'm not sure — maybe. All I know is that she asked me to come so we could talk. She said she's sorry about what happened between us." Dana felt sick when she saw the anguish that had transformed Ridley's face and the pain that had killed the spark in her eyes.

"And you're going?" Ridley asked.

"I have to go. I loved her once and I have to see if there's anything left between us. I need to do it for myself as much as for her." Dana closed her eyes. She was hurting Ridley and she hated doing it. She tried to think of something she could say to make her understand. "I'll never be free of her if I don't. You understand, don't you?"

"No, I don't." Ridley clamped her hand over her mouth but failed to stifle the tiny choking sound that escaped through her fingers. She took a few breaths and removed her hand from her mouth. "I didn't know you still loved her. I never would have thought—I mean I thought we..." A solitary tear trickled down Ridley's cheek.

"Please don't cry, Ridley. I shouldn't have told you this in here. I'm so sorry." Dana stood up, took Ridley's hand and pulled her to her feet. "Let's get out of here." She marched Ridley straight through the kitchen, out the back door and up the stairs without stopping to acknowledge anyone or deal with Tracy's bewildered expression as they hustled by.

Once they were safely inside her apartment, Dana put Ridley on the sofa and sat beside her. "Please try to understand. I need to see her and find out what she wants. More than that, I need to find out what I want. I can't get on with my life until I do this."

"What about us? I thought..." Ridley's body shook and she swiped at the tears she couldn't hold inside. "I thought we had something special and I thought you had feelings for me. I don't know how I could have been so wrong or such a fool."

Dana put her arm around Ridley's shoulder. "You're not a fool. I guess when I told you I didn't want to get involved with anyone and you pursued me in spite of it, I assumed you were willing to be with me on my terms. I figured why couldn't we have a good time together?" Dana cringed at the coldness of her own words. What had she become?

"What about being with me? What about making love with me?" Ridley glanced at Dana and then gripped her hands together in her lap and kept her eyes focused on them. "I heard all the things you told me, but after that weekend at the shore I thought..." Ridley closed her eyes for a short time and then stared at her hands again. "I thought you had changed your mind about me—about us. I never thought it would mean so little to you."

"It meant something to me," Dana said. "You know it did."

Ridley turned her sad eyes toward Dana. "Just not that much, right?" She sighed and ran her fingers through her hair. "Didn't you like kissing me and touching me?"

"You know I did. You're an incredibly attractive woman."

"Was that all it was to you? Just an attraction you couldn't resist?" Ridley's voice was calm now and her words deliberate. "I can't believe I'm hearing the same old story I've heard from other women. I'm too hot to pass up, but not someone who deserves to be taken seriously."

"I'm sorry." Dana reached for Ridley's arm.

Ridley pulled away. "So am I, because I let myself fall in love with you." Ridley studied Dana's dark eyes as if searching for something she'd lost along the way. "I love you."

"I should have known. I saw it in your eyes and felt it in your touch, but I suppose I didn't want to believe it or deal with it."

"Well, it's true and now we'll both have to deal with it. I've been in love with you since that night on the beach when we kissed for the first time."

The hurt in Ridley's eyes and the despair in her voice made Dana want to console her in some way, but she knew Ridley needed to be strong and she would not welcome what she might easily interpret as pity. Until Dana faced up to her past, her feelings would remain unclear and her future uncertain and right now, she had nothing to offer Ridley other than the truth. "I don't know what to say to you."

"I do. Please don't go back to her."

"I have to, but I don't want to hurt you." Dana felt her eyes fill. "Not you."

"Then don't. Stay here with me and don't go to her. Please."

"I've been so unfair to you. I wasn't..." Dana sighed and rubbed her forehead. "I mean..." Dana felt miserable. Her head ached and she was ashamed of herself. What could she possibly say that wouldn't make matters worse or hurt Ridley more? "I don't know what I mean."

"You don't know what you want, either." Ridley turned away.

"I have to agree with you on that point." Dana placed her hand on Ridley's knee and bent her head to capture her eyes, but Ridley would not meet her eyes and she would not let her in.

"Please let me try to explain."

"Don't bother." Ridley stood up without warning. "You've explained enough and I've heard all I can stand to hear. It's time for me to leave." Her voice quivered with emotion.

Dana followed her to the door. "Wait, please." She grabbed her arm.

Ridley shook Dana's hand off. "I have to get out of here." She threw the door open, bolted out of Dana's apartment and ran down the stairs without another word.

AFTER RIDLEY'S ABRUPT departure, Dana made a mad dash down the stairs to the kitchen. Tracy would still be busy and she wouldn't be able to talk to her yet, but Dana had to do something to occupy her mind or she would go crazy. They still had a few tables to serve and Dana went right to work. When the last customers departed and they closed their doors for the night she helped Tracy and the kitchen staff clean-up.

"Are you going to tell me what's going on now that we're alone?" Tracy asked as soon as Jimmy closed the door behind him. "You and Ridley tore through here like a human tornado and then about twenty minutes later, I saw Ridley running down the back stairs. Then you come storming in looking like you were going to flip out."

"I told her I was going to see Sarah."

"I guess she didn't take it well?"

"No, Tracy, I guess she didn't." Whatever temporary relief Dana had gained from working hard for the last two hours vanished into thin air with those words. "I was wrong."

"Wrong about what?"

"Ridley is serious about me."

"Dana...my dear friend. Anyone with one or two eyes in their head could see that." Tracy made a sucking sound through her teeth. "Sometimes..."

Dana held her hand up to silence Tracy. "Don't say it. Sometimes I'm a pig-headed royal pain in the ass with blinders on and I guess I didn't want to see what I didn't want to see."

"That about sums it up," Tracy said. "So, what did she say?"

"She said she's in love with me."

"I'm not surprised to hear that, but here's what I have a problem with. That kind of woman tells you she's in love with you and you're upset about it? That just doesn't make any sense."

"I'm upset because I don't know how I feel about her."

"Well, that's different. If you don't love her..." Tracy said.

"I don't know if I love her but I do know I care about her and I've hurt her. I'll never forget the look on her face as long as I live." Dana was more upset over this than she had expected she would be. Ridley was alone and hurting all because of her and she wondered where Ridley was and what she was doing. "When did I become so calloused and insensitive?"

"I'm not going to answer that because I don't think you're either of those things. You're just a little messed up right now." Tracy stepped closer and put her arm around Dana. "Try not to go to pieces on me. Everything will be all right."

"I wish I could believe that," Dana said.

"It's too soon to know, but I think it will."

"I hope you're right." Dana rested her head on Tracy's shoulder. "I don't know what to do. I've never been this confused and my whole world is turned upside down."

"Going to see Sarah is a good start. Maybe it will give you some answers and make you feel less confused." Tracy took her arm away and started to untie her apron. "I'm tired of standing. Let's get out of this damned kitchen and go upstairs where we can kick our shoes off and relax while we talk about this."

"Okay," Dana said. "I could use a beer. Do you have any?"

"But of course. That's a staple in my house." Tracy pulled her apron off and tossed it on the counter. "Come on, I could use one or two myself. We'll drink while we talk this out."

Chapty
Twenty-one

THE NEXT EVENING, curled up on the sofa in the same wrinkled pair of pajamas she'd worn since the night before, Ridley listened to her answering machine as it picked up another of the many calls she'd screened and ignored that day since she'd dragged herself out of bed early in the morning. She sneered at her recorded message. It sounded so upbeat and not at all like it came from the down-in-the-dumps lump of a human being she'd evolved into in just one day.

After the beep, she listened as Laurie left another message, one of several she'd left that day. The first one had come in the morning, the second during lunch and the third message about the time Laurie would have arrived home from work. After that, she'd left one every hour on the hour, each one more insistent and more concerned. This new message bordered on frantic.

"Ridley, it's me again. Where the hell are you? I'm getting really worried. Pick up the phone if you're in there. You weren't at work and I don't know if you're sick or what. This isn't like you. Come on, if you're in there, please pick up the phone. I tried your cell phone but you've got it on voice mail." After a pause, Laurie made one last plea. "Okay...maybe I'm overreacting or maybe you told me you were going somewhere and I forgot, but I want you to call me the instant you get my messages. I'll be home all evening."

Ridley felt guilty for ignoring her friend and letting her talk to a machine, but she couldn't bring herself to answer the phone. How could she talk to Laurie when she felt as though she had a huge knife wedged in her heart? Laurie didn't need to be dragged into her bottomless black hole of a day and what would she tell her? That she'd waited forever for a woman like Dana and it wasn't going to work out in her favor after all? Or maybe that she'd misread Dana's responses and misinterpreted her signals and she felt like an idiot?

The sound of the doorbell startled her out of her miserable thoughts. She waited and hoped that the unwanted visitor would give up and go away, but whoever it was began to bang on the door. Ridley got up and tiptoed over. She peered through the peep hole only to find Laurie's fun-house face looming an inch behind the hole as if she could somehow see into the apartment if she got close enough.

"Ridley! Open the door! I know you're in there," Laurie yelled from the other side. "Come on, open the door. I'm not leaving until you do."

Ridley opened the door and stood in the doorway. "Come in, Laurie."

"I knew it." Laurie hurried in and after Ridley closed the door, Laurie stood in front of her and gave her a thorough inspection. "I knew something was wrong. You look awful. Your hair's a mess and your eyes are all red. Are you sick?"

"Not physically, but I couldn't go to work. I..." Ridley struggled to speak as tears welled up and flowed down her cheeks. "I was too upset."

"Too upset? What happened?" Laurie took Ridley by the hand and walked into the living room with her. "I was so worried about you." Laurie sat on the sofa and brought Ridley down beside her. "Now tell me what happened."

Ridley dried her eyes. "My heart's broken."

"Now I'm really glad I came over. Karen told me not to worry but I know you and you would have told me if you were taking the day off and if you were sick you would have called me back. I told her something bad had happened."

"Oh, Laurie, I..." Ridley sat back. "I don't know where to start."

"Take your time. You'll tell me all about it when you're good and ready." Laurie put her arm around Ridley. "I've never seen you this upset. Why did you choose to suffer alone in here all day? You know you could have called me and asked me for anything. Why didn't you?"

"I wanted to, but I..." Ridley sighed. "I can't explain it. I almost picked up the phone every time you called, but I couldn't bear to talk to anyone."

"That's okay, but you know I'm there for you if you need me."

"I know." Ridley blinked a few times and rubbed her eyes. "My eyes burn."

"I'm sure they do. They're all swollen and red. Stay here, I'll be right back." Laurie left and when she came back she was carrying a folded washcloth. She sat next to Ridley and handed it to her. "Hold this on your eyes. I wet it and put some ice cubes in it. It's nice and cold."

Ridley closed her eyes and pressed it against them. "That feels good."

"How long have you been crying?"

"On and off since last evening." Ridley's inhaled breath hit a glitch in her throat and double clutched. "I've never cried this hard since my father died."

"I hate to say it, but you look like you just fell out of bed."

"I know. I was up until two o'clock in the morning and I didn't sleep much after that. When the alarm went off at six-thirty, I knew I couldn't go to work. I didn't have the energy to act like nothing was wrong and the thought of engaging in the usual chatter with the students and staff made me sick to my stomach."

"I don't want to push, but why don't you tell me how you got this way?" Laurie urged. "It might help to talk about it."

"It's about Dana. I'm in love with her."

"Are you serious? That's great!" Laurie blurted out. She smiled at first, but her smile soon faded as if she realized it might not have been the right thing to say. "Or not."

"Or not is more like it. Dana stole my heart like a thief in the night and now she's shattered it into tiny jagged pieces that will never fit together again. Even worse than that, I think I may have lost her forever."

"I didn't know you felt that way about her. I'd like to know why you didn't tell me, but I'll let it go for the time being because of the state you're in."

"Thanks." The corners of Ridley's mouth lifted a little. She hadn't told Laurie about the depth of her feelings for Dana in order to avoid this very situation, but now that it was out, she had no reason to hide and nothing to lose. "She's the only one for me. I love her more than I thought I could ever love anyone. I don't know if you recall what you said to me on the first day of school, but you were right. Love does come along when you're not expecting it."

"Love hurts, too, doesn't it? Did I happen to mention that?"

"You didn't have to." This time Ridley did smile, but just a little.

"Does she know how you feel about her? Have you told her?" Laurie hesitated. "You don't have to tell me, but have you two, uh..."

"Made love? Yes. And yes to all of those other questions."

Laurie didn't try to hide how happy she was about that answer. She grabbed Ridley and gave her a few quick squeezes, each one accompanied by a tiny squeal. "Forgive me. I know you're hurting, but that's the best news I've ever heard. You two make a great couple. Karen and I thought Dana and you were hitting it off, but we weren't sure. Let's just say we hoped."

"We're not going to be a couple," Ridley said.

"Why? What do you mean?" Laurie asked.

"Dana's not in love with me." Once Ridley said the thing she'd dreaded saying the most, it became easier to fill Laurie in on the events that had led to this point as well as everything she knew about the Dana and Sarah situation. "Dana left for Chicago today and I feel like my heart's been ripped out of my chest and thrown into the cargo hold of her plane along with the rest of the baggage."

"I'm sorry, Ridley, I really am. Are you sure there's no hope?"

"I'm sure." Ridley closed her eyes and turned her head back and forth. "She means the world to me and I'm not going to get over this any time soon, if ever." Then she stopped shaking her head and covered her eyes with the cold wash cloth.

"Why don't we focus on what we can do to make you feel better and then we can talk more about this. Have you had anything to eat today?"

Ridley shook her head. "I'm not hungry."

"Here's what we're going to do," Laurie said. "I'll run a hot bath for you and while you're soaking in it, I'll make you some eggs, toast and hot tea." She stood up. "When you get washed and dressed, you'll come out and eat."

"You make it all sound so easy."

"It is, and don't even think about giving me a hard time. If you keep this up, you'll get sick and I'm not going to let you make yourself sick."

Ridley surrendered. She was too weak to resist Laurie's loving care and it felt good to let someone take charge. "Okay. I won't give you a hard time."

"That's good, because you need some serious nurturing."

"I'm not very good at nurturing myself," Ridley admitted.

"None of us are. I'll call Karen and tell her I'm staying here tonight."

"You don't have to do that."

"I don't have to, but I want to. I can't bear to think of you over here alone, the way you feel. Either I stay here with you or you pack your things and come to our house."

"I'll come home with you." Ridley got up. No use arguing with Laurie once she'd made up her mind to something. "I really don't want to be alone and I know there's nothing I can do but wait. Are you sure I won't be in the way?"

"That's a ridiculous question." Laurie took Ridley's hand and gave it a yank so she'd look at her. "You're my oldest and dearest friend and I love you very much. Karen loves you, too. Besides, we can go in to work together. It'll be fun."

"You find fun in everything, even heartbreak." Despite her sorrow, Ridley felt her heart lighten a little, thanks to her friend. "That's one of the qualities I love the most about you and I can't tell you how much I appreciate what you're doing for me."

"So, go get your things together and I'll get your bath ready. While you eat, I'll call Karen and let her know you're coming home with me and when we get to my house, we'll discuss this Dana thing, with or without Karen. You can tell me any details you left out."

"Can I sleep in my favorite guest room?"

"Of course you can. Do you think you'll go to work tomorrow?" Laurie asked.

"If I get a good nights sleep."

"Don't hesitate to call out if you need to. You hardly ever miss work and you know if you go in you'll have to function like nothing's wrong. We both know those are always the days when all hell breaks loose."

"Yeah, I thought about that. But I also thought it might be good to go in. It would keep me from thinking about Dana."

"That's true. See how you feel in the morning. If you do decide to go to work, we'll have breakfast together before we leave and we'll ride in together." From the way Laurie's eyes lit up, you'd think they were going somewhere special.

"Sounds like fun," Ridley replied.

Chapter
Twenty-two

ON WEDNESDAY AFTERNOON, Dana borrowed her mother's car and drove into Chicago to visit Sarah. She had no trouble finding the place, a rambling old house that had been converted into apartments, located in a declining section of the city. She lingered in the hallway for a full minute while she searched for the courage to knock on the door to apartment 4B. She'd prayed for this moment and now that it was here and nothing stood between her and Sarah but an old wooden door, she wanted to do an about face and run in the other direction. With her heart wedged in her throat and her lungs so constricted they felt like they'd shrunk to half their normal size, she found the courage to form her right hand into a fist and raise it.

After the first set of knocks, she heard a muted flurry of activity inside and then after several knocks, each one a little louder, the door swung open. A combination of moderate weight gain, fatigue, personal neglect and perhaps a touch of depression thrown in for good measure had altered Sarah to the extend that Dana would not have recognized her if she'd passed her on the street an hour ago. A chubby toddler in pink pajamas, her face and hands visibly soiled, straddled Sarah's left hip.

"Sorry I took so long to answer the door, but I had to straighten the place up a little." Sarah ran her free hand over the surface of her hair as if to smooth it down. "I can't believe you're here. Did you have trouble finding the place?"

"No. Your directions were very clear."

"So, don't just stand there, come on in." Sarah moved aside.

"I assume that's Tori," Dana said as she squeezed past the two of them and entered the small, shabby apartment. She wondered what Sarah had done to straighten up because the place was a mess and she had to step over a teddy bear and a pile of toys.

"Yep, this is my daughter." Sarah grabbed the baby's chubby hand and waved it at Dana. "Say, hi to Dana, Tori. She's mommy's friend." The baby made a gurgling sound and buried her face in her mother's neck.

"Hi, Tori," Dana said, feeling more uncomfortable by the second.

"So, you got here this morning?"

"Yeah, just like I told you on the phone."

"That's right. You did tell me that. How's your family doing?"

"They're fine. My mother picked me up at the airport and I had lunch with her and got settled before I drove over here to see you. That's about it."

"What about your sister? How's she doing?"

"Fine, last I knew. She's busy tonight, but I'll see her tomorrow. Mom's having them all over for a family dinner." This small talk was becoming irritating. Sarah hadn't been interested in her or her family since they broke up and now she was full of questions.

"That's nice." Sarah struggled to hold Tori who had started to squirm and whimper. "She needs to go down for her nap. Let me put her in bed so we can talk in peace. I'll be back in a sec, so don't go anywhere." Sarah carried the fussing toddler down a long narrow hallway and into one of the back rooms.

Dana studied the dingy apartment and its sparse furnishings. It was obvious to her that Sarah and her husband weren't doing well financially, although a thorough cleaning and some tidying up would have made a big difference. A thick layer of dust coated every visible surface and the floor was strewn not only with toys, but with wadded-up clothing and God knows what else.

Some framed photos on the top of a bookcase caught Dana's eye and she made her way across the room to look at them. Several were of the baby and some were of Sarah's family, but one picture in particular caught her eye. Sarah was dressed in a white lacey dress and she stood next to Kevin who appeared quite out of his comfort zone in a baggy dark blue suit. Sarah held a small bouquet of flowers in her hands.

Sarah came back into the room and walked over to where Dana stood. She held her arms out. "You didn't even give me a hug," she complained in a whiny voice.

"I'm sorry." Although it felt inappropriate in view of the situation, Dana faced Sarah and gave her a fleeting hug with as little bodily contact as possible.

"It's good to see you," Sarah said after Dana let her go. "You look terrific."

Dana still held the picture in her hand and she lifted it so Sarah could see it. "Tell me about this picture. It leads me to think that you and Kevin got married. Did you?" She looked at Sarah and waited for an answer. If Sarah was married, why had she contacted her? What did she want from her?

"Yeah, we got married about a year ago. We had the baby and it kind of seemed like the right thing to do, you know? Besides, our families kept pressuring us to make things legal and tie the knot—for the baby's sake."

"You don't sound like you wanted to marry him."

"Geez, I don't know. I had my doubts, but I did it anyway."

"How romantic. Were you happy before you split up?" Dana asked more out of curiosity more than genuine concern.

"Happy? I don't know, I guess so." Sarah shrugged her shoulders. "Who's happy?"

Dana considered the question for a moment. She was happy. Lately, she'd felt especially happy any time she'd been with Ridley, happier than she'd been in years. "I don't know, but I sure want to be and I'm sorry to hear that you're not." She meant it in spite of all that had come to pass between them. It occurred to her right then and there that she couldn't remember ever having seen Sarah truly happy.

"Our marriage hadn't been going so good. Kevin was out of work most of the time and he got kind of depressed about it, you know? Sometimes he got mean. He had some good jobs, but he hated them and he either quit or he got into trouble. I tried to get him to go and learn a trade like welding or plumbing or something, but he said he hated studying and didn't want to go to school. I think he's just plain lazy."

"That's a shame."

"I know. Last summer, his brother got him a good job doing construction, but he got mad at his boss because of something he said and he hauled off and hit him. He broke the guy's nose and they arrested him for assault, but later they dropped the charges if he promised never to show his face around there again. Isn't that great?"

"Jesus, Sarah, did he ever hit you?"

"Not really. He just used to yell a lot, you know?"

"What do you mean, not really?"

"He almost hit me a couple of times, had his hand raised up and all, but he stopped himself just in time. It was my fault because I made him mad."

"That doesn't sound good." Sarah was talking like a typical victim. Dana had never known that about her, but then she'd never been abusive to Sarah. She wondered what else she hadn't known about her and feared she was about to find out.

"He wasn't always like that, you know? He used to be sweet until we started having money problems. I think his pride was hurt. It was tough on him."

"Why didn't you leave him?" Dana hoped Sarah's answer would not contain the phrase, 'you know', because if she heard her say it one more time, she might have to do something drastic like scream and stomp her feet.

"I almost left him a couple of times, but I couldn't do it, and it doesn't matter now anyway since he already left me. He said he was going crazy and he felt trapped. He couldn't stand the responsibility of supporting me and the baby."

"I know. You told me on the phone. Where is he?"

"He's staying with his parents."

"What about you? Aren't you working or anything?"

"No. That was one of the problems we had. I think he assumed I'd bring in a nice fat paycheck, being a chef and all, but I haven't felt like working since the baby was born. It's too hard on me and I'm not sure I like being a chef."

"You were a certified pastry chef. It would be a shame to throw it all away."

"I just want to stay home and take care of Tori. I just want to be a mother, you know? I don't like having to go to work every day and I never liked working in a restaurant. It's stressful and the hours are too much for me."

"You could make cakes or cookies or something here at home and sell them to restaurants or you could go to gift shops and specialty stores and ask people to display your baked goods and sell them. A lot of people have been successful doing that."

"I suppose I could, but that would be a lot of work, wouldn't it? And I'd have to buy all the stuff and..." Sarah frowned and quickly changed the subject. "Hey! Speaking of restaurants, how's yours doing?"

"Fine. We're full most nights and the reviews have been excellent."

"You must be making good money then, huh?" Sarah waited for a reply, but when she didn't get one, she asked, "Where is it?"

"The money?"

"No." Sarah put her hand over her mouth and giggled. "The restaurant."

Dana didn't laugh because nothing about their conversation amused her and she was getting angrier by the minute. She answered Sarah's question about the location of Café De Marco, but she didn't go on to tell her anything else about the restaurant.

"You always told me you wanted to open one there."

"I know and I'm glad I did. I love it there," Dana said, owning the truth of her statement. "Do you remember my friend Tracy?" After Sarah bobbed her head to indicate she did, Dana went on to tell her, "She's my sous-chef and she lives in my building."

"Are you and her together? I mean, is she your girlfriend?"

"She's my best friend, not that it's any of your business. Why would you ask me that? Since when did you become so interested in knowing about me?"

"I just wanted to know. I feel bad about what happened." Sarah took an interest in the floor and bent to pick up a dust ball. She rolled it into a tight ball and dropped it. "And I feel bad about what I did to you."

"You feel bad?" Dana laughed under her breath. "That's a good one. I thought we had a future and you were ruining it right under my nose. You treated me like I was nothing to you. When I found you in our bed making love with Kevin, my heart was broken." At last they were talking about the things that mattered and Dana thought something might get resolved.

"Shit, Dana, I never intended to hurt you," Sarah said.

"I thought I knew your intentions at the time, but you know what they say about the road to hell." Dana cleared a pile of clutter from one of the chairs, sat in it and squeezed her eyes against a burgeoning headache. All the energy had been drained from her body and she felt like a rag doll. "Look, Sarah, why don't you just cut to the chase and tell me why you asked me here? I've already had a long day and my patience is wearing thin."

"Uh, I..." Sarah stammered as she sat in another chair across from Dana's. She lifted her pleading eyes. "I thought I meant something to you once and I thought, you know, that you could help me and the baby out until we get back on our feet."

"Help you out how?" Dana asked, although she already knew.

"Well, I don't have enough money to pay the rent this month and I'm already two months behind. My parents gave me money a few times and they've flat out refused to give me anymore. They think I should get a job."

"Interesting thought. What about Kevin, or his family?"

"He's broke and his parents don't have a lot of money. They told him he could stay with them until he gets a job and that's all they were willing to do for him. I think he'll come back to me and Tori once he cools down."

"Let me see if I have this right. You want me to give you my hard earned money and then you want to wait and see if he comes back?"

"Well...yeah, that's right," Sarah confirmed.

Dana met Sarah's eyes. "And here I thought you wanted to resolve some issues and maybe talk about getting back together again." Did Sarah detect the sarcasm in her words? Dana had only been with Sarah a short time and that was all it had taken to convince her that she'd never go back to Sarah. Not in a million years.

Sarah's eyes were cold. "I'm not a lesbian, Dana. You should have figured that out by now. I'm sorry if I gave you the wrong idea, but I don't want to go back to that kind of lifestyle. I cared about you, but I never enjoyed the sex all that much. As far as I'm concerned, we were just experimenting like lots of young people do."

"You sure seemed to enjoy it well enough at the time, although looking back on it I'd have to agree that it wasn't the best sex I've ever had. It was limited and we were pretty immature." Dana paused to think about what she would say next. "So, let's get back to business, shall we? Just to make sure I heard you correctly, let me go over this. You asked me to come here so you could ask me to take care of you and your baby?"

"Just for a while, until I get back on my feet."

"You mean until you're through with me again?" Dana flicked a piece of something white from the arm of her chair. "And why would you think I'd want to do that?" At this point she was egging Sarah on, but she didn't give a damn. In fact, she was deriving pleasure from it.

"I don't know. I'd pay you back."

"Sure you would." Dana stood up and brushed off her pants. "What a waste of an afternoon. I don't know why I didn't see this coming."

"So you're not going to help me out?" Sarah asked.

"No, I'm not. I can't believe I ever had a relationship with someone like you in the first place. You don't know who you are or what you want and if you ask me, it sounds like you and Kevin are perfect for each other." Without hesitation, she walked toward the door, her eyes on the floor so she wouldn't trip over the clutter.

Sarah sprang up from the sofa. "Wait. You don't have to get so angry."

"You don't think so?" Dana stopped and turned. She knew her eyes were sharp and her tone sharper, but she was beyond being civil. "I do have some advice for you, though, and it's free of charge. Go live with Kevin's parents and let them take care of him and you and their grandchild. If that doesn't appeal to you, go home to your own parents. I am not willing to take care of you and some man's baby. If I ever decide I want a baby to take care of, I'll have one of my own with my lesbian partner."

"You don't even have a lesbian partner, do you?"

"Wouldn't you like to know? You have no idea what I do or don't have."

"This is just like you Dana. You were so sure you could turn me into a lesbian just because you got me to fool around with you, but it didn't work, did it? I always preferred men and I always wanted to get married and have children. You couldn't give me those things and I couldn't stand to go through life feeling abnormal."

"Lucky for you, you don't have to." Dana swept her hand across the front of her body in an all-encompassing gesture. "It looks like you've got everything you bargained for and more." With her hand gripping the door knob, Dana paused to say a few parting words.

"I'm glad I came to see you. I got the closure I needed and I finally got you out of my system. Thanks for showing me your true colors once again." She opened the door and stepped into the hallway. "One last piece of advice. If you need rent money, get a job and earn it...you know?"

Sarah stood in the doorway with her mouth hanging open. "Wait, I..."

"Don't call me or contact me again." Dana hurried down the hall and never looked behind her as she made a hasty retreat to her car. Relief and shame washed over her all at once. How could she have been with someone like Sarah? Something must have been seriously wrong with her to make her fall in love with a woman like that.

During the drive to her mother's house, she thought about being with Sarah. The sex had been tentative and groping at best and nothing like the passionate sex she'd had with Ridley. After seeing Sarah and listening to her, Dana knew that Sarah had never truly loved her and she doubted that she had ever loved Sarah. She had wasted so much time hanging onto something that had never really existed.

Even though they were hundreds of miles apart, she felt warm all over remembering the love in Ridley's eyes and the tenderness in her touch. It was something she'd never felt from Sarah, or from anyone else. The more she thought about Ridley, the more she realized she missed her.

As soon as Dana pulled into her parents' driveway and turned off the car, she doubled over with an attack of laughter as she pictured her life with Sarah and the baby. She pounded her fists on the steering wheel and guffawed so hard tears fell down her face. With each labored breath, she blew another memory of her past with Sarah right out the car window where it was carried all the way to Lake Michigan by the famous Chicago winds. It felt good to say goodbye.

As she sat behind the wheel of her mother's Toyota, she made a few decisions. There would be no more secrets and no more lies in her life. She would never be friends with anyone who didn't accept her for who she was and she would never be involved with any woman who wasn't sure of her sexuality. And she swore to tell her family she was a lesbian before she stepped on the plane that would take her home to Philly.

Chapter
Twenty-three

THE NEXT MORNING, Dana awoke to her parents' voices and the clanging of pots and pans. The aromas of coffee and bacon wafted over her nasal passages and made her stomach grumble with hunger. That's what got her out of bed. After a quick splash of warm water on her face and two minutes with her electric toothbrush, she threw on her jeans and a tee shirt and went downstairs.

Her father sat at the breakfast table reading the paper, so she went to him and planted a kiss on the top of his partially balding head. "Hey, Dad, what are you doing home? I thought you'd be at work."

"I decided to take the morning off to spend some time with my favorite chef," he said. "Next to you of course, my dear," he called out for the sake of Dana's mother who stood at the stove tending a couple of sizzling frying pans. "Maybe I'll go in to work later on or maybe I won't go in at all. We'll see."

Dana kissed him again. "Thanks for staying home this morning. It's been a long time since we've had breakfast together."

"Too long if you ask me," he replied.

Dana walked over to the stove and kissed her mother on the cheek. "Good morning, Mom. Speaking of breakfast, I'm famished. What are you making?"

"Nothing special, just eggs, bacon, home fries and toast. Get a cup of coffee and sit down and I'll have your eggs done in just a minute. You still like them done the same way you used to, don't you?"

"Uh-huh...over light, so I can dip my toast."

"That's the way your father likes his eggs." Dana's mother informed her of this fact as if she didn't already know. As soon as Dana had moved out of her parents' home her mother had started telling her things about her family like she was a total stranger who'd appeared out of nowhere instead of someone who'd spent the majority of her life living with all of them.

"I know that. We always have our eggs over light." Dana poured herself a big mug of coffee from the carafe on the counter and went to sit next to her father. She groaned after she took a big gulp of the aromatic brew. "Good coffee, Mom."

Her father let the top edge of his newspaper droop down and he winked at Dana from behind his reading glasses. "Like father, like daughter." He set his paper down and sized her up for a while until Dana's mother put their plates down in front of them. When her mother joined them at the table, he began to ask questions.

Once his curiosity was satisfied and they'd caught up on family matters, Dana knew it was time. She finished the last of her coffee in one gulp and cleared her throat. "Mom and Dad, I need to talk to you about something." Dana fiddled with her fork and pushed a little scrap of egg white around on her plate. "It's something important to me, something I need to tell you."

"What is it, honey?" Her mother's face appeared worried.

"Is something wrong, Dana?" Her father dropped the paper that he'd picked up again and pulled off his reading glasses.

Since she had their full attention and she'd run out of excuses, she told herself to get on with it. "There's been a lot going on in my life lately and I need to tell you..." Dana stopped and started all over again. "I know I should have told you this a long time ago because it's important. I hope you won't be disappointed in me."

"We're your parents. We could never be disappointed in you," her father said. "And we got the part about it being important, so why don't you just say whatever it is you have to say?"

"You know you can tell us anything," her mother added.

"This is ridiculous." Dana took a deep breath. "I'm gay. I'm a lesbian. That's what I wanted to tell you. I've known it since high school. I'm sorry I didn't tell you sooner. I wanted to, but I've been scared until now."

"Oh, honey, is that all?" Her mother was the first to respond. "I'm not surprised. In fact, I suspected as much a long time ago. In fact, I..."

"Damn it all to hell! Are you sure?" Her father stood up so fast he knocked his chair over, causing it to crash onto the tile floor behind him. His face was beet red, his eyes were bulging out of his head and he seemed to be holding his breath. He glared at Dana's mother. "You never said anything to me. I never thought she was a lesbian."

"Now, dear, take it easy. You're..."

Dana's father cut his wife off and addressed Dana. "I thought you just hadn't met the right guy or you were too busy to date." His eyes darted back and forth between Dana and her mother until they settled on his wife. "Why didn't you tell me about this since you'd figured the whole thing out? Why am I always the last one to know what's going on in this family?"

"Well, dear..." Before Dana's mother could even respond to her husband, he went back to talking to Dana.

"You're just confused. Why don't you talk to a therapist there in Philadelphia? I know they're expensive, but I'll pay for it if you can't afford it."

Based on the way he looked, Dana feared her father might blow a fuse. "Thanks, but I don't need to talk to anyone. Besides, any decent therapist would only help me to accept myself and I've already done that, so why spend the money? I know who I am and I want to live an open and honest life. I don't want to lie and I want my parents to know who I am and what's going on in my life. If I find someone I'd like to share my life with, I want you to know her and welcome her into our family. Maybe I'm asking for a lot, but that's what I want."

"Maybe you are," her father said. "And maybe it is too much to expect other people, including your family, to accept everything about you." He pounded his hand on the table in between every four or five words. "Some things are better left unsaid."

"I'm sorry, Dad. I'm tired of keeping secrets and I don't know how to do this except to just come out and tell you both the truth. Are you terribly upset with me?"

"I'm in shock, that's what I am. I wasn't expecting this kind of news out of the blue like this. Apparently, I'm not as observant as your mother is, but then I never was. She always has to explain things to me, especially these kinds of things."

"Now, dear," Dana's mother said. "I wasn't sure and it wasn't for me to tell you."

He ignored his wife and spoke to Dana. "Hell, I've been waiting for years to dance at your wedding, but I guess that's not going to happen, is it? For a minute there, I thought you were going to tell us you were getting married."

"I'm sorry, Dad. I can't change who I am."

"I know that, damn it." He glanced at Dana briefly as he lifted his chair from the floor and slid it back under the table. "I can't talk about this anymore, not right now. I think I'll go in to the office for a while, after all. I'll catch you both later." He waved behind him as he fled the scene.

Dana stood up. "I love you, Dad," she called out after him, not knowing what else she could say. She looked at her mother. "Should I go after him?"

"Let him go. He's not listening anyway. He handles things better when he goes off by himself. He has to think. Later, after he calms down, I'll talk to him."

"Thanks, Mom."

"Sit down. I have something I'd like to say."

"Okay." Dana sat at the table and her mother joined her.

"I've loved you since the first time I held you in my arms, even before that, and I'm not about to stop now. I don't think there's anything you could ever do that would ever change that. I want you to be happy and as far as I'm concerned, anyone you chose to love will be welcome in our home and in our family."

"That means a lot to me." Dana got up, walked around the table and threw her arms around her mother. "I love you too."

"Honey?" Dana's mother leaned back in her chair and looked up at her. "Have you met someone special? Is that why you're telling us this now?"

"You don't miss much, Mom. I have met someone." While she went back to her seat, images of Ridley flashed through her mind like a slideshow of digital photos. She saw herself kissing Ridley on the beach, she saw Ridley's eyes as they made love, Ridley's long eyelashes resting on her cheek as she slept and the downy fuzz along her jaw line, visible only in the morning sun. "Mom, she's really, really nice."

"I'm happy for you, honey. I'd like to meet her someday."

"You will and thank you for saying that." In her mind, she went back to the night they first met. At the time it hadn't entered her mind that Ridley would alter her life forever and yet, she'd started an avalanche of events that ended up changing everything Dana had accepted as her life. She pictured herself in bed with Ridley, their bodies joined like two fitted pieces of a puzzle and she felt her face grow hot.

She snapped out of it and forced herself back to reality as soon as she realized her mother was waiting for her to say something. "Do me a big favor, Mom. Don't mention this to Donna at dinner this evening. I'd prefer to tell her myself."

"I won't. I promise." Dana's mother said.

"And please ask Dad not to mention it."

"Don't worry, he won't bring it up. It would be too much for him to handle." Dana's mother winked at her. "Men are such cowards. Now, go and get us both another cup of coffee because I've got questions."

Dana got the coffee pot and brought it to the table. She filled her mother's cup to the brim and then her own. "What else are we going to do today?"

"Don't tell me you're spending the day with your mother?"

"That's the plan," Dana said.

"Well, that's a rare treat and I must say I'm delighted. First of all, we should plan the menu for tonight's dinner and make a list of what we need. Then you and I will need to go shopping."

"And then?" Dana asked although she knew what was coming next.

"And then I thought you'd help me cook. After all, we spent a small fortune to send you to culinary school and we should get some return for our money, don't you think?"

"I do think you should. I owe you big time and I'll start paying up tonight. We'll put on a fabulous dinner from soup to nuts that no one will ever forget."

"That's just what I had in mind. And I also hoped you could teach me how to make something seriously delicious that I've never made before."

"Me teaching you? That's a switch, huh, Mom?"

"Yes, but a welcome one. I can't wait to cook with my daughter, the chef."

"Thanks, Mom, but before we do anything, finish saying what you were going to say before about how you suspected I was a lesbian. How did you know and when and why didn't you say anything to me? I'd like to know."

"Okay. Want some more coffee?"

Chapter
Twenty-four

AS SOON AS Ridley and Laurie got to Laurie's house after work on Thursday, Ridley put her work bag down and made a decision. It had been two days since Dana had left for Chicago and Ridley was going insane not knowing what had happened. It was agony to wait and wonder and not know when Dana would return or if she would contact Ridley when she did. Even if Dana and Sarah were getting back together, Ridley wanted to know. "I'm going over to Café De Marco and see if I can talk to Tracy," she told Laurie. "She had to have heard from Dana and I want to find out what she knows."

"You should go," Laurie said. "Talking to her might make you feel better."

"I hope so. Maybe I can catch her before they open for dinner and she gets busy." Ridley put her work bag down by the door. "She might know what's going on with Dana and if there's no hope for me, I'd rather find out now."

"Let's hope that's not the case, but at least you'd know where you stand one way or the other." Laurie took her jacket off and hung it in the hall closet. "Will you be back for dinner? I hope so, because Karen has to work late tonight and I'd like your company. Besides, I'd like to hear what Tracy had to say."

"I'll be back in a couple of hours and I'll stay here again tonight if it's all right with you. But tomorrow I'm going back home after we get out of work. You've both been great, but I think I'm ready to tough it out on my own."

"Are you sure?"

"I'm sure."

RIDLEY RUSHED OVER to Café De Marco as fast as her legs would take her and walked around to the back. When she saw Tracy through one of the glass panels in the back door, she knocked and called out her name.

Tracy signaled for Ridley to come in.

"Hi, Tracy." Ridley saw Jimmy on the other side of the kitchen and greeted him as well. She closed the door behind her, entered the kitchen and walked over to Tracy. "Do you have time to talk to me, in private?"

"I thought I might hear from you at some point," Tracy said. She washed her hands, untied her apron and draped it across one of the islands. "Jimmy, do you mind taking over for me while we go upstairs and talk for a little while. We won't be long."

"No problem. You girls take your time."

"So what's on your mind, as if I can't guess?" Tracy asked Ridley once they were seated in her living room. "Forgive me for being direct, but you don't look good. You came to talk to me about Dana, am I right?"

"Yeah, you're right. I'm a mess, Tracy. I'm head over heels in love with Dana and I've already lost her. I'm afraid I can't compete with this Sarah person, whoever she is."

"Yeah, you can," Tracy said. "She's the one who can't compete with you, trust me on that one. Have you told Dana how you feel about her?"

"I told her how I felt about her when I was here for dinner the day before she left, but you probably already know that, don't you?" Ridley didn't wait for an answer. "I'm sure you also know that was when she told me she was going to Chicago to see her ex. She did tell you about all of this, didn't she?"

"She did, but I wasn't sure if it would upset you if I told you that."

"No, that doesn't upset me in the least. We all need someone to talk to. I told Laurie and Karen all about what was going on and I figured that Dana had talked to you since you're her closest friend."

"We talked after we closed the restaurant, but she didn't tell me that much. It was late and she had to get ready to leave at the crack of dawn the next morning. I suspected something was going on when she dragged you through the kitchen the way she did. You looked as if the world had just come to an end."

"It felt like mine had. She means a lot to me, Tracy."

"I can understand how you feel. Dana's a very special person."

"She sure is." Ridley got right to the point. "What's the story with her and Sarah?"

"Didn't she tell you anything about it?"

"Not really—not that much. I know about the spa in Pennsylvania and I know they had a relationship and broke up, but that's about it. And I know she still loves her."

"I don't think that's true. She just thinks she does," Tracy said.

"What do you mean?" For the first time, Ridley felt a spark of hope flicker inside. Did she dare to dream that Dana would come back to her after all?

"That was the first time Dana ever fell for anyone and she trusted Sarah completely. Why she fell for her or trusted her is anyone's guess. I hope you don't think I'm awful but I'm just telling it like it is. I've said all of this to Dana at one time or another."

"I don't think any such thing. Please go on."

"Well, love is blind as they say and her friends, including me, must not have warned her sufficiently about falling for straight women. Anyway, she didn't see the trouble ahead and when they broke up she never got over it. I'm convinced she wouldn't have been so enamored with Sarah if they'd stayed together longer."

"Why? Can you tell me more?" Ridley asked.

"Dana was crazy about Sarah from the start. God knows, Sarah did have a certain naughty girl sexiness about her and she was kind of cute. She could be charming and sweet when it suited her purposes, but she could also be needy and thoughtless. Dana never saw the bad things about her and she didn't want to hear it from anyone." Tracy paused as if remembering and whatever she thought about made her shake her head. "Sarah had a knack for upsetting Dana on a daily basis it seemed. Dana would call me all the time and tell me about the things she said and did. She was always up to something."

"Why did she stay with her if she was like that?" Ridley asked.

"That's a very good question, but you'd have to ask Dana because I have no idea. I doubt that she'd even have an answer for you. Why do any of us do stupid things or get involved with the wrong people?"

"Why indeed. But we all do, don't we?"

"Unfortunately," Tracy acknowledged. "You know what used to really bug me about Sarah? Whenever I saw them together, I got the impression that Sarah was ashamed to be in a lesbian relationship. More than once, I told Dana I didn't think Sarah was gay. I never saw her touch Dana in front of other people or show affection and if Dana tried to hold her hand or touch her in any way, she'd pull away. She..."

"That's awful," Ridley interrupted. "Sorry. Go on."

"So, you know they moved to the mountains, but they had other plans. All this was supposed to be theirs someday." Tracy moved her finger around in a big circle. "This house, the restaurant, all of it. They were going to move here and do this."

"Go on. What happened?"

"Dana and Sarah sometimes worked different schedules and one day Sarah had the evening off and Dana didn't. During her break, Dana went back to their living quarters to surprise Sarah, but it was Dana who got surprised. She walked in on Sarah and one of the young men from the maintenance department having sex, in Dana and Sarah's bed no less. They must not have heard her come in because they were really going at it."

Ridley sucked in a short burst of air. "Are you kidding me? That's more like a shock than a surprise and it must have been awful for Dana."

"I'll say. And it got worse. Sarah told Dana that she'd been seeing him almost from the time they got there. On top of that, Sarah was two months pregnant."

"What?" Ridley lifted her eyebrows and opened her mouth.

"You heard me. And as if that wasn't bad enough, Sarah told Dana she'd never really loved her, not that way. She loved her but only as a friend. Of course, Dana refused to believe it."

"Ouch." Ridley cringed. She could only imagine how much that had hurt Dana. It had never happened to her, but she'd heard similar stories from other lesbians. Now she understood why Dana had put up walls to protect herself and why she'd been so reluctant to let herself care about anyone. She also understood that it didn't mean Dana cared for her. "Those words are every lesbian's worst nightmare and when your lover leaves you for a man, that's another. What did Dana do after that?"

"Well, Sarah ran off into the sunset with her man and Dana went back to Chicago. She stayed with her parents until she got over the initial blow of what Sarah had done and then she moved to Philadelphia. To make a long story short, she called me and asked me to come with her and work for her and I jumped at the chance."

"That explains a lot," Ridley said.

"Maybe I shouldn't have told you any of this. I'm not sure Dana would have wanted me to, but I like you and I care about Dana and based on the situation it just seemed like the right thing to do. I hope it helps you in some way."

"It does, a little. At least it helps me understand her better and make some sense out of the things she's said and done. I feel for her...she's been hurt."

"And she's scared to death she'll be hurt again," Tracy added.

"I can see that now, but I'm not sure all the understanding in the world will change a thing if she doesn't want me. Dana either loves me or she doesn't and if she doesn't, I'll have to get over it and move on." As optimistic as Ridley's words sounded, she couldn't wrap her heart around them, not when her wounds were still so fresh and open.

"I'm sorry." Tracy said. "I know she was upset about hurting you and I think she cares about you, but I wouldn't want to speculate any further at your expense. What she told me was that she wasn't sure how she felt about you and I think she was telling the truth. Seeing Sarah might help her figure that out. That's why I encouraged her to go."

"Have you heard anything from her?" Ridley asked.

"She called me when she got there. She's supposed to come home on Saturday morning and I'm picking her up at the airport. I really don't know if she'll call again or just wait to talk to me when she gets here. She'll be busy with her family and she knows I'm busy."

"So you don't know how it turned out with Sarah?"

"No, but I hope it's over for good. I'm not a fan of Sarah's. In, fact I never liked her and Dana knows that. I do like you, though, and I think you're the best thing that's ever happened to her. I'd give anything to see you two together."

"Thank you, but I don't think that's going to happen."

"You never know. She might see Sarah for who she really is and if she does, she might be able to get in touch with her true feelings for you."

"If only you were right. The thought of losing her is killing me. No one's ever meant this much to me. Sometimes, when we were together I thought..." Ridley didn't finish her sentence. Sometimes she thought she saw her love returned in Dana's eyes, but your eyes can play tricks on you, especially when you want something so much it hurts.

"Well? What did you think?" Tracy asked.

"Never mind. I must have seen things that weren't there."

"Try to be patient with my poor, confused friend." Tracy got up and waited by Ridley's chair. "I really have to get back downstairs and help Jimmy."

Ridley got up and followed Tracy to the door. "I appreciate you taking time out of your busy day to talk to me and I'm grateful you were so honest. You've been more than kind. I guess I have no choice but to wait until she gets back."

"Give her some time to work things out."

"Do you think she'll talk to me when she gets home?" Ridley asked, hoping the answer would be yes.

"I'm sure she will. She would never want to hurt you any more than she has." Tracy held the door open for Ridley. "Come on, I'll walk you downstairs."

Chapter
Twent-five

ON FRIDAY AFTERNOON, Dana went to her sister's house for lunch. Wayne was at work, the kids were in school and her mother had a doctor's appointment she didn't want to cancel. For once, Dana and her sister were given the rare opportunity to talk privately without all the usual distractions. Donna and her family lived a short distance from Dana's parents in the sprawling megalopolis affectionately referred to by the locals as 'Chicagoland', a five thousand square mile area that encompassed the city proper and its constantly ballooning suburbs.

"I'm so happy we could get together, just the two of us. I've really missed you." Dana sat at the kitchen table watching Donna prepare lunch. "We don't see each other nearly enough since I moved to Philadelphia."

"I know and I've missed you, too. I loved the dinner at Mom's last evening. It was nice that we were all together again, except for brother dearest, of course. He couldn't very well come all the way from California. By the way, if that dinner was any indication of the food you serve in your restaurant, I can't wait to eat there. You're a genius."

"Actually, Mom made most of it. I only helped."

Donna raised her eyebrows. "Really? I never saw her cook anything like that."

"Well, I did come up with the menu, but she asked me to teach her how to make something new, so I did." A compliment from her sister meant a lot. "It is one of the dishes we serve at the restaurant, though, and since you mentioned it, I can't wait for you to visit. I know it's hard for you, but I hope you can come soon. My apartment's finished and I've got two extra bedrooms and plenty of room for guests."

"We'll come soon, I promise — whenever Wayne can get some time off. God only knows when that will be. Or better yet, maybe I'll leave Wayne home and give the kids to Mom and Dad and come by myself. What do you think of that?"

"That's a great idea. We could have so much fun," Dana said. It had been a long time since she and her sister had any quality time alone and she got excited as she thought about all the things they could do together. "Do you think you could pull it off?"

"I might be able to. Mom and Dad love to spend time with their grandchildren and spoil them rotten and Wayne will barely notice I'm gone." Donna paused and then took off in another direction. "Before I forget, did you notice how quiet Dad was last evening? He wasn't himself and I thought he acted like he was sulking."

"I'm afraid that was my fault." Dana took a sip of her iced tea. The time had come. Donna had given her the perfect lead-in and it made no sense to put it off any longer. After telling her parents, telling Donna should be a piece of cake.

"Your fault? I don't understand." Donna stopped chopping tomatoes and faced her sister. "You're Miss Perfect as far as he's concerned. What could you have done?"

"I told Mom and Dad something important yesterday. I would have told you last evening if we'd been able to talk without everyone hovering around and I can't tell you tonight because we're all going out to dinner. That's why I wanted to come over today. I wanted to spend time with you, but I also need to talk to you."

"You're not sick or in trouble are you?" Donna brandished her knife around in the air for emphasis. "Are you in love? Are you getting married?" The knife stopped about three inches from her right ear. "Oh my God, are you pregnant?"

"Good heavens, no. I'm not pregnant or getting married or in trouble with the law, although, come to think of it, I think it is against the law in some states." Dana told herself to quit joking and get on with it. She'd only have to say it once.

"Then what did you tell Dad that has him in such a tail spin?" Donna tapped the tip of her knife on the cutting board and stared at her sister. "Now I'm really curious."

"I'll bet you are. Just listen to me before I lose my nerve." Dana took a deep breath and began. "You're my sister and I love you."

"Good Lord, Dana, is it that bad?" Donna laid her knife down as if to make sure Dana knew she had her attention. "Why don't you just tell me?"

"I don't know how you're going to feel about this." Dana knew that once she said the words out loud, there'd be no taking them back and no matter what her sister's reaction was, she'd have to live with it for the rest of her life. "I..."

"Dana! Spit it out already, will you? The suspense is killing me."

"I'm a lesbian. There, I said it." Dana sighed with relief and then looked at her sister. She tried to read her sister's face but it was blank. "What do you think?"

"You're a lesbian?" Donna turned to her cutting board and laughed quietly to herself as she finished the tomatoes and put them in the salad bowl. "Is that all? You really had me worried there for a minute." She wiped the cutting board and started chopping celery on the diagonal. "This is hardly a news flash. I've been thinking you were for a while now. However, I am glad you finally came out and verbalized it. Just for the record, it doesn't make any difference to me as long as you're happy."

"You knew? How did you know and why didn't you say anything to me?"

"You never had any boyfriends and you never talked about men or showed any interest in them. I know you said you were too busy to date, but you would have found the time if it was something you wanted. I never asked you because it's not an easy thing to ask someone. I didn't know how to bring it up and I thought you should be the one to tell me. I also thought you would tell me when you were ready. It really didn't make any difference."

"Oh..." Dana said. "Mom said she knew it. You were both afraid to ask and I was afraid to tell you because I thought you might hate me or stop loving me. I love you all so much and I didn't want to lose my family."

Donna put the knife down and turned to Dana. "I would never stop loving you. We all love you and you will never lose your family."

"I'm so happy to hear you say that."

"I won't say anything to the kids unless you want me to, even though they would think you were cool. They talked about alternative life styles in school thanks to a very progressive teacher and they told Wayne and me all about it one night at dinner. They were very well informed and used all the proper words. Can you believe it?"

"God bless teachers like that," Dana said.

"Amen to that. Is it okay if I tell Wayne? We've already talked about it."

"You have? Okay, tell him if you want to, but don't tell the kids unless they figure it out or ask about it. I'll tell them myself when the time is right."

"You can tell them whenever you're ready to. You don't need to ask my permission. Just let me know if you do in case they have questions. We never discussed this with Danny, so I don't know what he thinks, if anything. Are you going to tell him?"

"Yes, I'll call him tonight."

"I like your plan. Fly in, lay it on the entire family and then fly away again. That's the way to do it. You don't have to stay around for the fallout and you get to escape." Donna opened a bag of hearts of Romaine and added it to the bowl.

"That's one advantage of living somewhere else," Dana said. "I'm so relieved to get this off my chest. I can't tell you how hard it was keeping a secret like this. One of the worst things was not being able to tell you what was going on in my life. "

Donna opened two cans of tuna and a can of pitted black olives. She drained them both and spread them around on top of the other salad ingredients. "Now I understand why Dad was acting the way he was. What happened when you told them?"

Dana went on to tell her sister the details of that morning and what her father and mother's reactions had been. "I don't have a clue as to what's going on in his head."

"Who does? Mom and I discussed the possibility you might be a lesbian more than once, but we never said anything to Dad and it never seemed to enter his mind."

"I can't believe you've all been discussing me behind my back."

"What are families for?" Donna shrugged her shoulders. "You have to remember. He's very conventional and he wants life to unfold the way he thinks it should. He's thrown off when it doesn't. You told him and that's all you can do."

"He also said he was disappointed I wouldn't be getting married."

"That's not the worst thing that can happen to a person, believe me." Donna made an odd sound with her mouth and then laughed to herself. When she was done, she asked, "Olive oil and Balsamic vinegar okay with you?"

"Yes, it's perfect."

"Are you serious about anyone?" Donna asked.

"That's another thing I wanted to talk to you about. You remember Sarah?"

"Of course I do. She was that chef friend of yours."

"We weren't friends, we were lovers." Dana gave her sister a condensed version of the story of her and Sarah including the reasons it ended and why she went to see her on Wednesday. "I just gave you the gist of it. I'm sick of going over it and she no longer matters to me."

"I'm sorry I wasn't there for you," Donna said.

"You could have been if I'd been honest with you."

"Well then, I'm not sorry."

"You know what amazed me the most when I saw Sarah?"

"No. What?" Donna popped a black olive into her mouth.

"I finally got to see her and I felt nothing except anger. I wasn't in love with her and I didn't even like her anymore. I'd been holding on to an idealized memory of her and I'd made her into the person I wanted her to be instead of the person she really was. I've been using that so-called tragedy to hide behind."

"Hold that thought." Donna added a small amount of thinly sliced red onion to the salad and brought it over to the table. "Here, help yourself and dish some up for me. I just have to get the rolls out of the oven." Donna tumbled the rolls into a basket and brought them to the table. "What were you hiding from?"

"Getting involved with anyone and making another bad choice," Dana answered. She took a bite of salad and chewed it. "This salad is delicious."

"Glad you like it. I had it once when Mom and I went out to lunch." Donna buttered a roll and took a bite. "I believe we have two choices in life. We either embrace life or we escape from it and I also believe you can't feel joy unless you can feel pain."

"I don't want a life without joy and I don't expect to live it without pain. Most of all, I don't want to be dead inside. Seeing Sarah made me realize something. I don't want to be with a woman who isn't sure about who she is and what she wants. I want to be with someone who loves me just the way I am, someone who wants me and needs me with her whole heart and..." Dana stopped talking and gasped. Her vision blurred as her eyes filled with tears.

"What is it, Dana?"

Dana covered her eyes with her hands. "Oh, my God."

"What's the matter?" Donna jumped out of her chair and stood next to her sister. She put her arm around her and rubbed her shoulder.

Dana raised her head and dried her eyes with her napkin. "I'm sorry. Something hit me so hard when I said that. I'm already in love with someone who's just like that. She's everything I've ever wanted."

"Tell me about her." Donna slid back into her chair. "What's her name?"

"Her name is Ridley Kelsen." Dana told her sister about how they met. "She's cute and nice and she's so kind and smart and sensitive and..."

"All right, that's enough. I get it." Donna smiled as she chewed a mouthful of salad. "She's completely wonderful and I can't wait to meet her. Does she love you, too?"

"She does, or I should say she did."

"She did? What does that mean?" Donna asked.

"I don't know if she'll want me after what I did." Dana told her sister more about her and Ridley, including what happened the last evening they saw each other. "How could I have done something like that to her? What have I become?"

"You'll be able to make things right."

"I don't know about that, but I'm going to try. The first thing I'm going to do when I get home tomorrow is to tell her I love her." Dana didn't know if Ridley would forgive her or want her back, but she was going to fight for her. "Why didn't I see this before?"

"Because you're human and you make mistakes just like the rest of us." Donna grabbed Dana's hand. "Don't be so hard on yourself.

Be grateful you were able to figure out what you want. Not everyone does."

"I want her. She's the nicest person I've ever known. I even like her mother."

"She has a nice mother?" Donna squeezed Dana's hand and let it go. "Then you definitely should go for it. There's nothing like a good mother-in-law. Aside from that, if she's half as wonderful as you say she is, don't let her get away. You'll never forgive yourself if you do."

"I know." Dana filled her fork with salad and shook it at Donna as she said, "You know what? I'm glad I came home. This visit has changed my life." A drop of dressing fell on the table and a little piece of lettuce flew off and landed on her sister's arm. Dana wiped up the dressing with her napkin and removed the piece of lettuce. "Oops."

Donna wiped her arm where the lettuce had left another drop of dressing. "You came out to your family, you got rid of an old flame and you had an epiphany. That's a whole hell of a lot for one family visit don't you think?"

"I'll say. They aren't usually that productive."

Chapter
Twenty-six

LATE SATURDAY MORNING Dana's plane landed at Philadelphia International Airport right on schedule. The moment she got off the plane with her carry-on bag, she scurried out of the terminal building to the pick-up and drop-off area. She spotted Tracy leaning against her car with the trunk open as she came through the automatic doors and called out to her. "Tracy. I'm over here."

Tracy waved to her in a way that indicated she should hurry up.

"I hope you haven't been here too long," Dana said once she got to the car.

"No, I just got here. Get in the car and let's get out of here." Tracy threw Dana's bag into the trunk, quickly closed it and hopped into the driver's seat.

"Thanks for coming to pick me up," Dana said as Tracy pulled away and joined the long line of cars leaving the always busy and crowded airport.

"Good thing your flight was on time. I had to go around five or six times and they were just about to make me go park in the high-rise lot." As she drove, Tracy glanced over at Dana several times as if appraising her. "It's good to have you back home. How was your trip?"

"It was amazing and I've got an awful lot to tell you." Dana began filling Tracy in on the highlights of her trip. She started with the Sarah visit, then told her about the coming out talks with her family and ended up with her conversation with Donna and how she came to realize her true feelings for Ridley. "I would have told you more about all of this on the phone, but I was really tired last night and I wanted to talk to you in person."

Tracy's smile stretched so far it looked as if it might hurt. "That was some visit and the best news I've ever heard. You need to know that Ridley came over to talk to me on Thursday. I didn't tell you about it when you called last night because you were beat and I thought it might upset you. I knew it could wait until you got home."

"She did? What did she say? How was she?"

Tracy went over the highlights of her conversation with Ridley. "She loves you, Dana, and in my humble opinion, she's the sweetest and cutest lesbian I've ever known, not counting you and me, of course."

"I agree, but what about Erika? Don't you think she's cute?"

"Yeah, she's cute, but she's a bit much. I've discovered she's the high maintenance type and way too intense for me. She's a drama queen if I ever knew one."

"Are things cooling down?" Dana asked.

"Let's just say she's not the one for me," Tracy replied.

"Are you okay with it?"

"I'm fine. I'm glad you finally came to your senses about Sarah."

"You were so right about her." Dana reached out and patted her friend's hand and then she leaned across the gear shift and planted a noisy kiss on Tracy's cheek. "I owe you big time."

"Hey, be careful. I'm driving here," Tracy said.

Dana stopped horsing around and got serious. "When I think of what I said to Ridley last Tuesday, I feel sick inside. I made it sound like she meant almost nothing to me. She told me she loved me and I brushed her off like she'd said it was a nice day."

"So you were an idiot. Now, what are you going to do about it?"

"When we get home, I'm going to call her and ask her to see me and when I do see her, I'm going to find out how I can make it up to her. I'm going to beg or grovel or plead or do whatever it takes to win her back."

"That might work." Tracy nodded her approval.

"It had better. How was everything while I was gone?"

As she turned onto the Columbus Boulevard exit ramp, Tracy told Dana what went on at the restaurant. She answered Dana's questions as they headed west on the city streets until she pulled up at the curb in front of Café De Marco. "You go up and call her, right now. I'll park the car and bring your bag up."

Dana rushed up the stairs to her apartment and reached for the phone. Her hands shook so bad she had to punch the numbers in several times before she got it right. Ridley's answering machine came on but Dana didn't leave a message. Instead, she tried Ridley's cell phone, but that went to voice mail. Again, she didn't leave a message. Ridley could be at the grocery store or visiting her mother or any number of places. She would try again.

Once she'd unpacked her things and freshened up, she called Ridley's apartment and her cell phone again and got the same results, so she changed and went downstairs to help Tracy. They were booked solid with dinner reservations and she'd been gone since Wednesday.

Every half hour she called Ridley both at home and on her cell, only to hear the same recorded messages. After a few attempts, she left a message asking Ridley to call her on her cell phone as soon as possible. By now, the need to reach Ridley had become an emergency of sorts and she felt she'd go crazy if she didn't connect with her soon. Her mind went wild wondering where Ridley was. Did she go away for the weekend? Was she at her mother's? Was she simply not answering the phone? Was she all right?

"Now I'm getting worried," Dana told Tracy as it got close to five o'clock and she still couldn't reach Ridley. "What if something's wrong?"

"It's Saturday. Maybe she went out for the day or she's away for the weekend. Why don't you call Laurie and see if they know where she is?"

"I think I will." Dana had Karen's number programmed into her cell phone and she wasted no time putting the call through. After several rings, Laurie answered the phone. "Hi, Laurie, this is Dana. I can't reach Ridley. Do you have any idea where she might be?"

"I'm so glad you called me. Ridley's been at the hospital all day. Her mother had a bad car accident early this morning."

"Oh, no! What happened?"

"Her car was hit by a truck."

"Jesus...how is she? Is she alright?"

"We're not sure yet. We were at the emergency room with Ridley this morning, but they were still evaluating her mother. We only know that she was unconscious at the scene and that she's alive. We hated to leave Ridley alone, but Karen got really sick all of a sudden and she had a fever and I had to bring her home."

"How was Ridley doing when you left her?" As soon as Dana asked the question, she knew what Laurie would say. She understood how much Ridley loved her mother and she was sure Ridley was beside herself with worry. The thought of her waiting alone at the hospital with no one there to comfort her was more than Dana could bear.

"She was out of her mind with worry."

"Have you heard from her?" Dana asked.

"Not yet and we can't reach her. She has her cell phone on voice mail and even though I left a few messages, she hasn't called us back. We even called the hospital, but they couldn't locate her. We'll just have to wait until she calls us."

"Do you think I should go to her?" Dana gestured frantically to Tracy to bring her a piece of paper and a pen.

"Could you? She's been in bad shape since you left. Maybe I shouldn't say this, but she's crazy about you and she's been heartbroken."

"I know and I'm sorry about that. I had some things I had to work out and if it makes you feel better, I'm crazy about her, too." Dana grabbed the pen and paper Tracy handed her and got ready to write while Tracy held the paper to keep it from moving around on the counter.

"We got directions on the Internet. Do you have something to write with?"

"Yes, tell me how to get there." Dana wrote the directions down as Laurie recited them. "Okay, I've got it. I'm leaving here as soon as I get changed."

"Thanks Dana. She needs someone with her. I've never seen her so lost."

"We'll call you guys later and let you know what's going on."

"Please do that and drive carefully, will you?"

Dana put the directions in her pocket and addressed Tracy. "I can't believe I'm leaving you alone again. I feel guilty and when things settle down, you're getting an entire week off and I won't take no for an answer. You've more than earned it."

Tracy waved her out of the kitchen, "Go. We'll be fine. We're used to it by now and no offense, but we're doing fine without you. The food's still excellent, the customers are happy and so far, we haven't had any problems. Tell Ridley I'm thinking of her and make sure you call me later and let me know what's going on."

"I will. I promise." In an instant, Dana was out the door.

Chapter
Twenty-seven

THE INTENSIVE CARE unit's family room looked the same as any other. Its walls were painted a third of the way up with bland hospital pastels while the other two-thirds was covered with heavy, geometrically patterned wallpaper. Groups of chairs attached at the base matched the colors in the wallpaper and lined the perimeter of the room. Ridley was certain the décor had been designed to help family members feel comforted, but in reality, the room had a coldness that jarred her senses. The stark white dropped ceiling and florescent lights didn't help. She'd been at the hospital since early that morning, sitting in one waiting room or another. People had come and gone, but at the present time no one else was there.

A television set mounted on the wall was set to a news channel with the volume so low that only an experienced lip reader could make out a word that was being said. Why did they choose a news channel Ridley wondered? Wasn't being here depressing enough without being forced to watch all the crap going on in the world?

On another wall, three vending machines stood in a row. The first one sold a grayish colored swill they had the nerve to call coffee, the second offered sandwiches of an indeterminate age wrapped in triangular cellophane packages and a variety of snacks. The third one contained beverages like bottled water, juice and soda.

Ridley felt smothered by the ghostly remains of too much pain and grief crowded into the lifeless room. She felt wired and exhausted at the same time. Her heart fluttered in her chest as she held her hands secured in her lap, slumped in her chair and closed her eyes. Where would she find the strength to get through this? She had barely recovered from the Dana incident and now her mother was injured and in the hospital.

While she sat there, she replayed the scenes of the day beginning with the phone call from the police that had jangled her out of a deep sleep. She'd had to rouse herself out of an anxious fog as she tried to comprehend the meaning of their words. The policeman told her that her mother's car had collided with a truck at an intersection not far from her home. The truck driver, who was miraculously unharmed, had checked on her mother and had found her unconscious. He called 911 and they transported her to the nearest hospital. That was all the police could tell her.

After she'd hung up from talking with the police, she called

Laurie. Her words came back to her as she remembered telling her the news. "Laurie, I'm sorry to call you this early, but something bad has happened."

"Ridley? What is it?"

"My mother's had an accident." Ridley told her everything she knew which wasn't much at the time. "She's in the emergency room at Bucks County Medical Center. I have to go there right away, but I wanted to call you and let you know before I left."

"God, Ridley, I'm so sorry." Laurie sounded wide awake now. "Do you need me to take you? I could get over there in a minute."

"No thanks. I'll have to stay at my mother's house so I'll need my car. Don't worry, I'll be careful driving. I have no idea why, but I feel surprisingly calm."

"You're in shock. You could pick me up and I could drive you in your car and then Karen could come and get me later on," Laurie suggested.

"No. I appreciate it, but I'll be okay...honest I will."

"Promise you'll call us if you need anything?" Laurie insisted.

"I promise."

"I'm really sorry to hear about your mother, Ridley. I know you've had a horrible week and now you have to deal with this. As soon as Karen and I get up and get ourselves together, we'll drive to the hospital. Just sit tight and wait until we get there."

"I will. Talk to you later." Ridley hung up, threw some extra clothes in a bag and ran to her car. Driving to the hospital was one of the toughest things she'd ever had to do and when she arrived at the hospital, the information desk directed her to the emergency room where she was told to wait until someone came out to speak to her.

A few minutes later, a tall woman in blue scrubs showed up. "I'm Anne Bower, the nurse in charge of the emergency room. The unit clerk told me you were waiting to talk to someone about your mother?" The nurse conveyed warmth and compassion and made Ridley feel like the most important person in the emergency room.

"Can you tell me how she is?" Ridley asked.

"Her vital signs are stable and she's in no immediate danger. The doctors are still evaluating her, so it will be a while before we know the full extent of her injuries."

"Is she awake? The police told me she was unconscious."

"She was conscious on and off by the time she got here."

"Will she be all right?" Ridley's voice quivered and tears trickled down her cheeks. She'd been running on adrenalin, but now she felt like she was crashing as the reality of the situation and the stress of the week caught up with her.

"Why don't we sit down?" Nurse Bower led Ridley to a chair and handed her some tissues from her pocket. She reassured Ridley that so far, none of her mother's injuries were life-threatening and then went on to explain more about the tests they would be doing. "Do you have anyone here with you?"

"No. I'm alone. Could I see her?"

"I don't see why not. I'll take you in for a few minutes."

Ridley followed the nurse into one of the cubicles that lined the walls of the ER. Her mother looked frail and her skin was pale against the pure white sheets. Her eyes were closed and she appeared to be asleep or unconscious.

"Why does she have that collar around her neck?"

"They put it on at the scene to stabilize her spine in case of injury. It's standard procedure. We did x-rays and the neurosurgeon is checking them as we speak. If he says there are no fractures or injuries to her spine, we'll remove it. You can touch her and talk to her."

Ridley took her mother's hand. "Mom, it's me, Ridley." Her mother's eyes fluttered open and Ridley felt certain their eyes met for a second. She felt her mother squeeze her hand. "I'm right here, Mom. Don't worry about a thing."

Later, Nurse Bower walked her back to the waiting room. "I'll talk to you as soon as we know more. We'll be sending her for tests, so you won't be able to see her for a while. Is there anyone who can come and stay with you?"

"A couple of my friends are on their way."

"Good. Just tell the girls at the front desk to let one of us know if you need anything."

AN HOUR LATER Laurie and Karen arrived with food and coffee. Ridley drank some of the coffee, but only picked at the food. As they sat in the waiting area, she updated them on her mother's status.

Although she'd slept well the night before, Karen felt excessively tired and she told Ridley and Laurie she had a scratchy throat and felt like she was coming down with a cold. Another hour passed and Ridley noticed Karen's face was flushed and she could hardly keep her eyes open. When she started getting chills and shaking all over, they all agreed she had a fever and should be taken home.

After Laurie and Karen left, Ridley continued to wait, convinced that time had failed to keep progressing with its usual precision. A couple of times, one of the nurses took her in to see her mother between tests and later in the afternoon, Nurse Bower came out to speak to her again. "I've got good news. Your mother's stable and we're going to transfer her to intensive care. One of our residents is coming out to talk to you before we move her." She patted Ridley's hand. "How are you holding up? Are you doing okay?"

"Not too bad for a nervous wreck."

When the resident came out, she gave Ridley an update. "Your mother was very lucky. So far, everything looks good. She did have a concussion but the CAT scan didn't show any other head injuries. She has two stable rib fractures. They'll be painful, but they'll heal over time. It must have been quite a crash. She hit the steering wheel, even with a seatbelt on, but her injuries could have been far worse if she hadn't been wearing it.

"The police said her car was totaled," Ridley said.

"I'm not surprised. We're sending her to intensive care so we can monitor her vital signs, her neurological status and her heart rhythm closely for the next day or so. She'll need special nursing care and close observation."

"What's wrong with her heart?" Ridley asked. "She never had any heart problems that I know of." This was the one thing the doctor said that worried Ridley the most since her father died of a heart attack. She felt her own heart begin to race.

"Based on her injuries we have to assume she could have bruised her heart muscle when she impacted with the steering wheel. It can produce the same clinical picture as a heart attack. The electrocardiogram we did was normal and we haven't seen any signs of damage to the heart so far, but it doesn't always show up right away. They'll need to do more cardiograms and lab tests before they can be sure she hasn't damaged her heart muscle. One of the cardiologists saw her and he'll follow her until she's cleared. She'll be on a heart monitor in case she develops an abnormal heart rhythm."

"I understand. Thanks for taking the time to talk to me and for taking care of my mother. She means a lot to me."

"Of course she does," the doctor said. "We're confident she'll make a full recovery. We called her primary care physician and he filled us in on her medical history. She's healthy and she's in good shape for a woman her age. All those factors are in her favor."

"Why don't you get something to eat or drink, or take a walk outside until she's settled in the ICU? It'll take some time. We'll tell the nurses that you're in the ICU waiting room. It's on the third floor. Just take the elevators in the main lobby and follow the signs when you get off. The waiting room is just inside the double doors to the right."

Ridley watched the doctor go through the ER doors. The thoughts of food made her queasy but she went to the coffee shop and forced down a muffin and a container of milk to calm the acids that were wreaking havoc on the lining of her stomach. It did help a little and she began to feel better for the first time since she'd gotten up.

After a quick trip to the restroom, she went outside and strolled around the well-manicured grounds. It felt good to inhale fresh cool air free of hospital smells. The sun hovered on the lip of the horizon, flaunting its fiery farewell, while random splatters of pink, orange and gray painted the indigo sky. Any other time, a gorgeous fall evening like this one would have made her feel in harmony with the world, but today the world seemed oddly detached and menacing. How could the outside world remain so untouched while her entire world lay in pieces at her feet like a heap of rubble?

No matter how hard she tried, she couldn't believe anything would ever be all right again. Not having to agonize over Dana every waking minute had been the only good thing to come out of such a wretched day. As she continued walking on the hospital grounds, the melancholy mood of twilight stirred up her emotions all over again and the full impact of Dana's words came back to haunt her. First she'd lost her and then she'd almost lost her mother and even though she had every reason to believe her mother would be okay, it had all been too much for her. Although she wasn't in the habit of praying, she lifted her eyes up to the heavens.

Since the walk was making her feel worse, she went back inside the hospital and took the elevator to the ICU waiting room where she submitted to the tedious task of waiting. After an indeterminate amount of time, one of the staff came out and took her in to see her mother.

A young man dressed in scrubs stood at the bedside, hanging a bag of fluid on a pole. He turned when Ridley entered the cubicle and introduced himself as her mother's nurse. He went on to explain all the wires, tubes and machines connected to her mother and fill her in on how she was doing. They talked for a while and then he put Ridley in a chair next to her mother's bedside and got back to work. "I'll be right here if you have any questions," he told her.

Ridley reached through the side rail and took her mother's hand. Gently, she shook it back and forth. "Mom, it's me, Ridley. Can you hear me?"

Her mother's eyes opened and she tried to smile as she turned her head toward Ridley. "There's my sweetheart," she whispered. "Chest hurts." She gripped Ridley's hand and closed her eyes again

"You had a car accident and you're in the hospital. You're going to be all right."

"Stay with me," her mother whispered.

"I will, Mom, as much as I can. If I'm not here in your room, I'll be outside in the waiting room. I love you very much and I won't leave you."

A tear escaped down Vicki's cheek and she held fast to Ridley's hand.

Ridley took a tissue from the bedside table and wiped the tear away. "The doctor's told me you're going to be all right. Just try to rest."

Chapter
Twenty-eight

DANA HESITATED IN front of the doors leading into the ICU waiting room. She couldn't wait to get home from Chicago, couldn't wait to see Ridley and talk to her and now, after she'd rushed to the hospital, she was afraid to go inside. Her apprehension made her question whether she should have come at all. What if Ridley didn't want her here? What if she hated her because of what she'd done and what if she turned away from her? "This is ridiculous," she muttered as she shoved the door open.

Ridley was the only one in the waiting room. She sat by the window with her eyes closed and her head propped up in the palm of her hand. When Dana came in, she slowly lifted her head to see who was there. Shock registered on her face and she blinked a few times.

"It's me," Dana said.

"Dana." Ridley leapt to her feet, but stayed in front of her chair. "What on earth are you doing here? How did you know where I was?" She moved forward a step or two.

Dana took a couple of steps into the room. "Laurie told me. I called you as soon as I got home from the airport and I called all day and left messages. When I didn't hear from you, I got worried and called Laurie to see if she knew where you were." She took a few more steps. The tension evident in Ridley's face and the desolation in her eyes broke Dana's heart. In the blink of an eye, she ran to her and put her arms around her. Her lips pressed against Ridley's forehead and her fingers stroked her hair. She kissed Ridley's eyes and cheeks and then her lips.

Ridley pulled her mouth away and buried her face in Dana's neck as she clung to her for dear life. "Thank God you're here."

"Please forgive me for taking so long to get here. I didn't know about your mother until I called Laurie or I would have been here for you hours ago."

"You're here now. That's all that matters." Ridley tightened her arms around Dana's waist. "Please stay with me for a while. I've never felt so alone. I won't ask you for any more than you feel you can give me, I promise."

Dana stepped back and gazed into Ridley's eyes. "You can ask me for anything. I'm here now and I have no intention of leaving you." She led Ridley to a chair and sat next to her. She put her arm around her and held her hand. "I'm sorry about your mother. How is she?"

"They tell me she's going to be all right." Ridley told Dana everything that had happened since the early morning hours when she'd first learned of the accident. "I've been out of my mind with worry. She's the only family I've got left besides my aunt and I don't know what I'd do without her." Ridley buried her face in Dana's shoulder, but this time she sobbed as if she'd run out of whatever strength had been holding her together.

Dana moved back in her chair and lifted Ridley's chin so their eyes would meet. "I want you to know something. She's not your only family. I'd like to be your family if you'll let me." Dana cupped Ridley's cheek in her hand and rubbed the last of the tears away with her thumb. "I want to be with you. I couldn't wait to see you and tell you how much I love you."

Ridley sucked in a tremulous breath. "You love me?"

"I love you more than anything in this whole world and I'm never going to run away again. I was just too stupid and stubborn to know it."

"Are you sure? Please don't say it unless you're sure."

"I'm sure. I'm totally and positively sure."

"What about Sarah? I thought..." Ridley sighed. "I mean you said you might go back to her and I thought I'd never see you or be with you again."

"Maybe I'll tell you all about Sarah some other time, or maybe it's not even worth talking about. She's history and that part of my life is over. I don't want her, I want you. I'm ready for a more mature relationship and I'm ready for you."

"I want to be with you more than anything," Ridley whispered.

"I know that and I'm sorry I hurt you. I didn't mean it when I said that being with you was just a superficial sexual thing and I'd give anything if I could take back the words I said to you last Tuesday—every one of them." Now Dana's eyes blurred with tears. "The only thing I should have said was that I loved you. I've loved you all along, but I was afraid to admit it."

"Are you still afraid?"

"I'm not afraid of anything anymore."

"I love you, Dana. When I turned around and saw you walk into this waiting room, it was like I'd been granted a miracle. Every day since you left I prayed you'd come back to me and today I prayed the hardest of all."

"Well, someone heard you because here I am." Dana brushed a stray piece of ornery hair away from Ridley's eyes and stroked her forehead. She wanted to touch her and hold her and make her feel all right again. When Ridley leaned down and rested her head on

Dana's shoulder, Dana wrapped her arms around her and held her close.

When the nurse came in and told Ridley she could come back in to see her mother, Ridley held Dana's hand and they stood up. "Can I take my girlfriend in with me?" Ridley asked him. "It would mean a lot to my mother and to me."

He looked at both of them, his eyes taking in the fact that they were holding hands, and he smiled as if he understood. "Sure. Come with me."

At the bedside, Ridley took her mother's hand and spoke to her. "Mom, Dana's here. She came as soon as she heard about your accident."

Dana took a hold of Vicki's other hand. "Vicki, it's me. How are you doing?"

Vicki's eyes opened and she smiled as she squeezed Dana's hand. "I'm still here and it's good you're here. My Ridley needs you."

"I'll stay with her. You just rest and get better," Dana said.

They stayed with Vicki about twenty minutes and then the nurse came in and tapped Ridley on the shoulder. "You know you're welcome to stay as long as you want to, but I think you should go home and get some rest. You've been here all day and you look like you're about to fall over. She's doing well and she should be fine overnight."

Ridley stretched and yawned. "Maybe I should."

"Give me your phone number and I promise I'll call you immediately if anything changes," the nurse said. "I'm doing a double shift so I'll be taking care of her all night."

Ridley wrote down her cell phone number as well as her mother's home phone on a piece of paper and gave it to him. "The girl at the desk taped these numbers to the front of my mother's chart earlier in case you lose this piece of paper. I want you to call me right away if she needs me, no matter what time it is."

"I will and don't worry we'll take good care of her." He attached the piece of paper to a clipboard he had on the bedside table.

Ridley brought her mother's hand to her lips and kissed it. "Mom, we're leaving. I'm staying at your house, so I'll be back in the morning. If you need me, tell your nurse to call me and I'll be here in a flash."

Vicki peeked at Ridley. "Go home sweetheart. You look tired."

BEFORE THEY REACHED the hospital parking lot, Ridley stopped and faced Dana. She held both of her hands. "I'm staying at my mother's. Can you stay with me tonight? I don't want to be alone.

I want to be with you."

"Tracy doesn't expect me back and I wouldn't leave you for anything." Dana let go of one of Ridley's hands and tugged on the other as she led the way. "Come on. We'll take my car and leave yours here. You're in no shape to sit behind the wheel of a car."

When they got to Dana's car, Ridley crawled into the passenger seat and collapsed. Her head fell back on the headrest and she rested a hand on Dana's thigh. She kept her eyes closed all the way to her mother's house except when she had to open them to give Dana directions. At last, the knife that had lodged in her heart had been removed and she could take a deep breath without pain. Her world made sense for the first time in days and now that her mother was going to be all right and Dana was beside her, she was struck with exhaustion.

Once they were inside Vicki's house, Dana said, "I promised Tracy I'd call her and if you'd like me to, I can call Laurie and Karen and let them know what's going on. I'm sure they're very worried by now."

"Why don't you do that? I'm too tired to talk to anyone. Tell Laurie I'll call her tomorrow." Ridley pulled her cell phone out of her pocket. "I do have to call Aunt Jean, though, before we go upstairs and get some rest."

"Are you hungry?" Dana asked. "I could fix you something to eat."

Ridley shook her head. "My stomach's all churned up. It's been one hell of a day and I'm way too tired to eat. What I need is a shower and then I want to get into bed with you and I want you to hold me all night. I can't think of anything I want more."

Dana stood in front of Ridley and cupped her cheek. "You don't look like you could even stand up long enough to take a shower. I'll take one with you. A hot shower would feel good and I don't mind going straight to bed when we're done. I've had a long, emotional day myself."

"That sounds good. Let's make those calls."

IN THE SHOWER, Dana washed Ridley's hair and soaped her body taking great care not to touch her in a way that was meant to stimulate. It didn't help, though, because at this stage in their relationship, just being close and naked soon left them panting with desire. Dana wanted Ridley with every fiber of her being and it took all of her resolve to keep from touching her. As soon as Ridley was washed, Dana finished washing herself and turned the water off. "Stay here, I'll get you a towel," she said.

"Just a minute." Ridley pulled Dana's wet, naked body to her and kissed her. "I love kissing you. I can't be in the same room with you and not want to kiss you, let alone make love to you, especially when we're both standing here naked and wet. I'm sorry I'm so tired."

"Don't be." Dana pressed a finger against Ridley's wet lips. "And as for the wanting, it's mutual. I want you so much, I can hardly keep my hands off you, but we'll get to that. We have plenty of time."

They stepped out of the shower and Dana pulled a towel from the rack. She spread it out on a bench in the bathroom and told Ridley to sit. After she wrapped another towel around herself, she got a third towel and dried Ridley's hair. "I love the color of your hair. It reminds me of autumn and I love your eyes. They're beautiful and they hold my world in them." The tension lines around Ridley's eyes had relaxed and it felt good to comfort her.

Ridley kissed Dana's cheek and stroked her hair. "I love everything about the way you look. I love your body and I really love your mouth. Those dimples and those luscious lips make me want to kiss you all the time." She pressed her lips to Dana's as if she just wanted to feel them. "So soft," she murmured when the kiss ended.

"Do you have any idea how sexy you are? It's a wonder I can think or talk when I'm near you." The air in the bathroom seemed heavy and too hot to breathe and Dana felt as though her entire body was on fire. "Finish drying yourself and let's go to bed," she told Ridley while she dried herself. When they were done they hung all the towels up and went into the bedroom hand in hand. "What do you usually wear to bed?"

"A tee shirt and panties," Ridley answered.

"Can I borrow something of yours?"

"Sure. Hold on a sec." Ridley rooted around in the dresser drawers and came up with a couple of soft, worn tee shirts and two pairs of panties. "I keep some extra clothes here in case I stay over. You should be able to fit in my stuff. We're about the same size."

"Do you have an extra toothbrush I could use?"

"My mother keeps some new ones on hand. I'll get you one."

"Just tell me where they are and I'll get it myself. You get in bed."

When Dana returned, Ridley was snuggled beneath the covers. Dana slid in between the sheets and gathered Ridley in her arms. "I'm so happy to be here with you and to hold you in my arms again. I love you so much."

Ridley lifted her head and moved up so she could brush her lips across Dana's. "I love you. I felt as if my world ended when you left."

"That's all over now. Let's try to forget about it and put it behind us." Dana pressed her lips to Ridley's and their kiss deepened. Ridley's mouth was like a cocoon of sun-warmed satin and Dana wanted to crawl inside it and never come out into the cold world again. She slipped her hand under Ridley's shirt, ran it up her smooth skin and tucked it between the soft pillows of her breasts. She felt Ridley's heart beating, her chest rising and falling and she allowed herself to fall into the same soothing rhythm. This was where she belonged. This was worth having.

"I want more. I can't..." Ridley had trouble speaking. "So tired."

"It's okay. Just go to sleep." Dana pulled Ridley closer. "Forgive me."

"Mmm...already have." Those were Ridley's last words.

Chapter
Twenty-nine

EARLY THE NEXT morning, the phone jangled them out of a deep sleep. Because she assumed it was the hospital, Ridley quickly sat on the edge of the bed and answered it before it rang a second time. "Hello? Yes, this is Mrs. Kelsen's daughter." Ridley listened for a minute. "Uh-huh. That's good. Should I come in now?" Ridley listened for another minute or so. "Okay, no problem. I'll be in later. Thank you for calling." Ridley hung up.

Dana turned in bed and placed a hand on Ridley's lower back. "Was that the hospital? What did they say? Is everything okay?" she asked during a yawn.

"She's doing great," Ridley said without turning around.

"How are you doing this morning?" Dana slid her hand under Ridley's tee shirt and rubbed her bare skin. "Do we need to go to the hospital right away? Is she asking for you?"

Ridley got in bed and rolled toward Dana. "That's a lot of questions." She held Dana's face and traced her lips with her thumb before she kissed her. "As far as how I'm doing, I think I'm back among the living. They told me it would be better if I waited until all the doctors made rounds and the nurses got her bathed and no, she's not asking for me."

"I guess we've got some time to ourselves." Dana lifted Ridley's shirt and cupped one of her breasts in her hand. "I feel good and rested, don't you?"

"I think I've recovered sufficiently." Ridley pulled her shirt over her head and threw it on the floor. Then she wiggled out of her panties and threw them aside. "I want to make love to you," she said as she helped Dana out of her tee shirt and panties. "I thought I'd never touch you again." Ridley kissed Dana until they were both struggling to breathe and then bent to kiss her breasts. With her hand she caressed Dana's entire body and when she reached between her legs, she gently parted them. "I need to touch you."

"Yes. I want you to...please." Dana's hips searched for Ridley's hand.

Ridley groaned as she felt how wet Dana was. She held her close as she made love to her and watched Dana's face change, her eyes close and her breathing become erratic. She stayed with her as she stiffened and cried out and then she held her close when it had passed. She knew she would never leave Dana. Life without her in it was unthinkable and unbearable. "I'm so glad you came back to me."

"I never left you, not really."

Ridley separated from Dana enough to meet her eyes. They were dark as the night and filled with a desire that poured into her and made her want to stay in bed with Dana forever and never stop touching her. "Pinch me and tell me this isn't a dream."

"If this is a dream, I never want to wake up." With her arms around Ridley's chest, Dana rolled them over so her body ended up on top of Ridley's. She straddled Ridley's firm thigh and wedged her own thigh between Ridley's legs.

Ridley opened her legs wider as Dana began to slide against her. She ached for relief from all the emotions of the last few days, all the pain and all the longing. They moaned together and moved together and fit together perfectly and before long, they cried out their release together.

"You're a wonderful lover," Dana said as she rested in Ridley's arms. "I never thought it could be like this. It's like you live inside me, inside my soul. We're amazing."

"You're amazing and I love you more than you'll ever know. We haven't known each other that long, but I feel like you're my soul mate. I've known it from the start." Ridley spoke through a haze of desire. She kissed Dana's eyes, her cheeks and mouth and then she laid a trail of kisses down the length of her body leaving no part of her un-kissed. When she reached the place she'd hungered for the most, she lifted her eyes. "I've missed doing this the most. I want to do this to you again and again and..."

"Oh, God," Dana cried as Ridley covered her with her mouth.

A COUPLE OF hours later, in spite of wanting to make love with Dana for the rest of the day and then some, Ridley climbed out of bed. "We'll have to continue this later. I hate to leave this bed and you, but we should get to the hospital. I'm anxious to see my mother and make sure she's okay. I'm going to hop in the shower. Want to join me?"

"If I join you, can I trust you?" Dana teased.

"Hell no." Ridley took Dana's hand and dragged her into the bathroom. "We're not in that much of a hurry and I'm not that strong."

After a long shower, they went into the bedroom to get dressed. Ridley reached into one of the dresser drawers and held out another pair of panties for Dana. "Here, you can wear these. Unless..."

"Unless what?" Dana's eyes twinkled.

"Unless you'd rather not wear any underwear at all? I'd find it terribly sexy knowing you didn't have any on."

"You don't say? Then I won't wear any panties." Dana threw the panties on the bed behind her and winked as she pulled her jeans on over her naked body. "I do have to wear a bra, though. I'm too self-conscious about going around in public without one."

"All right, if you insist, although, it would be a whole lot sexier to think of you without a bra or panties." Ridley pretended to pout as she pulled on her panties and jeans and then put on her bra. "I have to say I'm disappointed."

"You're not being fair. You're wearing underwear," Dana said.

"I'm visiting my mother. I have to be decent."

"Oh? And I don't?"

"No. Besides, she told me never to leave the house without clean underwear on case I have an accident and end up in the hospital and we are going to the hospital, aren't we?" Ridley grabbed Dana and hugged her playfully. "Are you hungry?"

"I'm always hungry for you, but if you mean for food, yes."

"I don't feel like making breakfast or doing dishes or trying to find my way around my mother's kitchen. Why don't we stop at my favorite diner on the way to the hospital? They have an interesting menu and they make the best home fries. I feel like I haven't eaten for days and I desperately need a good cup of coffee."

"So why are we poking around? Hurry up."

Chapter
Thirty

DANA GLANCED AT Ridley as they walked side by side down the long corridor that led to the ICU. Dana stopped about mid-way and grabbed Ridley's hand. "You look happy," she said as she studied Ridley's eyes. "And that makes me happy."

Ridley jumped into the depths of Dana's eyes. "I am happy. You're mine and my mother's going to be all right. What more could I want?"

Dana raised Ridley's hand to her lips. "The way your eyes burn into me, they melt me inside and I'm all flesh and blood and liquid desire."

"That's a beautiful thing to say." Ridley kissed Dana's fingers and raised her eyes to capture Dana's, again. "You seem to be able to take the heat."

"Hold that thought until we're alone again." Dana dipped the tip of one finger into Ridley's slightly open mouth and tugged on her bottom lip. "Right now we're in the middle of a public hallway and we have to go see your mother."

After checking in with the unit clerk, Ridley and Dana went to her mother's bedside. They were surprised to find Vicki out of bed sitting in a chair. Her color was much better and she was alert. Everything was gone but one IV and her nasal oxygen.

Vicki glowed when she saw them. "Here's my Ridley...and you brought Dana." Her voice sounded hoarse and her words came out dry and sticky. She motioned to the space by her chair. "Come over by me, girls, and sweetheart, give me some water, will you?"

Ridley held the plastic cup with the curved straw while her mother took a drink. "You look so much better, Mom." Ridley kissed her on the cheek.

"I think I'm on the mend," Vicki said.

"How do you feel this morning?" Dana asked.

"Like I've been hit by a truck," Vicki said, her words followed by a painful grimace.

"Mom..." Ridley and Dana looked at each other. "You were hit by a truck."

"I was?" Vicki winced as she started to laugh. She clutched a special pillow to her chest to brace her sore ribs. "Please don't make me laugh."

"Sorry, Mom." Ridley pulled up a chair next to her mother while

Dana sat on the edge of Vicki's bed. Ridley proceeded to tell her mother everything she knew about the accident and the events that followed. "Don't ever scare me like that again. I don't know what I would do if you weren't around."

Vicki took Ridley's hand in hers. "I'm not going anywhere just yet. I'll be around until you're good and sick of me." She touched her daughter's cheek. "I'm doing fine, so the doctors and nurses keep telling me. The cardiologist came in this morning. I must admit he was a little worried when he listened to my heart."

"He was?" Ridley asked. "Why? Was something wrong?"

"No, honey, but he was handsome enough to make it skip a beat or two."

"I guess you do feel better," Ridley said.

"You can't blame me for admiring a handsome man. I do that every now and then. One of these days, I might even do more than that if the opportunity presents itself. I'm not too far over the hill for romance, I hope."

"Of course you're not, Mom. I think you're lovely."

"Thank you, sweetheart."

"So, what did the cardiologist say?" Ridley asked.

"He said my heart's healthy and there's nothing wrong with it. I'm going to a regular room later as soon as they get a bed for me."

"Why are you still on the heart monitor?"

"I asked them that and they said you have to be when you're in the ICU. It's policy." Vicki took a long look at the two of them. "That's enough about me and my accident. Something has changed between you two. You both look radiant."

Ridley went to Dana and put her arm around her. "We're in love, Mom."

"Why, of course you are. That's what I see."

"What do you think, Mom?"

"Why, I think that's the best news I've ever heard. I'm happy for you both, I really am." Vicki held out her hands. When the girls took hold of them, she looked up at Ridley and said, "I so hoped for this." Then she spoke to Dana. "Welcome to the family. We're few in number, but we're a devoted bunch. A talented chef and a nice girl like you will be a wonderful addition and I'm very pleased to say the least."

"Thank you," Dana said. "I want you to come to my restaurant any time you want. Bring your sister or Ridley or anyone else you want to bring. I owe you and your daughter a lot."

"Whatever do you mean?" Vicki asked.

"Yeah, why would you owe us anything?" Ridley asked.

"Thanks to the two of you, I came out to my family when I was in Chicago."

"Why didn't you tell me?" Ridley asked.

"I wanted to tell you and your mother together. You're the one who pointed me in the right direction, Ridley, when you told me how you regretted not having told your father and then when your mother shared her feelings with me that time we went for dinner, I made up my mind that I would tell them the next time I saw them."

"Good for you, dear," Vicki said. "How did it go?"

Dana told them all about it. "I'm so relieved that's out in the open."

"Did you tell them about you and Ridley?" Vicki asked.

"No. I wasn't sure about us at the time and I thought it would be too much. I did tell my sister about her, though, and next time I talk to my mother, I'll tell her."

"I'm proud of you." Vicki's eyes drooped. "Push the bell for the nurse, will you? I'd like to get in bed and I think I need a pain pill."

Two nurses came in and asked Ridley and Dana to leave while they got Vicki back in bed and made her comfortable. They directed them to a small family room inside the ICU.

Ridley sat next to Dana in the empty room. "You are so hot," she whispered. "All day I thought about you naked inside those jeans and I wondered if you were wet and if you wanted me as much as I wanted you."

"We're awful. Your mother's in the hospital and all we can think about is making love to each other. I am wet and looking at you makes me wetter."

"Just knowing that turns me on even more. And we're not awful. It's wonderful to feel this way. It's a sweet, sweet torture."

Dana leaned forward, her voice low. "I can't wait to be alone with you."

With one eye on the door in case someone came in, Ridley placed the palm of her hand on Dana's cheek and ran her thumb back and forth over the soft skin. "Can you stay with me again tonight? Please say you can."

"Yes, but I'll have to go back home later tomorrow. I have to be up early on Tuesday to go to the wholesale markets and I need to get back to running my restaurant. I've taken advantage of Tracy long enough."

"I don't care as long as I know you're mine."

After fifteen or twenty minutes, the nurses sent one of the residents into the family room to talk to Ridley about her mother's progress. After that, she and Dana sat by her mother's bedside and talked to her for a while.

"You two don't need to spend your day watching me sleep. I'm fine," Vicki said once the pain pill kicked in and she started to drift in and out of sleep. "Go out and have fun together. Go have a nice dinner and get out of this hospital."

Ridley took her mother's hand. "I hate to think of you here alone."

"I won't be alone. My friend Arlene is coming and she'll be bringing Aunt Jean with her. I'm tired and sore and I think I just need to rest. Why don't you girls come back tomorrow? I'll have one of the nurses call you if I need anything."

"I'll call this evening and see how you're doing," Ridley said. "And I'll come to see you tomorrow. I'm not going home or back to work for another day or two."

Vicki nodded. "That will be fine. I'm very happy about the two of you." She glanced at Dana. "I'm glad you're staying with Ridley. Now, I've got two cheeks, so you each choose one and give me a goodbye kiss."

THEY DROVE IN silence, having no need for words. They knew where they were going and what they were going to do when they got there. Nothing else existed but the two of them, two people who needed to express their love for each other, not with words but with their hands, their mouths, and their bodies.

The instant they stepped inside the house, Ridley grabbed Dana and kissed her with a need and a hunger that had been building all day. She couldn't wait one more second. Dana's lips parted to allow Ridley access to the sweetness within. Ridley yanked Dana's shirt from her pants and touched the smooth skin at the small of her back. "I've wanted to touch you all day."

"You told me," Dana whispered.

Ridley slid her hands down the back of Dana's jeans and pulled her against her hips as she kissed her again. Wanting someone with this level of intensity was an entirely new experience and even this early in their relationship, she was hopelessly addicted to the feel, taste and smell of Dana. She was the most delicious, sweetest creature on earth and being with her was the very essence of joy.

Dana rocked her hips into Ridley's. "All day, I keep thinking of your mouth on me." She touched her trembling fingers to Ridley's lower lip. "Could you do that for me?"

Dana's question drew a low groan from Ridley. "Yes," she breathed. With one hand, she held Dana and with the other she unbuttoned Dana's jeans, slid the zipper down and reached inside. "I kept thinking about how wet you told me you were."

Dana's body shook all over and she cried out almost immediately. "Good lord, I've never done anything like that. I..."

Ridley held her until she stopped shaking. "You're so beautiful. Let's go upstairs before we end up on the floor."

HOURS LATER, DANA rested her head on Ridley's lower abdomen until their breathing returned to normal. When it did, she moved up in the bed, pulled the sheet and comforter up and cuddled underneath them with Ridley in her arms. "I love you," she said.

Ridley kissed her. "I can taste myself on you," she said against Dana's lips.

"I love the way you taste and I love making love to you that way," Dana said. "And I love the way you feel." She reached to touch Ridley again.

Ridley groaned. "Again? You're driving me crazy."

"Am I? You don't seem one bit crazy to me," Dana teased.

"Doesn't an incurable sex addiction count?"

"I suppose, but I don't see it as a problem, do you?" Dana brought her wet fingers up and rubbed Ridley's nipple to a hard peak. "We should enjoy it while it lasts."

Ridley moaned as Dana covered her nipple with her mouth. "Sweet-talker."

Afterward, Ridley said, "Do you have any idea how happy you've made me? You do realize it would be impossible for me to live without you now, don't you?"

Dana planted a gentle kiss on Ridley's lips. "I never knew it could be like this. You're the only one I want, for as long as you want me."

"Are you available for the rest of my life?"

"I don't know about that, but I am available for the rest of mine."

Chapter
Thirty-one

Almost a year later

"TRACY, I'D LIKE to know where the hell Jimmy is," Dana said as she flitted from one end of the restaurant kitchen to the other like a fly trapped in a lampshade. It was a Saturday and Tracy was busy preparing for the commitment ceremony and private party to be held at Café De Marco later that evening for Ridley and Dana. "He should have been here ten minutes ago and he needs to get started on the salads and appetizers."

Tracy stepped in front of Dana and grabbed her shoulders. In a firm, yet controlled voice she said, "I've had just about enough of you. You've got to get out of here before I kill you. Jimmy isn't due for another fifteen minutes and when he does get here I won't have you harassing the poor guy while he's trying to work. A lot of that stuff is already done and we have plenty of time to finish the rest."

"I know, but..."

"Uh-uh, no buts and not another word." Tracy wagged a finger in Dana's face. "You've got nine toes over the line and you'd better get up those stairs before that last toe goes over. And don't let me see your face in this kitchen again. The next time I see you, you'd better be in the restaurant with Ridley. It's going to be a wonderful party and if you're not happy with the way it turns out, you can fire me tomorrow, unless I decide to quit before then."

Dana started to protest, but the look on Tracy's face made her stop. Even though she could see Tracy was dead serious, she laughed to lighten the mood. "See that window? Keep your eye on it and if you see any pigs flying by you'll know you're going to be fired. Of course, if you do decide to quit..."

"Don't tempt me. Now, go and leave me alone or I swear I will quit and I won't wait until tomorrow. I have tons of work to do and you're getting on my last nerve, the one that was frayed when you came down here to pester me." Tracy pointed at the door. "Out with you!"

"All right, I'm going. Did someone put the sign on the door?"

Tracy glared at her. "Dana! For Christ's sake! We're not morons. Everyone knows we're closed tonight. No one has a reservation and the signs been there for weeks. Now, get upstairs and enjoy your special day with that gorgeous girlfriend of yours before I kill you."

"Uh-oh, I can see I've overstayed my welcome." Dana backed

out of the kitchen and headed upstairs to her apartment. Tracy was right. She should rest for the big event. As excited as she felt, she had no business getting in Tracy's way or interfering with any of the preparations.

"THERE YOU ARE, my love." Dana found Ridley perched on the edge of the bed. She was surprised to find tears streaming down Ridley's cheeks. She sat close to her. "What's the matter? I haven't seen you cry for ages."

"Your father..." Ridley dried her eyes.

"What did he do?" Dana asked with alarm. "Did he say something?"

"It's not what you think. I'm crying because he made me happy. We were talking and he told me he could see how much we love each other and he...he thanked me for..." Ridley blew her nose. "He thanked me for making you happier than he's ever seen you. He never said a word to me before about us being together and now he went and said something like that."

"Maybe he's coming around after all," Dana said.

"It seemed hard for him to say."

"It was, believe me." Dana kissed Ridley on the cheek.

"The rest of your family has been wonderful."

"Yeah, we're lucky, aren't we? Speaking of my family, where are they?"

"They were getting antsy so I suggested they go out and walk around South Street. They'll be back in a couple of hours."

"Did your mother call?" Dana asked.

"Yes she did. She and Aunt Jean will be here by five. She said to tell you how much she enjoyed meeting your parents yesterday and she also told me she invited your entire family to the shore next summer. And they said they'd come. And Donna and Wayne want to bring the kids."

"That house won't know what hit it," Dana remarked.

"And your mother invited my mother to Chicago. It seems they hit it off. They talked about going shopping and to some of the museums and restaurants."

"Are you serious? That's great."

"That's not all. Our mothers were talking about having a big family Thanksgiving next year in Chicago," Ridley said. "Your mother insisted."

"She loves big family dinners. What did your mother say?"

"She said yes and she seemed overjoyed." Ridley studied Dana with a curious look on her face. "By the way, where have you been? I hope you weren't downstairs bothering Tracy."

"Yes, I was, but she kicked me out." Dana crossed her arms, stuck out her bottom lip and pretended to pout. "I won't go down there, again."

"You'd better not. Just leave her alone."

"You should have seen the look she gave me. If looks could kill, I'd be dead on that kitchen floor right now instead of sitting up here talking to you." Dana's face brightened and she quit the pouting act. "Ridley, honey, the buffet's going to be luscious."

"Of course it will, but you need to stay out of their way and let them do this for you. This is your big day and you aren't in any condition to run the show."

"You're right. I'll behave myself," Dana promised.

"You don't have to behave in every way." Ridley touched Dana's cheek and fell into those familiar eyes. "I'm sorry we can't be legally married."

"So am I, but that doesn't change what we are to each other. We're married in our hearts and no one can take that away. Besides, I don't think we're going to have to wait that long. The laws are changing and the day is coming when we'll no longer be denied equal rights. I'm sure of it. Until that day, I say to hell with anyone who doesn't like it."

"If the law does change, will you still want to marry me?" Ridley asked.

"You bet, cutie." Dana kissed her.

"Karen's friend is a lesbian and an Episcopal minister. She's hearing our vows tonight and she's giving us a blessing. That has to count for something." Ridley put her arms around Dana and nibbled at her lips while her hand wandered. "I love you with all my heart. I should have had enough of you, but I still want more."

Dana took Ridley's hand and pressed it to her breast. "We don't have time and my family could come barging in on us any minute. That's all my father would need to see."

Ridley nipped at the tender skin on Dana's neck. "Promise you'll make it up to me? I'm available tonight and I've got nothing better to do."

"I'll ignore that last remark and I promise, my love."

"Hey, I almost forgot," Ridley said, changing the subject. "Your father wanted me to give you a rather strange message. He told me to tell you that you owe him a wedding dance. Does that make any sense to you at all?"

"It does. It makes all the sense in the world."

Another Janet Albert title to look for:

Twenty-four Days

Sometimes life forces us into uncharted territory, as Dr. Miranda Ross discovers when circumstances lead her to seek employment on a cruise line specializing in all lesbian cruises. Although she's single and surrounded by women, she has little time to socialize and even less inclination. She's made promises to herself, promises she intends to keep.

And keep them she does, until she meets the ship's head fitness trainer, Jamie Jeffries. Jamie has the kind of body and good looks most people only dream of and unfortunately, a reputation to match. The buzz on the ship is that she can have anyone she wants and often does.

Miranda fights valiantly to avoid Jamie and the unwanted attraction that seems to have a will of its own. She's strong and determined...but a lot can happen in twenty-four days.

ISBN 978-1-935053-16-3

MORE YELLOW ROSE TITLES
You may also enjoy:

The Sea Hawk
by Brenda Adcock

Dr. Julia Blanchard, a marine archaeologist, and her team of divers have spent almost eighteen months excavating the remains of a ship found a few miles off the coast of Georgia. Although they learn quite a bit about the nineteenth century sailing vessel, they have found nothing that would reveal the identity of the ship they have nicknamed "The Georgia Peach."

Consumed by the excavation of the mysterious ship, Julia's relationship with her partner, Amy, has deteriorated. When she forgets Amy's birthday and finds her celebrating in the arms of another woman, Julia returns alone to the Peach site. Caught in a violent storm, she finds herself separated from her boat and adrift on the vast Atlantic Ocean.

Her rescue at sea leads her on an unexpected journey into the true identity of the Peach and the captain and crew who called it their home. Her travels take her to the island of Martinique, the eastern Caribbean islands, the Louisiana German Coast and New Orleans at the close of the War of 1812.

How had the Peach come to rest in the waters off the Georgia coast? What had become of her alluring and enigmatic captain, Simone Moreau? Can love conquer everything, even time? On a voyage that lifts her spirits and eventually breaks her heart, Julia discovers the identity of the ship she had been excavating and the fate of its crew. Along the way she also discovers the true meaning of love which can be as boundless and unpredictable as the ocean itself.

ISBN 978-1-935053-10-1

Piperton
by Carrie Carr

Sam Hendrickson has been traveling around the Southwest for ten years, never staying in one place long enough to call it home. Doing odd jobs to pay for her food and gas, she thinks her life is fine, until fate intervenes. On her way to Dallas to find work for the upcoming winter, her car breaks down in the small town of Piperton. Sam's never concerned herself over what other people think, but the small minds of a West Texas town may be more than she bargained for - especially when she meets Janie Clarke. Janie's always done what's expected of her. But when she becomes acquainted with Sam, she's finally got a reason to rebel.

ISBN 978-1-935053-20-0

OTHER FORTHCOMING TITLES
from Yellow Rose Books

Soul's Rescue
by Pat Cronin

Talia Stoddard is an over-weight woman who has lived with this stigma, as well as being a lesbian, for most of her life. Kelly McCoy has been a fire fighter and paramedic most of her adult life for the city of New York. After 9-11, she relocates to Cincinnati, looking for a new start. Talia is getting her morning coffee in the atrium of the Winchester Building when a delivery truck crashes through the main entrance. She is about to step into the glass elevator to go to her office when the truck slams into her and part of the wall, pinning her beneath the wreckage. Kelly is one of the first fire fighters to arrive on the scene. Her small stature makes her perfect for confined rescues and she is sent into a void in the rubble to see if Talia is alive. She doesn't expect to find her soul mate. Years of being told that she's too fat, too tall, doesn't dress well enough, not to mention succumbing to the controlling ways of her ex-girlfriend, Talia doesn't believe that someone like Kelly could ever love her. Can Kelly help Talia move away from her past to start a new future? Can Talia ever believe that she could be worthy of the kind of love that Kelly is offering? *Soul's Rescue* is the story of finding love, healing the wounds of the past, and building a life that everyone dreams about, but few people ever find.

Available May 2010
ISBN 978-1-935053-30-9

Storm Surge
by Melissa Good

It's fall. Dar and Kerry are traveling — Dar overseas to clinch a deal with their new ship owner partners in England, and Kerry on a reluctant visit home for her high school reunion. In the midst of corporate deals and personal conflict, their world goes unexpectedly out of control when an early morning spurt of unusual alarms turns out to be the beginning of the shocking nightmare that was 9/11.

Available May 2010
ISBN 978-1-935053-28-6

OTHER YELLOW ROSE PUBLICATIONS

About the Author

Janet Albert was born and raised in Johnson City, New York. After working in Philadelphia for many years, first as a trauma and critical care nurse and then later as a school nurse for the school district of Philadelphia, she abandoned her life in the big city and now divides her time between the mountains of Northeastern Pennsylvania and the North Coast of Ohio. She lives with her partner of many years and their obligatory allotment of two cats. In addition to spending enormous amounts of time in front of her laptop writing, she enjoys reading, traveling, spending time in nature and delighting her family and friends with her cooking skills.

Because she's an avid fan of lesbian romance fiction, she hopes to make a contribution by writing the kinds of stories she enjoys reading. She also hopes to add to the increasing number of books that celebrate and affirm the lives of lesbians. After all, it seems as if there are never enough of them (books, that is, not lesbians). On second thought...maybe both.

VISIT US ONLINE AT
www.regalcrest.biz

At the Regal Crest Website You'll Find

- The latest news about forthcoming titles and new releases

- Our complete backlist of romance, mystery, thriller and adventure titles

- Information about your favorite authors

- Current bestsellers

Regal Crest titles are available directly from our web store, Allied Crest Editions at www.rcedirect.com, from all progressive booksellers including numerous sources online. Our distributors are Bella Distribution and Ingram.

Breinigsville, PA USA
28 April 2010
236960BV00003B/53/P

9 781935 053279